SING THE RAGE

Peter Palmieri

Sing the Rage

ISBN-13: 9781657124769

Sing the Rage

For Marino

2·3·20

To Nancy,
    the kind of reader writers
    dream about.
                    All the best,

                    Peter Pal...

Sing the Rage

We everlasting Gods ... Ah, what chilling blows we suffer — thanks to our own conflicting wills — whenever we show these mortal men some kindness.

The Iliad

3

CHAPTER ONE

Major Balakin

4 OCTOBER, 1991 — ODESSA, UKRAINE

Svetlana Medvedeva hobbled across the cramped kitchen, grimacing with every step as though she were walking on hot coals. She poured her daughter a cup of coffee, let out a woeful sigh and muttered, "At this rate, you'll never shoot a man."

Seated at the kitchen table, Lyudmila Medvedeva avoided her mother's gaze, keeping her eyes focused on the plate of dumplings and scrambled eggs set in front of her, her appetite quickly waning. She resigned herself to yet another one of her mother's grillings but this time she would not be rattled. She would deny the old lady that satisfaction.

"My dear sweet child," Svetlana continued. "But, what am I saying? You're twenty-six years old! Not such a child anymore."

So it was going to be that conversation again!

Her mother might have enjoyed a stellar career as an inquisitor with the Interrogations Unit had she wanted, Lyudmila thought. Even as she pushed sixty, the woman could give people gooseflesh with a simple glance, make the hair on their neck stiffen with a few well-chosen words. Words like, "My dear sweet child."

Lyudmila's uncle Boris said it was all because Svetlana had been hit by lightning as a child. It had left a permanent electrical charge in her spine. She had even been examined by a specialist at the time — a professor from Moscow, no less — who had taken x-rays of her head, run batteries of tests. The professor concluded that little Svetlana's body had become a repository of static electricity. It was all very scientific.

"Twenty-six years old," Svetlana resumed, "and you've never had to change a dirty diaper. And even worse! Not once have you fired your service revolver at a man."

Lyudmila took a sip from the steaming china cup and grimaced. "Mama, why do you still drink chicory coffee? Austerity is over. You can buy Arabica beans from all over the world now. Tell you what. I'll go to Privoz Market after work. Get you some Colombian dark roast. You'll like it."

"Change the subject," her mother said and pulled a pack of cigarettes out of her apron pocket.

"What was the subject? Diapers? Guns? I'm confused."

The older woman turned on the gas stove, bent down, and lit her cigarette directly from the burner. She turned the fire off and exhaled a blue plume of smoke in the general direction of the range hood. She licked her lips and cleared her voice. "Your grandmother was only twenty-four during the siege of Odessa."

Lyudmila rolled her eyes. "My grandmother again!"

"Did you know, my child, listen to this, she was so tricky, your babushka, she would prop mannequins against tree trunks, or sometimes tie red ribbons on high branches to distract the Nazi soldiers. Then she'd pick the bastards off with her sniper rifle, one by one, like little doves. Clipped many little birds' wings that way."

"Well, mother," Lyudmila said, "in case you haven't noticed, these days there aren't so many Nazis in the streets of Odessa looking to be shot."

Svetlana smiled a menacing smile. "Don't think I've given up yet," she said. "I still have hope."

"For what? My career? Or on becoming a grandmother?" Lyudmila said.

Her mother chuckled. "Well, at least now you're going to learn how to change a dirty diaper."

* * *

Lyudmila had lost count of the number of diapers she had had to change since that breakfast

in her mom's cramped kitchen two weeks ago,
though she had yet to learn to execute the
operation flawlessly. Or so claimed the ward
supervisor, a woman with a ruddy complexion,
whose starched white uniform and stove-pipe chef
hat made her look more like a supermarket
butcher than a nurse. And Lyudmila couldn't help
but think that this odd undercover assignment in
the nursery of a small military hospital was some
kind of punishment despite her lieutenant's
assurances that the operation was of a particularly
sensitive nature. It was a commission that, if
handled discretely, might even lead to a modest
promotion. Her grandmother, the war hero, was,
without a doubt, turning in her grave.

Tuesday morning, Lyudmila arrived at the
ward and started the important ritual of scrubbing
her hands, carefully moving from fingertips to
elbows, using the harsh iodine disinfectant that
left her skin smelling like an old lady's dirty
laundry. Meanwhile, on the other side of town,
Major Borya Balakin had long finished his
morning ablutions.

The day the Major chose to snuff out the life of
his only-begotten son was appropriately gloomy,
not that it mattered to him one way or the other.
After washing his neck and his feet, he recited his
morning prayers, then broke a three-day fast with
a meal of smoked sardines, a slice of stale rye
bread, and a cup of sour black tea which had

grown tepid in its clay mug.

Unlike prior missions the former Soviet Army officer had embarked on, this operation demanded more spiritual preparedness than strategic planning. So for three days, Borya Balakin fasted. He meditated under the frozen gaze of a gilded portrait of Saint Spyridon and read from his Bible.

After breaking his fast, the Major took shears to his overgrown beard. He shaved his jowls clean with a dull razor that nicked his skin. Then, he combed his hair with the dregs of an ointment he scraped off the bottom of an amber jar with a spoon. Finally, he put on his Army uniform only to find that the jacket drooped over his emaciated frame like an over-sized lamp-shade. Had he tried it on sooner, he could have re-sewn the buttons to make it fit more snugly. It was too late now.

As he marched to the bus stop, Borya Balakin caught a glimpse of his reflection in the plate-glass window of a coffee shop. He stopped to look at himself and muttered, "What if I take them all?"

* * *

Lyudmila was bottle-feeding baby Misha when the ward supervisor marched in and said, "I wouldn't waste my time with that one."

Misha was the runt of the litter. He was a baby that looked rather unremarkable from the tip of his toes to the bridge of his little nose. His eyes were his betrayal. They were void of emotion, unable or unwilling to fix on any mark. And if one removed his cotton skull-cap, the underlying problem became evident. The baby had no forehead, almost no head to speak of, to put it bluntly. A shallow promontory rose above his eyebrows, leading to a plateau that sloped back to the nape of his neck.

Lyudmila had taken a liking to Misha. Compared to the other six babies, all strapping infants with rosy cheeks and pale blonde hair, greedy and demanding at every feeding, Misha was docile, peaceful, undemanding.

"Where are their parents?' Lyudmila asked the ward superior.

"They are orphans."

"All boys," Lyudmila observed. "The same age."

The ward superior started to walk away, then stopped and turned. Through clenched teeth, she uttered, "Mind your business, comrade nurse." She left the ward in a huff.

It was all very strange to Lyudmila, this nursery for orphaned boys in a secluded ward of a military hospital, with an armed sentry at the door, and an undercover policewoman impersonating a nurse to provide an additional layer of security. Security against what? Against whom?

Lyudmila was dying for a cigarette by now. She held up the bottle to the yellow light streaming in through a muslin-draped window.

"Only sixty milliliters this time, Misha," she whispered. "You'll have to do a lot better than that if you want to keep up with the monsters."

The female police officer put down the bottle and patted the infant's back until he let out a feeble belch, swaddled him in a blanket, and lay him in his crib. Lyudmila then ambled up to another nurse, a frizzy red-head whose face was fiercely covered in freckles and said, "I'm going for my break. See you in ten."

The Ukrainian Army private standing by the door straightened his spine in a subtle show of servility as she walked into the outer corridor. For a moment, it made Lyudmila think the Army did know of her presence in the ward, but her lieutenant had repeatedly told her that was not the case. No one knew of the presence of the National Police in the hospital. No one could possibly know. No, the private was just another broken soul.

Lyudmila stepped onto the concrete patio overlooking the hospital's power plant, reached under her gown for a pack of cigarettes, grazing the butt of the Walther PPK tucked into her hip holster — the same gun James Bond used. A perfect weapon for a secret agent, she thought.

She was half-way through her second cigarette when the Army sentry from the ward walked out onto the deck, and meekly asked her, "Do you have an extra smoke, comrade?"

Lyudmila pulled out her pack of cigarettes, taking extra care not to let the soldier catch a glimpse of her gun.

"Why aren't you at your post?" she asked the Army grunt.

"My relief came," the soldier said. He was just a boy with big ears that stuck out like clamshells. The soldier chuckled. "First time I'm relieved by an officer."

"Say again?" Lyudmila said.

"I was relieved by a Major, can you believe it? In an old-school uniform."

Lyudmila dropped her cigarette and grabbed him by the lapels. "What kind of old-school uniform?"

"I don't know . . . It looked Soviet. It's okay. The major showed me credentials."

Lyudmila cursed, pushed the soldier back, and unfastened her handgun from its holster. She sprinted toward the nursery, shedding her bouffant cap along the way. She ran up the two flights of stairs, taking three steps at a time, gasping for air by the time she reached the last floor. She pushed on, racing down the empty corridor, the empty hall where an Army soldier should have been standing guard, and kicked the door of the ward open with the heel of her boot. In a smooth motion, she had practiced countless times, Lyudmila brought her gun up in a two-handed grip.

A man in a Soviet Army uniform was standing over Misha's crib, smothering the infant with a pillow.

"Back away, or I shoot!" Lyudmila shouted.

The man looked at Lyudmila with a bewildered expression. But his grip on the pillow, which engulfed the entirety of the baby's face, remained firm.

"Back off!" Lyudmila's muscles tightened. There was a tingle in her wrists, which made the policewoman think her hands might start to shake.

"It must be done," the man in the uniform said.

She squeezed the trigger just once. Heard the distinctive pop. Felt the familiar nudge of recoil, and saw the intruder fall backward, landing in a seated position with his back against the wall. For a moment, the two looked at each other in silence. The man on the floor looked as surprised as Lyudmila by the turn of events.

"I thought maybe you'd miss," the man said in a calm voice. "My coat is too big, you see."

Like an idiot, Lyudmila felt compelled to study the man's coat to check it for size. A dark stain was forming on the fabric over the left shoulder.

"Shut the hell up!" she shouted, upset at herself for taking that stupid cigarette break.

Lyudmila kept her gun aimed at the man as she slinked to the side of the crib to look at Misha's lifeless body.

"Is he dead?" the man asked. Blood was dripping down the inside of his sleeve and onto his hand now

"You bastard. What do you think?"

The man sighed. "Let us pray then. Let us pray the others perish too."

CHAPTER TWO

Private Arkadi Orlov

11 MARCH, 1992 — KYIV, UKRAINE

"What about the second time you died?" asked
the American. Mr. Henry Snodgrass from Akron,
Ohio, sat behind his government-issued metal
desk. He wore a haughty smile on his pale lips
and maintained a stiff pose: his back straight, his
shoulders forward, his chin lifted just enough to
give his listless eyes the necessary angle to look
down on Arkadi Volkov.

The man had an insolent expression, Arkadi
thought, ripe with the presumption of power. An
appearance that would have gotten the
American's windpipe crushed before lights-out at
the Black Dolphin, just to teach him a little lesson
in manners.

"Yes, what about it?" Arkadi Volkov said. He
looked at the American's neck, stared at the man's

prominent Adam's apple, studied the mid-line
notch on the top lip of the thyroid cartilage.
Arkadi spied a patch of black stubble that glided
over Mr. Snodgrass's hyoid bone as the man
talked, the remains of a careless morning shave,
and imagined how that tiny island of prickly hair
might feel against the palm of his calloused hand.
Arkadi smiled back, innocently at Mr. Snodgrass.

"Well, frankly, Mr. Volkov, the paperwork in
your file is . . . unconventional," the American
said. "Your dossier has one birth certificate and
two death certificates."

Arkadi turned his head to look out the fourth
story window of the U.S. embassy. The vastness
of open space past the plate glass was utterly
disorienting — yet one more thing he would have
to re-acclimate to. Perhaps it was just the light
playing a trick on his eyes. The sky was glazed in
a gray sheen, just a shade paler than the cinder
blocks of his old prison cell. The glare made it
impossible for Arkadi Volkov to discern whether
the condominium towers of the Bdzhilka Market
were one hundred meters away as the crow flies
or many kilometers off in the distance.

Indoors was an entirely different matter. He
was able to work out the exact number of steps it
would take to lunge at the man sitting behind the
desk. How much force he'd have to exert to snap
that pencil neck. Not that he wanted to. To his
delight and relief, Arkadi felt collected, unruffled

by Mr. Henry Snodgrass's boorishness.

Yesterday was a different story. On the two-mile march back to the hotel, after Arkadi knocked out a half-drunk cab driver with a well-placed uppercut, Miss Natasha had pleaded with him not to kill anyone at the American embassy tomorrow, "If you can manage."

"That cabbie asked for it," Arkadi said in his defense.

"That's beside the point," Natasha replied.

"I know how to handle myself," Arkadi said, sulking.

"We all think we do," said Miss Natasha, "until we're put in one of those situations where we're backed up in a corner, and we just snap. We have no control over the devils that live inside our souls. And we all have devils."

He couldn't argue with that line of reasoning. For years, Arkadi had been forced to live each day surrounded by demons. Real demons with bodies covered in poorly etched tattoos, the bleeding black ink made from a mixture of burnt wood and spit. They were devils, every last one, each living in a constant state of heightened vigilance. Ready to strike out at the pettiest slight, like wild dogs guarding scraps of food. But Natasha was right: it was those inner demons that gnawed on a man's soul.

Arkadi had asked Natasha, "You really think I can't sit through a thirty-minute interview without killing someone?" He shook his head and chuckled, even as he was needled by self-doubt. Today was different: he was brimming with new-found confidence. The solution came to him as he lay sleepless on the hotel floor before day-break. All he had to do to get through the interview was act subservient. Surely, a former private in the Soviet Army, even one with a record blemished by a few episodes of insubordination, would still remember how to play the part. Outside the confines of the gulag, subservience was the most practical stance when dealing with small men intent on displaying their authority. This, more than anything, he had to keep in mind.

"Mr. Volkov, are you listening?" Mr. Snodgrass said.

Arkadi leaned back in his chair, crossed his legs, nonchalantly licked his thumb and scratched off a white fleck of dust caked on the insole of his black leather ankle boot — a handsome boot just one size too large, as stiff and ill-fitting as the rest of his clothing.

"I'm sorry," Arkadi said, exaggerating his Russian accent. "My English not so good. You can repeat?"

"I said, your dossier has one birth certificate and two death certificates."

Volkov straightened to peer over the desk. "You have my birth certificate?" he said, in an accent approaching Queen's English. "That's smashing

17

good news, old chap. I should very much like a fac-simile if you don't mind." Acting subservient was harder than he thought. He had lost the knack for it.

The embassy man removed his glasses, tossed them onto his desktop and fixed his eyes on Arkadi, shot him a look which was undoubtedly meant to intimidate. Still, Arkadi noticed a slight tremor in the American's shoulders: perhaps a shudder of revulsion.

Arkadi was taken aback by the American's reaction to his outward aspect.

I really must do something about my appearance when I get to America.

Arkadi had always been considered handsome by the fairer sex. Tall, well-built, with piercing eyes and an infectious smile, he might have been a Russian Kevin Costner with the proper acting lessons. Now he felt like a wreck.

The clothes were clearly not the problem, though they did make him look somewhat like a well-dressed scarecrow. The donated items he had received were clean and more than adequate, selected with enough slack in their seams that he might grow into them as he regained his weight. They had been chosen by Miss Natasha with the prudence a grandparent might use when shopping for apparel for a growing child. He especially liked the way the bomber jacket looked, with its cracked brown leather, fake shearling collar, and over-sized brass zipper. Tough-guy fashion. Very American, Arkadi thought. It would suit him well in his new surroundings. But Arkadi was so malnourished that his cheekbones jutted out like those of a wooden marionette. And his teeth and gums were an unmitigated disaster. Miss Natasha impelled him to double his intake of fresh fruit and beseeched him to replace his morning coffee with a glass of unsweetened juice squeezed from Turkish lemons. "I'll drink the juice," Arkadi had countered, "I'll eat the blessed lemons whole if I must, peel and all. But my morning coffee stays."

"I'm glad you find this all very amusing," Mr. Snodgrass said. "Do you care to offer an explanation?"

"Which part?"

"The death certificate."

"Which one?" Volkov asked.

"Let's start with the first one." The American held up a document printed on thick yellowing stock.

"Ah. That must be from March 18,1989."

Henry Snodgrass reached for his reading glasses. "Penal colony number 6, Federal Penitentiary Unit, Orenburg region."

"Better know as the Black Dolphin prison," Arkadi Volkov added. "Are you familiar with it?"

"Cause of death, blunt head injury."

"A prison riot," Arkadi said. "Nasty business."

The American looked up from the document with a scowl. "What were you in for?"

Arkadi Volkov uncrossed his legs and wiped the front of his pants with his palm. "Insubordination. Refusing to follow the order of a superior. But don't worry. It was just a misunderstanding. The Army decided they wanted me back. So I was exonerated. I even got a promotion."

"Why the death certificate?"

Arkadi sighed. "The Black Dolphin has a reputation to uphold."

"Two weeks later, you were promoted to Junior Sergeant of the Soviet Army, and you were assigned to a unit in the Crimea under a different name: Lazarus Orlov. Did you pick the name?"

Arkadi shook his head. "A lieutenant from Odessa did. The only officer in the whole Red Army with a sense of humor. Sadly, he's no longer with us." Arkadi made a cursory sign of the cross.

The American shuffled the papers. "Later, Junior Sergeant Lazarus Orlov dies in an Army prison in Sevastopol, Crimea in December of last year. Cause of death..."

"A broken heart," Arkadi said.

"The death certificate says Typhoid Fever."

Arkadi Volkov shook his head. "He died of a broken heart well before that." It felt natural to refer to his past self in the third person.

The American removed his reading glasses and set them back on his desk. He flashed Volkov a sardonic grin. Volkov smiled back, his palms starting to tingle as blood rushed to the muscles of his hands. The American was pushing his luck. Arkadi wondered if there was a Mrs. Snodgrass at home somewhere, in an embassy apartment; little Snodgrass children with tiny pencil necks in some private Kyiv school, pestering their teachers with a unique brand of congenital insolence. How would they react if they received the dreadful news that Mr. Snodgrass, husband and father, had crashed through the plate glass window of his office somehow?

Subservience, Arkadi reminded himself. It would all be over in a matter of minutes now.

"You don't honestly expect me to process your application, do you, Mr. Volkov? Or is it Orlov? Or have you picked up a new name in the last few weeks since getting out of prison?"

Arkadi Volkov erupted in a fit of laughter. It was a deep, hearty laugh. One of those infectious laughs that bring tears to the eyes. Mr. Henry Snodgrass allowed himself a chuckle.

Arkadi wiped the tears from his cheeks with the back of his hand, sniffed and let out a long sigh. He leaned back in his chair, crossed his legs, and fixed his gaze on the black lacquer telephone sitting on the American's desk.

"Mr. Volkov. Your application for political

asylum, as it stands, is rejected. I suggest you..."

Arkadi Volkov cracked his knuckles so loud that Mr. Snodgrass winced. Arkadi said, "I suggest you sign the papers, Mr. Snodgrass, and seal them with your pretty little stamp. You have a pretty little stamp, don't you? All good bureaucrats do."

"And I suggest you get used to the idea of settling down in Kyiv."

"The Ukrainian government doesn't want me. They will deport me to Russia. And the Russians will kill me."

"You should be used to it by now, Mr. Lazarus. Who knows? You might even get another promotion."

Arkadi Volkov's smile vanished. He redirected his gaze to the black telephone. He stared at it until it rang.

The American picked up the phone. "Snodgrass speaking." The bureaucrat quickly straightened in his chair. "Yes, sir. As a matter of fact . . ." Poor Mr. Snodgrass looked like he was going to be sick all over his desk — purple blotches cropped up on his cheeks, the corner of his left eye twitched rhythmically. "No sir . . . Yes, yes, I understand." Snodgrass kept the telephone receiver pressed to his ear and slowly allowed his gaze to slide over to Volkov. "Absolutely. Yes, sir. Consider it done." He carefully placed the telephone headset back on its cradle.

Arkadi turned and looked out the window. A thin smile returned to his face. One hundred meters. Two hundred tops. There was a break in the clouds which allowed a column of sunlight to shine right through. The change in lighting seemed to aid his depth perception. He probed the gaps between his teeth with the tip of his tongue. Perhaps he could stroll on over to the Bdzhilka Market, pick up more lemons, soon as the interview was over.

"It seems you have friends in high places," Mr. Snodgrass said. Volkov didn't reply. "Your application has been fast-tracked by the ambassador himself."

"See?" Arkadi said. "You get to use your pretty little stamp after all."

The American flipped the manila folder shut emphatically, trying to reassert some sense of authority. "Come back next week. Your paperwork will be ready then."

"I will come for my paperwork tomorrow," Arkadi said. "I have a flight reservation to Houston, Texas, Friday morning."

"Friday the thirteenth," Snodgrass said. "I guess you're not superstitious."

"Arkadi Volkov got to his feet, headed for the door. As he reached for the handle, the American asked him, "Why Texas?"

The Russian turned, pulled up the collar of his jacket, winked at Mr. Snodgrass, and said, "All my exes live in Texas."

CHAPTER THREE

Patricia

19 MAY, 2005 — DALLAS, TEXAS

Just one PowerPoint slide left. Dr. Patricia West took a moment to survey the audience before pressing the advance button on the tiny remote control, which would bring her lecture to its closing remarks. The faces that looked back at her were unreadable. Patricia West couldn't discern if they expressed disagreement, confusion, surprise, apathy, or sheer boredom.

She told herself that at this point, it didn't matter. She had gotten through her lecture without fumbling words, without interjecting the ubiquitous, "Uhm," before each phrase as some speakers do, and without exposing the fine tremor of her hands, which might be misinterpreted as nerves. She wasn't at all anxious. The invitation to speak at the American Society of Pediatrics annual meeting had been a complete surprise, but an event of no consequence, as far as she was concerned. It would have no impact on her middling career. She accepted the invitation merely as a personal challenge, and only because the conference would be in Dallas this year, just a four-hour drive from her home in Central Texas. Tomorrow, she'd be back at her mundane job, sludging through an overbooked appointment schedule consisting in large part of children with runny noses and cough and upset tummies. How the article she had penned, titled, "Unconscious Bias in Medical Diagnosis," which had been published by a relatively obscure medical journal, caught anyone's attention remained a mystery to her.

Patricia West pushed the button of the remote, and the last slide appeared on the screen. She reached toward the podium to deposit the remote on its sleek, laminated surface when her right hand started to shake, the uncontrollable quiver growing in momentum with each pulse of her wrist. Patricia tried to rush the act but released the remote control a moment too soon, bouncing the small appliance off the edge of the podium. She managed to bobble it before snatching it out of the air. She exhaled slowly and finally set it down in a slow, steady two-handed delivery. A low murmur rose from the audience. There was stifled laughter. Someone uttered, "Good catch!"

"In conclusion," Patricia West said, raising her voice a notch, "the diagnostic process is a minefield of cognitive pitfalls. We doctors often fall prey to a wide variety of unconscious biases, which can seduce us into latching onto a diagnosis far too soon and induce us to downplay, ignore, even bend evidence accumulated thereafter to fit our a priori conclusions. Thank you for your attention."

Patricia West stepped back from the microphone and cleared her throat as the gray-haired mediator who had introduced her walked up to the podium, clapping his hands. The man shook Patricia's hand and resumed his applause. He leaned toward the podium.

"Thank you, Dr. West, for introducing us to a most intriguing topic. And a controversial one, to be sure," he said. "Surely, we have some questions for Dr. West? If you'd be so kind as to use one of the microphones. Yes, up here in the front row."

A man in an ill-fitting camel-hair blazer walked to the microphone stand at the front of the center aisle, reached into his trouser pockets with both hands as if he were searching for loose change, and rolled on his feet while maintaining his head steady, like some kind of inverse bobblehead doll. "Dave Lasky," he said, "UCLA." After his introduction, his voice rose an octave. "Forgive me, Dr. West, but you paint a rather grim picture of the current state of medicine as it is being practiced in your estimation. You seem to be implying that we are all a bunch of numskull incompetents at best. And at worst, we're no different from crooked cops that plant evidence to nail down a wrongful conviction."

There was a murmur in the audience. Patricia West re-adjusted the height of the microphone on the podium and thought it best to wait a moment until things settled, but the chatter only grew louder. Before she had a chance to provide her rebuttal, there was a loud tapping of one of the hallway microphones, followed by ear-splitting amplifier feedback.

"Begging your pardon," a silky voice with a lilting drawl chimed in. "Oliver Flynn, Austin Children's Hospital. That's Austin, not Boston, as you might have inferred from the accent." The room broke out in laughter.

The speaker was a man dressed in an impeccably tailored white suit with a teal bow-tie and matching pocket square. He seemed to be in his late fifties or early sixties but sported a mischievous boyish mien, accentuated by the wispy bang of thin blond hair that drooped over his forehead. "If I might take the liberty of rephrasing the question from my esteemed colleague from California, in words a fellow Texan might appreciate-"

"It wasn't a question," Dave Lasky from

UCLA said. "It was an observation. A statement of fact."

"Okay, then. You observed. You stated. Looks to me like you're done," Oliver Flynn said. "Take a load off, cowboy." Oliver Flynn redirected his attention to Patricia West. He smiled, flicked his head to jostle the hair from his brow. "Now, Dr. West, if, as you say, we are all liable to being boondoggled by these biases, and if cognitive mishaps are inevitable, well what in tarnation is a good doctor to do? What should we teach our students and residents?"

Patricia West nodded. The question was a fastball right down the middle of home plate. All she had to do was swing hard and hit it out of the park. "We can start by using an explicit process of metacognition, that is, we have to think about how we are thinking."

Patricia West was wheeling her suitcase toward the main exit of the convention center when a voice called out to her. "Dr. West? Oh, Dr. We-est!" Patricia turned to see Oliver Flynn ambling toward her, a broad white felt hat riding askew on his crown, a mauve umbrella with stitched leather handle drooping from his forearm. He was carrying a monogrammed leather satchel that seemed to belong to a more genteel era.

"Hell of a talk you gave back there," Flynn said.

"Way to stand up to the slings and arrows."

"I had a little help," Patricia said. "Thanks."

"You stood your ground. You were simply fabulous," Oliver Flynn said. He reached out his hand, "Oliver Flynn."

Patricia shook his hand. "I know who you are, Dr. Flynn. You're the chairman of Pediatrics at Austin Children's."

"And I know who you are, Dr. West. Still down in New Braunfels, are you?"

If Patricia showed any sign of perplexity, Oliver Flynn ignored it. "Yes sir, I am," she said, wondering how the chairman from Austin knew where she lived and practiced.

"Heading out to DFW?"

"Actually, I'm heading to the parking lot. I drove to the conference."

"Is that a fact?" Flynn said. "Driving back to New Braunfels, are you?"

"Yes, sir."

"You'll hit Austin right around evening rush hour. I-35 will be like molasses."

"I'm not in too much of a hurry," Patricia said.

"Well, that's good to hear," Flynn said, "Because I'm in a bit of a bind. You see, I was booked on a ten am flight to Austin this morning, but I decided to stick around to hear a lecture on cognitive biases in diagnosis. Don't get me wrong: the talk was worth the price of admission, but now I have to go on standby." Oliver Flynn closed his eyes and shook his head in horror. "Lord knows when I'll get home tonight."

There was a moment's hesitation. Then Patricia said, "I'm driving through Austin. I can give you a lift."

Oliver Flynn jutted his chin. His eyes brightened. "Now, that's a swell idea. I'd be mighty obliged."

And Patricia West immediately got the sense she had been taken in.

They were on the I-35 overpass crossing the Trinity River when Oliver Flynn said, "Remember how I told you I was in a bit of a bind?"

Patricia glanced over at her passenger. He smelled nice. Patricia couldn't be sure, but she thought the scent was Chanel number 5. Dr. Flynn looked pensive, but Patricia couldn't help but think that every facial expression the man adopted now involved a touch of burlesque.

"You mean, how you missed your plane?" Patricia said.

"Oh no, no, no," Oliver Flynn said. The man let out a protracted sigh, shook his head. "No, the problem I have, you see, is that we have Grand Rounds on Monday, and our invited speaker, a heavy-weight from Cincinnati — I'm not going to mention her name — dropped out with less than one week's notice. Left us flapping in the breeze in our long-johns. Damn shame if you ask me."

"What are you going to do?" Patricia asked, out of politeness.

"Well, I'm going to have to scramble to find a replacement. Lord only knows how I'll be able to pull that off on such short notice. Ah, it's hopeless."

"I'm sure one of your faculty can rustle up a talk." Rustle up? When did Patricia West ever use that expression? Was she altering her speech as a way of expressing empathy or simply to ingratiate herself with the man? It was yet another manifestation of cognitive bias exposed. She'd have to note it down for future reference.

Flynn seemed to ignore the comment altogether. A moment later, he snapped his fingers and widened his eyes as though an idea had just dawned on him. "I know. Why didn't I think of this sooner! *You* can give the talk. The very same talk you gave today. Don't need to change a single syllable."

Patricia West had the distinct impression she was being hood-winked. That Flynn had, in fact, planned this escapade all along.

"What do you say, partner?" Flynn said.

"I'm supposed to go on vacation next week," Patricia said.

"Where to?" Flynn asked.

"Aransas Pass." It was only a half-lie. In truth, Patricia's plan was to drop off her son, Alex, with her parents at their beach house for a week of fishing, boating, and swimming. She planned to retreat to her home, do some much-needed house cleaning, drink Earl Grey tea by the pint, and curl up with Jane Austen in the evenings. Traditional vacations did not agree with Patricia West.

"Aransas Pass? Well, that's just a hop, skip, and a jump away. Our Grand Rounds is at noon. You can be waist-high in Gulf waters, sipping banana daiquiris before sunset. You like banana daiquiris?"

Patricia chuckled at the way Flynn put it.

"Now, how does that sound?" Flynn asked.

"It's just a little sudden — unexpected."

"How long are you going to be down there? A week? Two weeks?" Flynn said. "Dr. West, I'm not embarrassed to say that Austin Children's budget is wholesome enough to permit us to shell out what I think is a downright lavish honorarium for our speakers. None of this freebie stuff like the American Society for Pediatrics. This little Grand Rounds will cover all your vacation expenses in Aransas Pass and then some. Besides, you've already done all the grunt work for the speech. And just between you and me, it would be a real satisfaction to see our little dollars take residence right here in Texas rather than fly all the way to Cincinnati, Ohio."

"Thanks, but it's not that."

"Then what is it?" Flynn said. "Ah, I get it. You have to check with your significant other.

Understood." Flynn winked and crossed his arms.

Patricia changed lanes to pass a slow-moving truck billowing out black exhaust. A minute later, she said, "Noon, you said?"

"Twelve o'clock," Flynn said. "Two-thousand dollars plus meals and travel expenses."

Patricia waited for a beat as if she had to think about it. "Yeah, okay. I'll do it."

"Well, hot damn!" Flynn said. "I'm glad we got that out of the way. Now we can get down to brass tacks."

"There's more?"

"First, I want to come clean with you. I didn't miss my flight. My flight was scheduled for the afternoon. Heck, the only reason I came to the conference was to listen to your talk."

"So you're stalking me," Patricia said.

"My darling, you're not exactly my type — surely you've figured that out by now — but you're damn right I'm stalking you." Flynn glanced at his wristwatch. "I figure I have about two hours and forty-five minutes before you jettison my achy bones at the lonely doorstep of my small but tastefully decorated home. That's less than three hours to convince you to accept the position of residency program director at Austin Children's Hospital.

Patricia chuckled. "This is a joke, right?"

Flynn held up three fingers in salute. "Scout's honor."

"I'm just a clinician. A run-of-the-mill general pediatrician," Patricia said. "I have no experience in academics."

"Five articles published in academic journals in the last two years? Could have fooled me. Yeah, I read them all. Also read your book, *Bedside Manners*. You might say I've been following your career in earnest for some time now."

"So you're the one that bought my book," Patricia said.

Flynn smiled. He said, "Check your royalty report at the end of the quarter. I ordered a hundred more copies direct from your publisher to distribute to faculty and residents. It has officially become required reading as of last week."

"I just don't understand."

Flynn started rubbing the cuticles of his manicured hands. "Since coming to Austin Children's three years ago, I've been shaking up the joint pretty well."

"Word is you've done a remarkable job," Patricia said.

"We're growing by leaps and bounds," Flynn said. "But growth has its perils. Medicine is a hazardous profession, and doctors in training are a special kind of menace. Tell you the truth, the interns don't worry me so much. Sure, they're ignorant, but they know they are. That keeps them cautious. But that steep learning curve betrays them. At some point in their second year of residency, they've learned so much they start to think they know it all. That's when they become dangerous. By their third year, most of them have committed a few harrowing missteps that bring their feet back to the ground. The sensible ones will learn to accept and even embrace their mediocrity."

"Are you saying you consider all the residents in your program mediocre?" Patricia West said.

"All great apes of the biped variety are, Dr. West, regardless of career choice. Human genius is a rare commodity, indeed."

"And your solution is?"

"Smooth out the process. Get the poor sods to recognize their limitations sooner. Help them settle into a sustainable level of mediocrity."

Patricia West scoffed. "I see. And that's why you're interested in hiring me. I happen to embody that sustainable level of mediocrity you want your residents to aspire to. That's a hell of a sales pitch!"

Flynn smiled. "Well, I'm glad I'm hooking you," he said. "Look, I'm not going to wheedle you, Dr. West. That's just not my style. Please, don't misunderstand me. I think there's nothing wrong with mediocrity. It does not preclude the occasional flash of brilliance when a particularly challenging situation presents itself. The beauty of humanity lies in the fact that ordinary mortals are

capable of heroic acts. There are many perils to
being chairman of a growing program, the worst
one being to appoint the wrong people to
positions that matter. Luckily, I have a bit of a
knack for spotting character. I'd like you to be part
of our leadership team."

"You don't even know me."

In a somber voice, Dr. Flynn said, "I know you.
I know you fair enough. Don't worry, I won't fall
for the cognitive pitfall of assuming you are warm
and tender and agreeable because you have
beautiful pale blue eyes that remind me of my
dear aunt Sophie. I know you through your
writing, which is as good a way of knowing
someone that I've ever come across." He shifted
his weight in his seat and said,

"There are going to be people from the hospital
board coming to listen to your Grand Rounds
talk. Think of it as a kind of dress rehearsal. Show
them what you showed me at your lecture today,
and you're home free."

"Dr. Flynn," Patricia said.

"You can call me Oliver."

"Dr. Flynn, I think you're getting ahead of
yourself."

Flynn rolled his shoulders. "Patricia, the last
thing you want is to put up with me jabbing for
two and a half more hours trying to talk you into
it. Take the damn job. You'll be glad you did." He
waited for a beat before adding, "It will help fill

that void."

CHAPTER FOUR

Jamie Lee

Jamie Lee Foster was leaning over the
bathroom sink brushing her left upper molars
when the doorbell rang. Sunday morning, it had
to be those annoying church folk making their
rounds through the neighborhood. The "NO
SOLICITING" sticker she had taped to the
window of the front doorway had already been
peeled off twice, no doubt by one of the more
zealous members of the congregation. She could
kick herself for neglecting to tape on a new sign.

Jamie Lee didn't budge. The last thing she
wanted to do on her day off was to wrangle with
someone who had the pluck to judge what was
best for her soul. Besides, she had eighteen more
strokes to go on the outer surface of those left
upper molars, counting them down now, the
toothbrush at a steady 45-degree angle to the
gums.

She got to the end of the set and stopped brushing. With toothpaste still in her mouth, she straightened her shoulders and admired her reflection in the mirror. She turned slightly and flexed her abs. Pink lace bra, black straight-leg rayon trousers, nine-millimeter Glock riding high in the holster of her right hip — she liked the way she looked.

The doorbell rang a second time. Jamie Lee wondered if she should traipse over to the front door just like she was, shirtless. Maybe she could even shed her trousers. Clip her Glock on a lace garter, open the door in her skivvies, and her pink silk robe, which only reached mid-thigh. Slip on some high heeled stilettos, while she was at it, to make her bare legs look just a little longer. It'd be worth doing just to see the look on the faces of those darn church people. Except it might not go down too well with the chief if word got back to headquarters, which it always did whenever she did something half-witted.

Trouble always seemed to have a way to find her, even when she wasn't trying too hard. It had been that way for as long as she remembered. Ma used to call her a congenital rabble-rouser. Pa would just smile and say she was her little firecracker.

Now Pa knew how to handle church folk. One morning, she must have been eleven or twelve, she was sitting on the cedar boards of the front porch with her father. Jamie Lee was whittling away at a beautiful piece of basswood, Pa sitting on his favorite Shaker rocker, the ash gathering on the Winston hanging from the corner of his mouth. A gaggle of parishioners walked up the buckled concrete path — Pentecostals preaching the gospel of health and wealth. The prophets of profit, Pa called them. The leader was a tall lady, all bones and joints wrapped up in a lavender skirt with a matching tweed blazer, a yellow hat that looked like an upside-down fruit bowl pushed down on her head.

After introducing herself and her two minions, she came right down to business. The woman asked Pa, "Sir, if you don't mind me asking, how much do you smoke?"

"Just about enough, I reckon," Pa said.

"How much is enough?"

"Two packs a day," Pa said. "Most days, three."

"And how much does that set you back?" the woman asked.

"A buck and a quarter."

"Each pack?"

Pa nodded. "Uh-huh."

The lady flashed an I-thought-so glare at him, rummaged through her handbag, and fished out an electronic calculator, one with over-sized keys which she probably got in the mail as a gift for ordering a magazine subscription.

She said, "Let's see, three packs a day, that's

three dollars seventy-five, times thirty makes one-hundred and twelve dollars and fifty cents each month."

"Sounds about right," Pa said.

"In one year that comes out to ..." The woman's jaw dropped, her eyes bugged out. "Why, that's one-thousand three-hundred and fifty each year."

Pa shifted in his seat. "Is that so?"

"Sir, how long you been smoking?" She was getting worked up now. Let a twang creep into her speech.

"Going on thirty years," Pa said.

The woman went back to tapping on her calculator. "Without adjusting for price fluctuations and inflation, that means you've smoked yourself out of — sweet word! More than forty-thousand dollars over the course of your life."

Pa grunted and leaned forward, squinted his eyes in feigned curiosity. "Them numbers sure add up fast, don't they?" he said.

The woman said, "Had you invested that money in a diversified portfolio, with the power of compounding interest over thirty years, why, you could have bought yourself a little aeroplane by now!"

Pa leaned back, took a last deep drag of his cigarette, and squeezed the stub out on the worn leather sole of his boot. He said, "Ma'am, have you ever smoked?"

"Not a single stinking puff in my entire life," the churchwoman replied in an indignant tone.

"Is that so?" Pa said. "So lady, tell me something, where's *your* aeroplane?"

The doorbell rang yet again. Jamie Lee rinsed her mouth, slipped on a blouse, and yelled, "Hold your horses!" as she walked across her living room, still buttoning up, trying to subdue an impish grin.

Turned out, it wasn't church people after all. Her across-the-street neighbor, Olga, was standing on her doorstep looking sheepish, a cardboard shipping box in her arms.

"Miss Olga," Jamie Lee said in surprise.

"Good morning, detective. Sorry to intrude."

"Something the matter?"

Olga straightened her shoulders. "I am moving," she said. She was trying hard to sound cheerful.

"Oh," Jamie Lee said. "Where to?"

A blank look fell on the woman's face, as though she hadn't expected the question or even considered the matter. "South," she replied.

"Is this sudden?"

Olga chuckled, but it seemed a little prod might tip her over into tears. "Very sudden, but a long time coming." To Jamie Lee, the phrase rang a dissonant note: an American idiom pronounced with a distinct Russian accent — it came off sounding like a classically trained musician playing the banjo.

"Here," Olga said. She raised the cardboard box. "This is for you."

"For me? What is it?"

"I can't take it with me," Olga said. "I would like for you to keep it."

Olga flipped back one of the cardboard flaps. Jamie Lee peered inside. It was filled with small, framed religious icons painted in oil and gold leaf.

Jamie Lee said, "Miss Olga, they're beautiful, but I can't take these from you."

"Please."

"They look like they're precious."

"More than you can imagine," Olga said.

"The thing is, I'm not exactly devout. Isn't there someone else-"

"I trust them in your hands." There was a determined, solemn look in the woman's eyes. "And maybe one day you will look at them in different light, yes?"

Jamie Lee studied the pained expression of her neighbor's face. "Olga, is something the matter?"

Olga pursed her lips, shook her head as if trying to rid herself of a yearning, perhaps the urge to say something she might regret. "I liked it here so very much. This neighborhood, it was home. And such nice neighbors."

In the last four years, Olga and Jamie Lee had spoken maybe half a dozen times, and now the lady was entrusting her to safeguard a box of heirlooms while remarking on the virtues of their neighbors, all of whom she apparently trusted even less.

Jamie Lee said, "If something was the matter, if something was not quite right, you would tell me, right?"

"Of course, my dear. You are detective woman."

Olga gently lay the box in Jamie Lee's hands and started walking away. She stopped, turned, and said, "I hope one day, please God, you will look at the pictures in different light."

CHAPTER FIVE

Alex

Leave it to Alex West to be late for the first time on the last day of school. On most school mornings he'd be waiting for Patricia to pick him up, sitting on an Adirondack on the front porch. Today, when Patricia pulled up to the curb in front of her ex-husband's house, he wasn't there. She'd have to wait. Honking her car horn might provoke Marcus into a confrontation. Ringing the doorbell might have even less pleasant consequences.

The shared custody agreement had been a sham right from the start. Marcus had insisted on it just to spite Patricia. She went along with it, trying to appease him, thinking that it might open the way to a more conciliatory relationship. But of course, it didn't. What would happen if she really did take the job in Austin? She wasn't seriously considering it, now, was she?

Patricia West slipped the gear-shifter in park and leaned her head back on the head rest of the driver's seat, eyes closed, listening to the idle of the car engine. She began to focus on her breathing, trying to clear her mind, if only for a couple of minutes. The ringing in her ears had grown louder over the past few days, and this morning that annoying fluttering of the left upper eyelid was back. But her hands were steady. She gripped the steering wheel firmly to validate this last fact, and rubbed her left thumb over the spot where Marcus, had managed to dig his nail into the leather covering one week after purchasing the car for her. She liked the feel of the gouge. It's presence somehow comforted her, provided a feeble sense of permanence. She sometimes wondered if it qualified for what the Japanese called Wabi-Sabi: the world view where imperfection was at the heart of beauty.

Patricia opened her eyes, growing a tad impatient, and turned to look at the shiny new car parked in Marcus's driveway — a snazzy, red little Audi convertible with temporary plates. Marcus West loved his toys, even as he bitched about how he was never earning enough money, *and don't for a minute think I'm paying for Alex's college tuition.* Marcus West had paid his own way at A&M working two part-time jobs. The hero.

When Patricia had told him over the phone that she'd been invited to give grand rounds in Austin on Monday, he replied, "Great. Now you expect me to drive Alex all the way to the coast."

"Relax," Patricia said. "I'll drive him down in the evening after I'm done." The way the conversation was going, she didn't see the need to let him know about the job offer. It was all pie-in-the-sky anyway.

"I'll just do it, so you don't have to gripe to your little lawyer friend," Marcus said before hanging up on her.

A fan from somewhere under the hood came to life making Patricia flinch. She looked at the orange dial on the dashboard. It read 7:45. She craned her head to look at the front door. No sign of her son. He was really pushing it, now. She tapped tentatively on the horn once, not hard enough to make a sound. Then a second time. This time the horn blared, louder than she had hoped. Right on cue, the passenger door of the car flung open, Alex hopped in and shut the door.

"What are you honking the horn for?" Alex said. He spoke in an even tone, as though the question was merely to satisfy his curiosity. It was rare for Alex to expose any annoyance, or other emotion, for that matter, when speaking to his mother.

"Where were you?" Patricia asked.

"Hail to your grace!" Alex answered. "I was in the garage."

The greeting Alex selected was from King Lear.

Patricia and her son had worked out a secret language, based on greetings from Shakespeare plays, to communicate not just their hellos, but an assessment of the situation they were in. *Mistress, what cheer?* (The Taming of the Shrew) was Alex's way of signaling he was bored, without sounding rude to potential hosts. *Bless thee, bully doctor* (The Merry Wives of Windsor) meant that he wished to be left alone. *Good even, Audrey* (As You Like It) meant all was well whereas *Peace be to France* (King John) meant something was wrong. And *Welcome to Rome* (Antony and Cleopatra) signified imminent danger. Time to leave, fast! They had never had to exchange that greeting, but Alex insisted it should be included in their repertory. *Hail to your grace,* the words Alex had greeted her with this morning, meant, "Mom, you're being bossy." Patricia was obligated to answer with the appropriate retort to acknowledge that she got the message before the conversation could proceed.

"*I am glad to see your Highness,*" she said. "What were you doing in the garage?"

"Coming out to the car."

"You always come through the front door."

"What's the difference?"

"You're going to be late for school," Patricia said.

"Then what are you waiting for?"

Patricia reached over to smooth out a tuft of unruly hair that dangled over the boy's brow. He turned away from her. "Let's go, already."

She sighed, slid the gear shifter to drive and eased away from the curb. Drove to the end of the street and turned right past the front yard of a German cottage where, on a wooden swing hanging from the blackened branch of a gnarly oak, sat a stained cloth doll with yellow bows in its hair, its terrifying painted eyes gazing absently at the sky. The sight always made Patricia shudder.

"Late on your last day of school ..." Patricia said.

"They don't give perfect attendance ribbons in high school, mom," Alex said, with no malice in his voice, no intention of disrespect, in that humdrum sober tone which was his trademark.

"Well, you survived your first year of high-school!" Patricia said.

Alex turned to her with a puzzled expression. "You thought I might die?"

"It's just an expression, silly," Patricia said, wishing she hadn't picked those words. She remained quiet as she maneuvered the car down the hill and reached the highway.

"Dad got a new car?" Patricia asked.

Alex shook his head. "New girlfriend."

"Oh. What happened to Jenny?"

"Jinny." Alex corrected her. Then shrugged.

"What's this new one like?"

Alex said, "She wears leopard-skin thong

underwear."

"Alex! How would you know?"

"I found a pair between the sofa cushions."

"Oh jeez, honey! I'm sorry about that."

"I don't care."

But Patricia knew things like that affected her son, affected him deeply, if only by shoveling more rubble on the heap of confusion that was his pubescent mind. She understood now that Alex sneaked out the garage door only to avoid the embarrassment of coming face to face with the owner of those roving panties.

"Hey, mom," Alex said. "You know those people in the commercials?"

"What commercials?"

"You know, commercials on TV — all those people in commercials. You know how they're all happy all the time? Are people really happy like that? I mean, in real life. Like they buy a new car, right? Or life insurance, or whatever, and now they're all chill and happy and popular." He was smiling, becoming animated, as if he had really put his finger on something.

"The drug commercials are the worst," Patricia said. "They always start with some fake patient who can barely get around because he's got some dreadful disease, something chronic and pernicious. But as soon as his impossibly attractive doctor prescribes this new medicine, guess what? He's meeting beautiful people at a fancy cafe', all smiles and looking oh-so-confident. Next scene, he's sitting at a bonfire on the beach with his girlfriend, and a bunch of cool friends are dancing around them, doing the limbo, and they all roll with laughter. As if all he ever needed for health, fulfillment and joy was a stupid little pill."

"It's all fake, huh?" Alex said.

"It's how commercials work. They have to create this false sense of need, this itch that only their product can scratch. And they try to convince you that only after you purchase their product will you attain happiness and tranquility, in a beautiful home with loving friends and family. The truth is, what people really need to be happy in the first place are those loving friends and family; not a new car, or a new life insurance policy, or a pill from a sharply dressed doctor in a fancy modern office."

"Yeah. I thought that was all fake." Alex was looking at the highway up ahead. "There's no pill that will make you fit in." Before Patricia could reply, he said, "What about the cool kids in school? Are they as happy as they look or is that fake too?"

A lump rose in Patricia's throat. She wanted to reach over and grasp her son in a bear hug. Most days, it was his reticence, his detachment she found unnerving, but then she'd catch a glimpse of the silent sorrow lurking in the deep, cold waters of his soul, and it made her feel so helpless, so inadequate as a parent. She managed to answer in a stolid voice. "No. Most of those kids are deeply unhappy."

"They're actors? Like the people in commercials?" Alex said.

"That's right."

"I thought so," Alex said.

They drove about a mile without saying a word. Then Alex asked, "Mom, you remember what the weather was like the day I was born?"

Patricia could feel her face grow flush. "Where did that come from?"

"I was just wondering," Alex said.

"Yeah. It was a beautiful sunny day."

"Are you sure?"

"Of course I'm sure." Patricia let out a nervous laugh.

"But how can you be one hundred percent sure?"

"Because I remember driving to the hospital and there wasn't a cloud ... Alex, it was the day you were born. You think I'd forget?" Patricia said with a strained smile.

"Did you know Carson Taggart was adopted?" The smile faded from Patricia's face. "He told me so. He was adopted. From some other country, Russia or something."

"Carson is one of my patients," Patricia said. "You know I can't discuss confidential information."

"Yeah," Alex said. "I figured you already knew, just never told me."

Patricia pulled into the parking lot of South Lake High School, stopped at the curb. Alex hopped out of the car, turned and poked his head back in.

He said, "Don't worry about me surviving my last day of school, Mom. *Good even, Audrey.*" *All is well*, Alex passed on in code.

Patricia blew him a kiss and provided the only acceptable reply, "*God ye good even, William.*"

CHAPTER SIX

Kyle

The rusty Ford F-150 gunned through the intersection north to south an instant after the traffic light turned red. Comal County Sheriff's Deputy Bobby Briggs was behind the wheel of the cruiser, which was idling in the westbound lane. His partner, Kyle Wagner, was riding shotgun.

"D'ya see that?" Bobby Briggs said.

"Mm-hmm."

Bobby Briggs reached for the dashboard switch box with the toggles for the siren and flashers, but Kyle Wagner caught his wrist.

"Let this one go," Kyle said.

"But that was blatant!" Bobby Briggs said as if the traffic infraction had been a personal affront.

"We got a warrant to serve," Kyle said.

Bobby Briggs put his hand back on the steering wheel, accelerated through the intersection smoothly. "Damn right, we do," he said. He kept glancing at Kyle, smiling, like a damn schoolboy with a secret."

"Okay, what is it?" Kyle Wagner said.

"I was wondering, wanted to hear your opinion on the matter. You think Lee Harvey Oswald was able to fire off three shots in five-point-six seconds with a crummy bolt-action Carcano?"

Kyle nodded. He hated talking conspiracy theory crap. It never ended. "I don't see why not."

"Course, you wouldn't have needed three shots. Ain't that right? What's the motto in sniper training? One shot, one kill?"

Kyle Wagner didn't reply.

"You think you still got it?" Bobby Briggs prodded.

"Got what?"

"You know, the ability to hit a target a thousand yards away on the first try."

Wagner looked out the passenger window.

"I don't see why not," Bobby Briggs persisted. "Once a HOG, always a HOG."

"I'm not a Hunter of Gunmen anymore. I'm not a sniper."

"Then why you still wear that bullet around your neck. That's your HOG's Tooth, ain't it? Kind of a graduation present? You know what I say? I say, once a sniper, always a sniper."

There were some things Bobby Briggs would never understand. For example, he couldn't understand that Kyle Wagner couldn't just

remove that necklace as if it were a store-bought
charm. And it wasn't for sentimental reasons. It
would have been tempting fate. Every Marine
sniper has a bullet with his name on it — the
round destined to end his life. As long as Kyle
wore that bullet around his neck, the one that had
his name on it, he would be invincible. Or so went
sniper lore. And there was no use telling Bobby
that what dangled on his chain was not the 7.62 x
51 millimeter NATO-issued round he had
received on graduating sniper school, but a 7N1
load he had removed from the chamber of a
Dragunov rifle. A Russian-made weapon that had
belonged to an Iraqi Army sniper Kyle managed
to kill after playing cat-and-mouse for the better
part of a morning on February 27, 1991, in the
terminal of the Kuwait International Airport. This
was indeed the round which would have killed
him: the bullet with the name, "Kyle Wagner"
written on it. Even now, removing it from his neck
was sure to bring bad karma.

"Maybe, we'll get to see," Bobby Briggs said.

"See what?"

"I brought my hunting rifle with me. A
Browning BAR with a 4X scope."

"It's not hunting season, Bobby."

"Just thinking, if old man McClish decides to
get slippery when we serve him-"

"What? We shoot him?"

"He's caused trouble before. Doesn't hurt to

have some artillery."

"Bobby, just drive."

The radio crackled. "Unit 51. State your location, please."

Kyle Wagner picked up the transceiver. "Unit 51 here. We're on highway 2673, westbound approaching South Access, over."

"Kyle?" The dispatcher's voice was shaky.

"What's the matter, Helen?"

"There's an active shooter situation at South Lake High School. You're the closest unit."

Kyle flipped the lights and siren on. "How many shooters is that?"

"We can't be sure. But it looks like there's hostages locked up in the gym."

"Okay, we're on it, Helen." He pointed at the intersection they were approaching. "Turn right at the light."

"I heard her," Bobby said.

"That hunting rifle of yours is loaded?" Kyle asked.

"So now you're glad I brought it."

CHAPTER SEVEN

Dr. West

"What you're telling me is that you're not going to do nothing for my baby."

Patricia West forced herself to smile. "Of course we'll help your child. All I'm saying is David does not need antibiotics. He's got a cold, a viral upper respiratory infection. I'd like to go over some things you can do at home to-"

"This here cough always turns to bronchitis. You should know that. It's in his record."

It was a heck of a way to start the day. But it was the last day at the office before her vacation. She wouldn't let Mrs. Becker ruffle her feathers.

"If there's any sign he's not getting better," Patricia said, "or if anything changes in the coming days, we'll be more than happy to re-evaluate things."

"I'm not going to waste my time and come back down here so you can charge me another copay. I know my child. I'm his mother. He needs an antibiotic." The woman was becoming increasingly agitated, acting as if her civil rights were being infringed upon.

Patricia pressed her lips together and nodded. "Okay, I'll tell you what-"

"And don't give me none of that pink stuff. My child's resistant to it. He needs a shot. Dr. Perkins always gave him a shot."

Dr. Harry Perkins, that grinning dunderhead who retired not a day too soon. Unfortunately, there were still many physicians like him in private practice: hand-holding mountebanks who distorted standards of care and skewed patient expectations.

There was a knock on the door of the exam room. With any luck, it was Flora, her nurse, coming to rescue her. The door opened before Patricia could say, "Come in."

To Patricia's surprise, it was Myrna, the office manager. She looked stunned, bewildered.

"I'm sorry, Dr. West," Myrna said. "There's an emergency. We need you right away."

Patricia got to her feet, excused herself with Mrs. Becker, and stepped out of the room.

Myrna grabbed her by her lab coat sleeve, pulled her a few feet down the corridor before turning to face her. "Okay, Dr. West. Now try to stay calm."

"Jesus, Myrna, what the hell is going on?"

"I just got off the phone with Dr. Fisher in the emergency room. He said they were notified by the Sheriff's department that there's a school shooting in progress." She paused, nodded once. "At South Lake High."

"Oh my God! Alex!"

"Now, there are no confirmed fatalities-"

"I've gotta go," Patricia said, peeling off her lab coat.

"Where? You can't go there."

"Where's the crash kit?"

"Dr. West ..."

"There might be some injured kids. We're the closest medical office. I can help."

"Paramedic crews are already on their way."

Patricia jogged up the hall, tossed her lab coat on the counter of the nurse's station, and flung open the cabinet doors where a gray plastic suitcase holding emergency supplies was stowed. "So am I."

CHAPTER EIGHT

Carson

The assistant principal, a Navy veteran, it would turn out, was waiting for the Sheriff cruiser to arrive in the parking lot by the gym, completely exposed, clinging to a walkie-talkie. Bobby Briggs and Kyle Wagner hopped out of the vehicle as it was still recoiling from the jolt of the sudden stop. Bobby pulled out his side-arm as Kyle ran to the rear of the vehicle to retrieve the hunting rifle. There was a box of ammunition on the trunk floor. Kyle ripped it open, grabbed a handful of cartridges, and stuffed them in his pocket.

Mr. Doherty, the assistant principal, jogged over to Bobby. "He's barricaded himself inside the gym. The front door is locked. The rear of the building has a fire door that can only be opened from the inside.

Bobby said, "You said, 'he.' Is there only one shooter?"

"Best we can tell," Doherty said.

"A student?"

"I'm afraid so. Strangest things, the shots are spaced out — only one at a time. As if the shooter is ..."

"Executing them," Bobby added.

"Three shots so far," Doherty said. "There are about a dozen kids in there. If we don't hurry ..."

Kyle Wagner walked up to the two men, rifle in hand. "Is there any other way to access the building? Windows? Skylights?"

"There are domed skylights on the rooftop."

"How do I get up on the roof?" Kyle asked.

"There's a metal access ladder on the back of the building."

"How about the other buildings?"

"They're in lock-down," Doherty said.

"What's your name?" Kyle asked the assistant principal. "Doherty. John Doherty."

"John, I want you to position yourself at the front of the building, behind some cover. If any kids start running out that front door, you direct them toward the parking lot. Bobby, you'll take the back door. I'm going up on the roof."

The hollow sound of a gunshot rang out.

"Jesus!" Kyle said. "Let's go."

Kyle and Bobby ran to the back of the gym, a boxy two-story white stucco affair. Kyle strapped the rifle on his back and started climbing the ladder. Bobby grabbed his pant leg.

"Kyle, what do I do if the shooter comes out?"
Kyle said, "He won't be coming out."

There were three domed skylights on the roof.
They were made of tinted Plexiglass, their
aluminum frames bonded to a stucco-covered
raised frame with what looked like layer upon
layer of tar. There was no way to jar the covers
open. Kyle peered in through the first skylight. He
counted ten kids, sitting on the floor of the gym,
all in matching t-shirts and shorts, their backs
pressed against the bleachers. A single boy was
kneeling at mid-court, hands behind his back, his
head lowered in a posture of submission. The
shooter, who was the only boy dressed in street
clothes, paced around the kneeling boy,
occasionally flailing his handgun in the air. At the
free-throw line lay the bodies of three boys, side
by side, on their backs. One might have thought
they were taking a nap were it not for the dark
pool of blood that spread over the parquet floor
from beneath them.

The shooter seemed to be lecturing the boy at
mid-court. No, Kyle decided; he was holding
court, like some self-appointed judge. Soon, a
verdict would be reached. And the sentence he
would issue was sure to be death. Kyle had to act
fast.

He grabbed Bobby's rifle by the barrel, hoisted
it over his head, and slammed it down onto the

skylight, smashing it to bits. He took cover just as gunfire erupted from below.

Kyle waited for the shots to finish. He shouted, "This is the Sheriff's department. Drop your weapon and lay face down on the floor."

A screeching voice responded, "I'm not finished! Justice has not been carried out!" There was a bone-chilling rage in the boy's voice. He sounded possessed.

"Son, it's over!" Kyle shouted. "Drop the gun." He jogged over to the second skylight, stood back a couple of feet so that he could look inside without the shooter noticing him. The shooter hadn't moved much. He was still standing over the boy kneeling at center-court. He was just a kid, for crying out loud, in blue jeans and an over-sized canary yellow t-shirt, his baseball cap worn backward.

The kid with the gun shouted, "Where was the police when justice was needed? Where were you?" Kyle placed the rifle on his shoulder, sighted his target through the Plexiglass, and waited. He whispered, "Come on, kid. Put the gun down."

"This is your fault!" the shooter yelled. "You could have let this cup pass me by. Now it's too late. This trial is over. We, the jury, find Tommy Feldman guilty as charged." The shooter turned and pointed his pistol at the kneeling boy's head.

Kyle Wagner pulled the trigger. The round

went through the Plexiglass and found its mark between the boy's eyes. The boy with the gun fell to the ground, lifeless.

There was silence, as if the world were too stunned to take its next breath. Then the children inside the gym, the survivors, got to their feet and stampeded for the back exit.

Bobby Briggs had the good sense to have each kid lay face down on the moist lawn behind the gym as Kyle made his way down the metal staircase. The last kid to come out appeared to be unhurried. He seemed remarkably calm and had the good sense to keep the back door open until Kyle was able to secure it so that it wouldn't shut.

"I'm going to have to frisk you, son," Kyle said to this boy.

"Sure."

Kyle found no weapon, didn't really expect to, but something was unsettling about this kid. Maybe he was in shock.

"Are you okay, kid?" Kyle asked him.

"I'm fine. The shooter wasn't after me," the boy said. "He was only after the guys that killed Ashley Watson."

"Say again?"

"This girl Ashley killed herself last week. She was bullied to death. He only went after those boys. The rest of us were supposed to be witnesses."

"Did you know him, the shooter?"

The boy nodded. "He's a patient of my mother. She's a pediatrician. His name was Carson Taggart."

"What's your name?"

"Alex. Alex West."

"Alex, do me a favor. Stay right here, okay?"

Alex nodded.

Kyle entered the gym. Back in the Marines, a Lieutenant Colonel had once told him, as a compliment, that he had a real gift for killing, even called it a blessing from heaven. For Kyle, it was a hard position to accept that the most exceptional talent he had been able to develop was that of murder from afar. Now he would force himself to witness the devastation he had wrought, sear the image in his memory and carry this burden for the rest of his days. It was, at best, a shoddy act of penance.

He walked up to the lifeless body of Carson Taggart, knelt down, used his fingers to pull the boy's lids over his vacant eyes. *What a waste!*

He had talked to old-timers, snipers from Vietnam who had pulled the trigger on child soldiers, kids only thirteen or fourteen. And that was war. Those guys came back stateside and were never the same. How could they be?

Kyle unfastened the top button of his shirt, grabbed his necklace, and yanked it off with a clean jerk. He stared at the bullet in his palm for a moment, then stuffed it and the chain in his shirt pocket. It was time to be vulnerable. No one deserved immortality. Least of all him.

He continued to study the still boy. He had attractive features: a delicate nose, cherubic lips, a faint cleft in his chin. Then something caught his eye: a spattering of snow-white hair the size of a silver dollar over the boy's right temple.

CHAPTER NINE

South Lake

Patricia trailed behind two ambulances as they made their way into the school parking lot. They coasted past the parked cars, sirens off, proceeding with no urgency. Perhaps it had all been a misunderstanding. Maybe there had been no shooting after all. The entire scene appeared too mundane, too ordinary to suggest otherwise.

She parked by the curb in a red zone, snatched the gray crash-kit from the passenger seat, and started jogging onto the school campus. A sheriff's deputy called out to her.

"Ma'am! You can't be here!"

"I'm a doctor," Patricia said.

The deputy stepped in front of her, his arms held out as if he was trying to corral her. "There are no injuries to tend to."

"So, there was no shooting."

"I said there are no injuries to tend to."

Patricia's heart sunk. "My son ..." Her voice cracked. "My son is here."

The deputy said, "I need you to step back until we process the scene."

"Mom!" Patricia heard Alex's unmistakable voice. It was the most beautiful sound she had ever heard.

"Alex?" she cried out.

"Mom! Over here!"

Alex was next to the gym, standing alongside an officer with a rifle slung on his shoulder. Patricia's eyes welled up with tears. She started toward her son. The deputy stiffened his arm to stop her, but she pushed it aside and broke out in a sprint. Alex didn't seem to know how to react. Patricia dropped the crash-kit, plunged on her son, and gripped him in a bone-jostling embrace.

Alex patted her back with a flat palm.

"Are you alright?" Patricia asked.

"*Good even, Audrey,*" Alex replied. Then he added, "It was Carson," he said.

"What?"

"He killed three boys."

"Where is he?"

She looked up and saw the officer with the rifle walking toward the other deputy, keeping a wide berth between himself and Patricia. He walked with a somber cadence, his demeanor very much like an honor guard at a military funeral.

"He's dead," Alex said, confirming what she

already deduced. "Can we go home now?"

* * *

That evening, Patricia and Alex dined on take-out pizza, sitting on barstools at the kitchen counter. Alex slid a slice a pizza over the rim of the box onto a plate and began cutting it into tiny pieces with knife and fork while Patricia scooped up a large triangle in her hand, folded it lengthwise and took a bite. She chewed slowly, looking at her son as he methodically sliced the pizza into geometrically pleasing shapes, finally placing the knife on the counter to switch the fork to his other hand. Alex drove his fork into a piece of crust and lifted it up to his mouth.

Her son was the only person she knew who ate his pizza crust first. Had Marcus seen Alex eat this way, he'd have embarked on yet another discussion about the roles of nature versus nurture in child development. Marcus West, the accidental father, who on the phone earlier today managed to express the bare essential concern over the school shooting — "That's horrible, but Alex isn't hurt. That's all that matters," — before plunging another barb about having to drive his son to Patricia's parents' beach house in the morning as if he didn't have a million other things to get done this week.

"Your dad is driving you to Aransas Pass tomorrow morning," Patricia said. "Need help packing?"

"You're busy," Alex said. "I'll do it."

"I'm sorry," Patricia said. "I know I told you I was going to take you."

"It doesn't matter."

"I can call the chairman in Austin in the morning, cancel my talk."

"Why?" Alex said. "You said they're paying you a lot of money for a talk you already gave."

"It doesn't feel right."

Alex said, "Mom, it doesn't matter who drives me to grandpa's house."

"I'll help you pack. Do you know what you're going to take?"

"I'll put my junk on my bed," Alex said. "I'll let you put it in the suitcase. Things never fit when I do it."

And that's how they always reached a compromise, swooping in on a tangential approach, with pragmatism trumping emotion. But tonight it left Patricia wanting.

"So, you were in the gym when it happened?" Patricia said.

Alex nodded.

"You want to talk about it?"

Alex shrugged. "If it makes you feel better," he said.

Patricia took another bite of pizza, took the time to think. She had never been able to read her son. That wasn't true. When he was a toddler, she could practically read his mind. She could guess

what he wanted from the slightest expression of
his chubby face. The fog set in around the time he
started school and never cleared.

"You were in the gym," Patricia said.

"Yeah. It was pretty loud."

"You must have been scared to death."

"Not really. I knew Carson wasn't going to hurt
me. I was more, like, surprised, you know, that it
actually happened."

"What made you think he wasn't going to hurt
you."

"Well, two things. First of all, he told us all he
was doing justice for that girl, Ashley Watson."

"That's the poor girl who had the drug
overdose," Patricia said.

"It was a suicide," Alex said.

"We don't know that for sure."

"Only the grown-ups don't know. All the kids
at school knew. Those boys Carson killed; they're
the ones that teased and bullied her till she
couldn't take it anymore."

"So Carson was close to her," Patricia said.

"I don't think he really knew her."

"Then why..."

"He had this thing about injustice," Alex said.
"It's like he couldn't stand it. Made his blood boil.
He told me about it once."

Patricia studied her son, searching for clues to
what emotions may be roiling under the surface.
A preoccupation with injustice: it was a phrase

she had not explicitly associated with Carson Taggart, that she had never entered in his medical record. Yet now that Alex mentioned the word, "injustice", it seemed to provide a plausible link for her patient's worsening temper outbursts. Patricia felt the urge to peruse Carson Taggart's medical record one last time before the inevitable subpoena would come in from the medical examiner's office. If she went to the clinic early enough in the morning, she'd be able to do so and still make it to Austin well before noon.

"What was the other thing?" Patricia asked

"What?"

"You said there were two things made you think Carson wasn't going to hurt you."

"Oh," Alex said, chewing with his mouth open. He swallowed. "A couple of weeks ago, he came up to me at lunchtime. He sort of started asking me stuff."

"What kind of stuff?"

"About you and dad. How life was at home."

"Why do you think he was asking?" Patricia said.

"I don't know. I'm not psychic," Alex said. "Anyway, he said we were like brothers, we had so much in common, even the same birthday." Alex laughed. "You ask me, I think the same birthday is the *only* thing we have in common. But he said, no, we were like brothers, and that I didn't have to ever worry about the other kids

74

messing with me 'cos he would always have my back."

"He said that?"

"Uh-huh."

Patricia reached for a napkin, dabbed the corner of Alex's mouth.

"I'm so sorry you lost a friend," she said.

"Yeah, well, that deputy had no choice. Carson was about to shoot Tommy Feldman in the head."

CHAPTER TEN

Brother Balakin

The abbot told the officer he would find the holy man in the monastery's basement chapel. The Junior Lieutenant of the Russian Army smirked at this display of superstition. "He is a holy man now? I shall ask him to recount his miracles on our drive back to the Kremlin."

"Our brother does not talk," the abbot said.

"A vow of silence? There's no such thing when it comes to matters of national security."

"Just the same, it may be wise not to engage him on your travels," the abbot said

"Really?" The smirk giving way to a sneer.

"It would be best for your..." The abbot paused. He was either searching for the right word or reconsidering whether he should finish his admonition.

"Tranquility?" the officer interjected impatiently.

"... soul."

"Stop wasting my time, old man." The Junior
Lieutenant reached the end of the hall, the abbot
scuttling in his wake. As the soldier began to
descend the stairway, the cleric grabbed him by
the sleeve, turned him around, and traced the sign
of the cross on his forehead.

"May God protect you," the abbot said.

The chapel was a damp, cold cellar, round stone
arches spanning its low walls, lit only by the
flickering candlelight of a wrought-iron
chandelier. The monk stood at the far end of the
tabernacle wearing a charcoal Podriasnik cassock
held together by a plain brown leather belt. His
sleek black hair was tied in a bun at the nape of his
neck. In one hand, the monk held a hundred-knot
prayer rope; in the other, a cross made of what
looked like twisted railroad spikes. He did not
turn as the officer's footsteps clicked on the bare
slate tile floor. Instead, the monk knelt, his torso
bending forward in a single fluid motion until his
forehead kissed the floor.

The officer stopped, clicked his heels, cleared
his throat. The monk did not move. Above the
bowed figure glittered the gilded icon of a haloed,
balding, bearded man. The officer recognized it as
one of several saints his late mother worshipped:
St. John the Theologian.

"Major Balakin," the Junior Lieutenant called
out. The monk did not move. Perhaps the man

had gone deaf in that hell-hole of the Crimea. The officer had heard stories. "Comrade! They have sent for you." The army officer waited half a minute before taking a tentative step forward. As he did so, the monk sprung to his feet, made the sign of the cross, and pivoted.

The Junior Lieutenant stumbled back. The monk was taller than he had anticipated. His gaunt face was framed in a wild, wavy beard that reached below the collar. The holy man glared at the officer with the piercing eyes of a madman. For a moment, the officer thought he was staring at the very ghost of Grigori Yefimevich Rasputin. The Junior Lieutenant shuffled aside as the monk swept past him without saying a word, then followed him out the chapel's only entrance. Followed him up three sets of stairs, down a narrow corridor of wood-plank doors, saw the cleric enter an apartment at the far end of the passage and pull the door shut behind him.

The Junior Lieutenant marched to the door and began pounding on it with his fist. There was no response.

"Major Balakin, I have a car waiting."

Still no sound. He knocked again, in a more respectful rap, placed his ear on the door to see if he could make out a sound.

A putrid voice that sounded so close it felt to the soldier as though the monk's lips were pressed up to his ear said, "Five minutes."

The Junior Lieutenant recoiled. He stepped back until his shoulders were pressed against the stone wall of the corridor. His body began to shiver. The hall was so frigid it was a wonder these monks didn't all catch their death of cold. He tried rubbing his hands together, held them up to his mouth, and cupped them so he could blow warm breath into them. Still, his shoulders shuddered. There were voices down the corridor, the distant creaking of a door hinge. Silence again.

By now, he was only too happy to start driving back to Moscow. The old monastery was starting to give him the creeps.

Then he heard it: a soft sobbing. It seemed to be coming from the holy man's garret. Holy man? What nonsense! This was just another sinner made of flesh and blood, a former major of the Red Army, discharged in utter disgrace. Or was he still active? A sleeper agent of sorts, who answered only to the highest officials whose bureaus were housed in the most secure recesses of the Kremlin. Officials who, in turn, responded to a single authority. He had heard conflicting stories.

The door flung open. A figure stepped through the doorway. The Junior Lieutenant could scarcely believe he was looking at the same man he had seen in the chapel. Major Borya Balakin stood in his Russian army dress uniform, his hair shorn, his face shaven, the skin of his jowls and chin speckled with seborrheic scales and bleeding nicks. He clutched a small, pale-blue cardboard suitcase with rusted metal latches. Balakin nodded and said, "I am ready."

CHAPTER ELEVEN

Aubrey

Aubrey Hurst had known James Preston Tully since seventh-grade science class. Back then, they had both been relegated to the cellar of the Junior High School hierarchy. Little Jimmy was a runt compared to the other boys. Aubrey was devastatingly freckled, her frame still clinging to more than a few stubborn pounds of baby fat. Aubrey and Jimmy ate lunch together in those days, at a corner table of the cafeteria, off in the land of misfit toys, as Aubrey would say. Meanwhile, Jenny Smolek and her minions sat at the other end of the room, in the light of a plate glass window. The table of the anointed.

"Look at her," Aubrey said one day, looking up from her tray of limp vegetable lasagna.

"Who?" Jimmy said.

"Jenny Smolek. Who else?"

"What about her?"

"She is the sun. And all her little friends? Those are her planets, orbiting around her."

Jimmy said. "You must be Neptune then."

"You kidding? I'm not even a planet. I'm just an asteroid. A hunk of rock and ice in a wide eccentric orbit. I only get to enter the solar system once every hundred years."

"Some orbiting hunks of rock become comets and light up the night sky," Jimmy said, blushing.

Since that day in the lunchroom, Jimmy grew seven inches and filled out nicely in the shoulders. The other kids stopped calling him Jimmy. As the freshman standout of the varsity water polo team, he was known as JP. It was Aubrey, however, who underwent a more radical transformation. That baby fat melted away, revealing a nicely toned tummy. But mother nature wasn't done with her. By the start of freshman year in high school, she had developed supple, perfectly shaped breasts that even Jenny Smolek glared at with envy.

Despite her remarkable transformation, it was JP who had become that comet, shining brighter than Aubrey could have ever imagined. But he had not forgotten what it was like to have been an outcast. Still shy and reticent at his core, recently, he had shown potent flashes of indignation, possibly nourished by the memory of past slights. For Aubrey, that mix of bashfulness and grit, decency and fierceness, was beyond noble; it was downright sexy.

When he invited her to go fishing — an activity she had zero interest in — she immediately said yes. When he confirmed it would be just the two of them in his dad's snazzy motorboat, equipped with a cozy below-deck cabin, she went out and bought a new bikini: a cute little number that would have given Aubrey's mom a coronary if she'd have seen it. The top was composed of two tiny turquoise nylon triangles, cut short on the bottom end to better reveal the lower curvatures of her breasts. The whole thing was held together by spaghetti straps that tied behind the neck. Judging from her gear, there was only one specimen Aubrey Hurst was aiming to reel in on this fishing trip, and he had no scales or gills to speak of.

"I can't believe you've lived in Galveston all your life, and you've never gone fishing," JP said as they made their way up the boardwalk.

"Maybe I've been saving myself for the right guy," Aubrey said.

"Har, har," JP said in a flat voice. Right on cue, his face turned red.

They walked up the wood plank ramp to Lazy Dayzee's Bait & Tackle Shack, JP swinging a Styrofoam cooler by his side. They entered the shop, barely noticing the man who followed them in.

As they walked down the central aisle of the cramped shop, JP asked Aubrey, "You need sunscreen?"

"I came prepared."

"Chewing gum?"

"Check."

"Beef jerky?"

"Gross."

"Potato chips?"

"I wonder. Do you think they sell condoms here?" Aubrey said.

JP put a finger in front of his mouth to hush her.

"Don't worry, dude," Aubrey said. "I told you I came prepared."

"Let's get the bait and get out of here," JP said. As he slid open the door to a refrigerator, a loud clattering sound to his left made him turn. He just managed to catch sight of a dozen fishing poles which had been hanging from a wall-mounted display come crashing to the floor. An ashen middle-aged man with wild hair was flailing, trying to catch the last few poles as they toppled over. He was dressed in an odd mish-mash of clothes: a well-pressed printed shirt, baggy khaki shorts, white sports socks, and polished black loafers. Now he was bending over comically, trying to lift a pole off the floor, but it wasn't budging as the heel of his loafer was firmly planted on its handle.

JP smiled at Aubrey. She sucked in her cheeks like a fish and crossed her eyes. JP walked over to the man and started picking up the fishing poles off the floor.

"Oh, thank you! Thank you very much!" the man said in a thick accent.

"Going fishing?" JP said as he hung a couple of poles back on the wall display.

"Yes, yes! I go fishing." The man laughed. "These poles, they are so big."

Aubrey moved in behind JP. This was too rich to miss. "Guess you're not used to having a big pole in your hands," she said.

JP elbowed her gently in the ribs.

"No," the man said. "At home, I use cork and line."

"Cork and line?" JP said.

"Yes," the man said. "You know?"

JP picked up the remaining poles, selected one out of the bunch and handed it to the man. "Try this one out for size," he said.

The man took the fishing pole in his hands, ogled it with venerating eyes, and gave it a quick flick of the wrist. "Oh, my friend. You have a good eye, eh? This is very beautiful for me. Maybe you give me more advice. What bait I should use?"

"It depends. What do you want to catch?" JP said.

"I don't know. In Greece, I fish St. Peter, mackerel."

Aubrey said, "You're Greek?"

"I am Cypriot. You know Limassol?"

JP said, "I don't think we've got mackerel here. We have grouper, snapper…"

"Snapper," the man said. "Is good?"

"Snapper is good eating," JP said. "Lots of bait you can choose from. Sardines, mullet, pilchards…"

"I don't know pilchards," the man said.

JP stepped over to the bait fridge, pulled out a plastic container, and popped the lid off, held it out for the man to see. "Pilchards," JP said.

"Oh, oh, oh, I know this fish," the man said, wagging his finger. "In my country, we eat this pilchard." He laughed. "Is good eating!"

Aubrey said, "Maybe this whole fishing thing is a waste of your time, then. You can just eat bait and call it a day."

"Ah, but I want to be on the beautiful sea," the man said. He inhaled deeply. "Smell the seawater, yes?"

"I think you're going to do just fine," JP said. He grabbed Aubrey's elbow and started leading her toward the cash register.

"And excuse me? Sorry for one more thing," the man said. "Where you go fishing, find this snapper?"

JP pointed out the shop's window. "Out there. In the water."

The man looked at JP, slack-jawed, then let out a guffaw. He tapped his temple with his finger. "I understand. You have secret fishing place, yes?"

JP said, "There's fish everywhere here, mister. There's no secret."

"And where I find a nice fishing hat like you have?"

The guy was becoming a nuisance. Aubrey snatched JP's Houston Astros cap and slipped it on her head. "This is my hat, actually," she said. "Bought it in New York City."

JP pulled the cap off her head, quickly put it back on. Aubrey thought it was silly how self-conscious he had become over a small patch of white hair that had recently popped up on his crown. Once, she ran her fingers through his hair, and JP brusquely asked her stop, as though he was afraid she might make the patch spread somehow.

The creepy man's smile went stale. "I shall go to New York then, one day." He made a slight bow. "I hope you and your sister catch much fish."

JP paid for the bait, some snacks, and a couple of bottles of water. They exited the shop and headed for the dock.

Aubrey locked her arm around JP's waist. "I ever tell you you're my favorite brother?"

"Poor guy's a foreigner just trying to get by," JP said. "He's out of his element."

"Cypriot," Aubrey said. "Rhymes with idiot."

JP reached down and pinched her butt. "Be nice, baby sister."

Summer break hadn't officially started, and there weren't many crafts out on the bay. JP maneuvered the boat out of the dock with great skill, headed out Offat's Bayou, pointing out to Aubrey the pyramid at Moody Gardens off to their left, then throttled out into West Bay. There was no reason to venture out too far with no other boat for miles around, so soon, he cut the engine and set anchor. He showed Aubrey how to bait a fishing hook, how to cast a spinning reel, and check the tension on the line before placing their poles in the stainless steel tackle rack at the stern of the boat.

They sat on the padded bench, JP handing Aubrey a bottle of water.

"So now what happens?" Aubrey asked.

JP shrugged his shoulders. "Now, we wait."

"Wait?"

"We can eat some snacks."

Aubrey handed the water bottle back to JP, got to her feet, and put her forearm across her bikini top. With her other hand, she reached behind her neck and unfastened the bow in the spaghetti straps.

"I've got something else in mind," she said.

JP's Adam's apple lurched.

Aubrey's forearm came down, letting her bikini top fall onto the boat's fiberglass deck. She put her hands on her waist and struck quite the pose, cocking her hips, letting JP get an eyeful of those perfect boobs before turning on her heels and stepping down into the below-deck cabin. JP didn't have to be begged to follow her down.

Considering it was their first time, it wasn't an altogether awkward or inelegant bit of love-making. Aubrey had managed to slow JP into a pleasing and manageable tempo and was approaching the promise of a sustained climax when JP clumsily lurched to the finish line. Still, it was better than she had dared to hope for. Perhaps it helped that they were on a boat, adrift at sea. It took a lot of pressure off knowing no one was about to walk in on you, the cramped, dim quarters limiting their exposure and range of movement. And the fact they were detached from civilization had helped to unfasten their inhibitions. If that was the case, Aubrey had no doubt: island castaways had the best sex.

"You want to try again?" Aubrey said. "This time, let's pretend you're Robinson Crusoe, and I'm your girl Friday."

JP laughed, still breathless. "I think you're mixing your metaphors."

"We need to test your resilience. Time your refractory period."

"Refractory period?"

"See how quick you can get it up again, you big dope."

"Like a science experiment?" JP said.

Aubrey traced her finger down the center of his chest. "To get a baseline. Might be important for you medically one day."

JP laughed. He sat on the bunk, slipped his bathing trunks back on. "Okay, start counting. I'm going to check on the lines, and I'll be right back."

"You take too long, your hands better smell like red snapper. Or else I'll think you're double-crossing me."

JP shook his head. "You're one crazy chick."

"I'm your comet. Remember?"

"Yes, you are," JP said. He leaned down and kissed her.

JP stepped out on the deck. Audrey reached down to pick his t-shirt off the floor. She held it up to her face, took in his scent. She stood up and slipped the shirt on. The hem reached down mid-thigh. This was going to turn him on for sure. It was self-serving to the max, but she wanted that baseline to be set as short as possible. She had lots of plans for her and JP, plenty of things she wanted to try out on him.

She heard his voice coming from out on the deck. He was talking to someone. She stepped up the bottom two steps of the gangway and peered out the cabin. Some thirty feet away, off the boat's starboard side, was that idiot the Cypriot in a metal dinghy. He was bent over in a wide stance, ass in the air, yanking the pull start of a small outboard motor like some banshee on crystal meth.

Aubrey muttered, just loud enough for JP to hear, "You've got to be fucking kidding me."

"What happened?" JP called out to the Cypriot.

The man let go of the pull start. He yelled back, "I turn engine off. She don't want to turn on again."

"Did you run out of fuel?" JP said.

"Eh?"

"Out of gas. Are you out of gas?"

"I don't know," the man said. "Where is gas gauge?"

Aubrey said, "The surface of the world is two-thirds ocean, and we gotta run into this creep again?"

JP smiled. He told Aubrey, "I think you can stop counting. We don't want to get a false baseline." He opened a compartment in the hull, reached in, and pulled out a coil of thick rope. "I'm going to toss you a line," JP yelled at the man in the dinghy.

The first toss, the guy tried to catch the rope but missed badly.

Aubrey said, "Catching doesn't come naturally to people from soccer-playing nations. We could be here all day."

JP reeled the line back in. The second toss, the man caught it, but as JP started pulling, the guy almost fell overboard, face-first, and let go of the line.

"I want you to tie the rope to your boat," JP called out.

"Yes, yes. I understand," the guy said, doubled over, wiping sweat from his brow.

The third time was the charm. The guy managed to catch the rope in a sort of klutzy embrace, the line slamming against the side of his face. He managed to tie it somehow in an unconventional but effective knot to a cleat on the bow of the dinghy's hull. JP pulled the dinghy toward him, tugging the line hand over fist.

"I think I eat pilchard tonight," the man called out. "Like your sister says."

"Girlfriend!" Aubrey shouted back. Damn right, she was his girlfriend. It was official now.

"Keep your hands clear, now," JP said as the two vessels came together. "Permission to come aboard, captain?"

"Of course," the creep said, with a slight bow complete with a little roll of the hand.

Aubrey looked on, just her torso poking out of the covered cabin. She suddenly felt too exposed, wearing only JP's t-shirt, no bra or panties underneath, this creep just a few feet away.

JP stepped onto the dinghy, stooped down to inspect the outboard motor.

"Well, there's your problem right here," JP said. "The fuel valve is in the off position."

He had barely finished uttering the phrase that the man picked up a wooden oar, swung it hard, landing a blow on the back of JP's head. Aubrey froze, unable to scream, unable to breathe as JP writhed on the bottom of the dinghy. The man lifted the oar again, this time plowing it down edge-wise, smashing JP's skull. JP lay motionless now. The stranger dropped the paddle.

Aubrey began to hyperventilate. She managed to yell, "What the fuck are you doing?"

The creep pounced aboard the motorboat. He had his hand on her neck before she could even think of moving. Her chest was heaving, but only a thin whisper of air was trickling to her lungs.

She wanted so much to speak. She wanted to say, "I'm sorry," as if this was all some sort of punishment for her sins. As though this man were not her executioner but her confessor, and with the proper contrition, all would be forgiven. She'd be allowed to live, and JP would rise up from that dinghy with a mournful smile. She stared deeply in the stranger's blank eyes.

I'm so sorry.

The man's eyes softened. They welled with tears. Somehow, he had read her mind. Softly, he said, "I know you're sorry, my child. So am I."

He brought up his free hand to cover Aubrey's eyes and, with a final thrust, crushed her windpipe.

CHAPTER TWELVE
Finn & Espericueta

Jamie Lee Foster entered the East 8th Avenue Police Station from the east entrance, where the five-story brown brick building connects to the Austin City Prosecutor's Office. As she approached the homicide division, the automatic glass door flung open, and she had to hop to one side to avoid being run over. Ethan Simmons, an assistant in the District Attorney office, pushed through the doorway, leather briefcase in hand.

"Top of the morning," Jamie Lee called out.

Hardly a nod from Simmons.

She shook her head and walked in, turned right past the situation room to the large shared office, which was the lair of the homicide detectives. In a corner cubicle, detectives Mike Finnigan and Ramon Espericueta were sitting, staring at a computer monitor. Espericueta was repeatedly tapping on a keyboard to stop and replay a loop of video.

"What was Sparky snooping around here for?"
Jamie Lee said as she settled in her cubicle, across
from them.

Mike Finnigan swiveled in his chair. "Good
morning, Detective Foster. The real question is,
what are you doing here, on such a fair day? The
first day of your summer vacation, I might add."

"Thought I'd take a look at the cold case files."

"On your holiday?" Finnigan said. "Seems to
me you should be relaxing on a tropical beach,
sipping rum-based drinks from large tumblers
garnished with fresh fruit and paper umbrellas,
bronzing your well-toned calves as you gaze out
onto turquoise waters."

"Unwinding," Ramon Espericueta added.

"Never mind my calves," Jamie Lee said.
"What did Sparky want?"

"Assistant DA Simmons came to view security
camera footage from a local Greek eatery."

"The Magic Gyros?" Jamie Lee asked.

"Aesop's Tables," Finnigan replied.

Jamie Lee shook her head. "Too heavy on the
onions, that place. Gives me gas. Why's Simmons
interested in Greek food?"

Finnigan said, "His interest is not at all of the
epicurean variety. There was a fatal shooting at
the restaurant last night. A sad and sordid affair."

"Disturbing," Espericueta said.

"Caught on camera?" Jamie Lee said.

"Detective Espericueta and I have been replaying the tape all morning," Finnigan said. "I dare say, the incident has managed to jar even the leathery sensibilities of two old homicide sea-dogs such as we are."

Espericueta said, "Shocking."

Jamie Lee said, "Let me take a little look-see." She pulled up a chair between the two men and sat square in front of the monitor.

Mike Finnigan said, "The camera is mounted on a ceiling tile in the northwest corner of the main dining hall. It has a fish-eye lens that pretty well captures the entire restaurant service area. Notice the time stamp: six-o-eight p.m. The main door opens and in comes a young lad."

"He's looking around shifty-like," Jamie Lee said. "Seems nervous."

"Jacked," Espericueta said.

"Enter stage left, Mr. Florakis," Finnigan said. "Chef de cuisine and restaurateur. Now pay attention."

Jamie Lee leaned forward. The video showed the young man pulling a kitchen knife out of a rucksack. He lunged towards Mr. Florakis, who stumbled backward, lifting his arm in self-defense before falling flat on his back. The youth with the knife straddled the man and stabbed him with a fury that made her recoil. "Jesus! What's this guy on?"

"Wait for it," Finnigan said.

Mr. Florakis batted at his aggressor with open palms. The young man lifted the kitchen knife again, grasped it with both hands this time, and seemed set to plunge it in his victim's chest when a third person came into view, a woman, who lifted a handgun and repeatedly shot at the young man until his body crumpled onto the floor.

Finnigan stopped the tape.

Jamie Lee exhaled through pursed lips. "Now, that's something you don't see every day."

"Deo Gratias," Finnigan said.

"Toxicology on the kid?" Jamie Lee said.

"Negative," said Espericueta.

"Negative? Did you see what I just saw?"

Finnigan narrowed his eyes, took a deep breath. In a lyrical voice, he recited, "Oh goddess, sing the rage of Peleus' son Achilles, that brought countless ills upon the Acheans ..."

Espericueta leaned into Jamie Lee. "Homer," he said in a low tone as if to append a footnote to a somber sermon.

"Motive?" Jamie Lee said.

"Revenge," Finnigan said, "Mr. Florakis there had an illicit relationship with the boy's mother, a Miss Candy Benson, formerly Mrs. Candace Roberts, age 46, divorced, hairdresser and beauty consultant at Raphael's Coiffeur on West Koenig Lane. Wednesday evening, Miss Benson returns home with a busted nose and a hell of a shiner."

"Fractured zygomatic arch," Espericueta said.

"Compliments of Mr. Florakis," Jody Lee said.

"Bingo!" Finnigan said.

"Does the boy have a name?" Jamie Lee said.

"Tommy Roberts," Finnigan said, "Age 14. An honor student at McCallum until last semester when family members, teachers, and friends started noticing increasingly erratic behavior."

"Such as?"

"Violent outbursts," Finnigan said. "Refractory to counseling."

"Was there some kind of triggering event for his change in behavior?"

"Not that his mother can identify. She chalked it up to hormones."

Jamie Lee leaned back in her chair. "So, what's the final score?"

"One dead boy," Finnigan said. "Mr. Florakis is in surgical intensive care at Brackenridge, condition upgraded. Looks like he'll pull through."

"The shooter?"

"That would be Mrs. Florakis," Finnigan said. "Imagine having to live with the knowledge that you killed a boy — the son of your husband's mistress — to save the life of your cheating spouse. There's no coming back from that. The stuff of Greek tragedies, if you'll pardon the pun."

"Deeply ironic," Espericueta said.

Jamie Lee said, "So, what did Sparky decide?"

"District attorney Simmons determined that no

charges will be filed against Mrs. Florakis, who acted within the legal definition of self-defense."

Jamie Lee smirked. "Even a broken clock is right twice a day."

"Video speaks for itself," Finnigan said.

Espericueta nodded. "Case closed."

A desk phone rang. Espericueta picked up the horn and handed it to his partner.

"Homicide. Detective Finnigan speaking." Finnigan's expression hardened. "Mmm-hmm. Who's the uniform at the scene? Officer Stoner? Good. He knows the drill. Address?" he said as he reached for a pencil and notepad. "Mmm-hmm." He scribbled an address and tore the paper from the pad. "Right. We'll be there in ten."

Mike Finnigan hung up the phone and stared at the address he had taken down.

"Detective Foster," Finnigan said, "don't you live in the Chestnut neighborhood?"

"Yeah. Over on Ulit."

"I thought so. I hate to break this to you, but a body's been found on Ulit Avenue. Looks like a suspicious death."

Jamie Lee stiffened. "What's the address?"

Finnigan handed her the piece of paper he had just written on."

Jamie Lee looked at the number. She consulted her mental map of the street, double-checked the number before shaking her head. "Oh, no. That's Miss Olga's house."

CHAPTER THIRTEEN
Olga

When they turned onto Ulit Avenue, Jamie
Lee Foster's first impression was that the street
hardly looked like the scene of a crime. Sure, there
were two squad cars parked off the curb, along
with a van from the forensic science bureau, but
the street scene was otherwise downright serene.
Her own bungalow across the street from Olga's
house seemed cheerful, unscathed. Strange how
even a seasoned homicide detective could fall prey
to the fallacy that violent crime only happened to
other people.

Jamie Lee told Ramon Espericueta to go ahead
and park in her own driveway. He pulled in
slowly, with a deference akin to taking your shoes
off when entering someone's home. Mike
Finnigan hopped out of the car first, tucked his
shirt inside his belt, and tipped his head at the
other two detectives before the three walked

across the street to Miss Olga's home.

Ty Stoner, the uniformed cop, stood guard by the front door, his thumbs hooked to his belt. He greeted the detectives and quickly started the briefing he must have been practicing for the better part of the last fifteen minutes. "The victim's name is Olga Belenkova, sixty-two years old, widowed. The local mailman, one Henry Clay, was the one that found her. He was on his route, saw the front door propped open, so he called her name twice, and entered the home when there was no answer, fearing the worst."

"Fearing the worst?" Finnigan interrupted him.

"Olga Belenkova was a diabetic," Ty Stoner said.

"How would the mailman know?" Jamie Lee asked, peeved by the fact a relative stranger knew about this facet of Olga's life while Jamie Lee, her neighbor for four years, was utterly unaware of her medical condition.

"He delivered her diabetic supplies to her," Stoner said. "Test-strips and such."

Mike Finnigan nodded as he crossed the threshold of the front door. "No signs of forced entry?" he asked.

"None at all, sir," Stoner said.

Mike Finnigan walked across a small vestibule and entered the living room where he suddenly stopped. The body of Olga Belenkova was reclined on a pale green couch, her head turned slightly on a cloth cushion, her eyes closed, her shoes set tidily on the floor. On a TV table sat a chipped porcelain teacup with dark leafy dregs. No saucer.

"I thought she was sleeping," Finnigan said. "Didn't want to wake her."

"Peaceful," Ramon Espericueta said.

"Standing here, I don't see any obvious injuries," Finnigan said. "Why do we think foul play was involved?"

"The dog," Jamie Lee Foster said before Ty Stoner had a chance to reply.

The uniformed cop looked at her as though she were psychic. "The dog," he repeated.

"Would you care to elucidate?" Finnigan said.,

"She had this dog," Jamie Lee said. "Darn thing would yap at everyone. Where is it?"

"The kitchen," Stoner said.

"Where's the kitchen?" Jamie Lee asked the uniformed cop.

"How long have you been neighbors?" Finnigan said. Jamie Lee ignored the question.

"Back that way," officer Stoner said. "Careful, the floor's slick."

A crime scene investigator in white booties was taking pictures of the kitchen floor, its black and white checkered linoleum stained by a lake of congealed blood. The dog, a black and white spotted mongrel with a pointy snout and a white-tipped bushy tail, lay on the floor, its throat cut clean across.

"Odd-looking pooch," Finnigan said. "What breed is it?"

"Never asked her," Jamie Lee said. "I always took it for a border collie."

"Wrong tail," Espericueta said.

Finnigan turned to officer Stoner. "Have we recovered the implement used in this canicide?"

"I beg your pardon?" Stoner said.

"Weapon used to kill the dog," Espericueta said.

"Oh. Kitchen knife. It's in the sink."

Finnigan leaned to look into the sink. He pressed his lips together. "Mmm-hmm. We will most definitely need an autopsy on Mrs. Belenkova. That door leads to the back yard, I presume?"

"Correct," Stoner said.

"The door was unlocked?"

"Yes, sir."

Jamie Lee said, "That seems like our likely point of entry. Perp comes through the back door, the dog jumps him — I think we can safely presume the suspect is a male by the condition of the dog — perp fights off the dog, grabs a kitchen knife, slits the dog's throat and then…"

"Then," Finnigan picked up, "the perp brews a nice cup of tea for the victim. The two sit and chat for a while until the victim suffers a major coronary. Or alternatively, she slips into a diabetic coma as she's waiting for the mailman to deliver her supplies, at which point, the perp, clearly feeling a tad embarrassed, exits out the front door, leaving it open."

"The storyline kinda fizzles out at the end, don't it?" Jamie Lee said.

"Don't take it too harshly," Finnigan said. "That's a common problem with stories."

"Act three let-down," Espericueta said.

"Truth is," Finnigan said, "until we determine Mrs. Olga Belenkova's cause of death, it will be impossible to establish the precise nature of the crime committed here."

"Besides canicide," Ty Stoner said.

"Beyond canicide," Finnigan echoed, pleased by the fact that the young officer had learned a new word.

Jamie Lee scanned the living room. In one corner, a low bookshelf was stacked with hard-covered titles. Framed photographs sat on its top-shelf. A gilded icon of the Virgin Mary adorned one wall.

"Wait, something's not right here," Jamie Lee said.

"Something's out of place?" Finnigan said. "How can you tell? I'm guessing you've never set foot in this house." He said it matter-of-factly, not in a judgmental way.

"Miss Olga came to my home this morning to drop off a box full of Russian religious pictures, like that one on the wall except smaller." She pointed to the icon of the Virgin Mary on the far wall. "She told me she couldn't keep them cause she was moving."

"Moving where?" Espericueta asked.

"South. That's what she said."

"That's odd," Finnigan said.

"Look around," Jamie Lee said. "Nothing's packed, no moving boxes, no nothing."

"She tells you she's moving," Finnigan said, trying to make sense of it, "gives you some items, religious icons. Items which, at the very least, I would guess, have significant emotional value. Later the same day, her dog is brutally killed, and she dies of yet undetermined causes. And her home shows no sign that she was in the process of relocating."

"How does any of this make sense?" Ty Stoner asked.

"We best take a closer look at those icons she gave you," Finnigan said to Jamie Lee.

"They're in a box across the street."

Espericueta said, "*Vamonos!*" and headed for the front door.

Jamie Lee and Finnigan followed him.

"Any special instructions?" Ty Stoner called out as they were making their way down the front yard path.

"Get toxicology on the dregs of the teacup!" Finnigan shouted back.

CHAPTER FOURTEEN
Duke

The first time Patricia West saw Duke Taggart, he was on her TV screen. In the commercials, he wore a black Stetson and a buckskin coat with fringes on the chest, rode a pinto along a cactus-studded ridge, sunset in the background, while a western-sounding soundtrack, an Ennio Morricone inspired motif complete with a whistled melody, played as a backdrop. A voice-over in a severe and menacing tone said, "Injured by a company eighteen-wheeler? Time to call the Duke!" Then a close up of the rider, the attorney staring into the camera with steely eyes, telling the viewers in a subtle Texas drawl, "Those big insurance companies have New York lawyers on their side. Who's on your side? I'm Duke Taggart, and I'll fight for every penny you deserve!"

When she met him in person for the first time, he was wearing a Fila tracksuit, a Dallas cowboy cap, and two-hundred-dollar sneakers. Patricia's ex, Marcus, was involved in a new commercial real-estate development with Taggart at the time, and the lawyer had invited the couple to his hundred-acre ranch for a barbecue. The underlying reason for the visit, what Marcus had described as a once-in-a-lifetime opportunity, was that the Taggarts, having failed to produce an heir for their sizable estate, decided to pursue the adoption route. They were scheduled to pick up the infant in less than a week and had yet to find a suitable pediatrician. For Patricia, this was nothing other than a job interview.

Gloria Taggart brought out a platter of catered brisket while Duke poured red wine in glasses you could fit your fist inside of. "Sorry if this is store-bought," Gloria said, "but I've been so busy getting the nursery ready, I haven't even started packing, never mind cooking."

"We're heading out to Odessa on Friday," Duke Taggart said.

"Odessa, Texas?" Patricia asked.

"Odessa, Ukraine," Duke Taggart answered with a smile. "We didn't want to take any chances with the local kids. We've done our research. You know what the number one reason for putting a baby up for adoption is in this country? Maternal drug addiction. Truth is, there's only two ways to go. You want a little girl? Get yourself a Korean. Smart as tacks, they are. Put a little violin in their hands, and with the right teacher, you're almost guaranteed a chair in the Boston Philharmonic. With boys, it's always harder. You don't want to go too ethnic. Boys always have a tougher time fitting in. They have to excel in academics as well as sports. So your only option is to turn to European stock. But that's always been a supply-side challenge. Until now." He lifted his wine glass and said, "To parenthood and healthy babies!"

Gloria, Marcus, and Patricia raised their glasses in turn. Patricia took a tiny sip of wine, set her glass back on the table gingerly.

"One thing I never got around to asking Marcus," Duke Taggart said, looking at Patricia, "do you have children of your own?"

"Not yet," Patricia said.

Duke Taggart brought his wine glass under his nose, swirled it, and took a long whiff. "A childless pediatrician … There's nothing wrong with that, I suppose. But I can't say I ever bought steaks from a vegetarian butcher. Don't know how reassuring it would be to get parenting advice from someone who's never been a parent."

"You might have a point," Patricia said. "But lawyers are often asked to defend criminals, and I imagine not all lawyers are-"

Marcus kicked her under the table. "The truth is," Marcus said, "we're not able to have children of our own."

"Is that so?" Duke Taggart said, surveying Patricia the way a horse rancher inspects a horse for sale, surprised by how deceivingly fecund she appeared.

"We've been thinking of adopting ourselves," Marcus said. "Haven't we?" he said, turning to Patricia.

"Oh, I think that's just wonderful," Gloria Taggart said. "I'm so excited I have to pinch myself sometimes."

"Boy or girl?" Duke Taggart asked Patricia.

"I don't think we've gotten that far," Patricia said.

"Cause if you want a boy, there's no time to lose. Gloria and I came across this once-in-a-lifetime opportunity. A select group of male orphan infants of very sturdy constitution, certified to be in excellent health. By the Ukrainian Ministry of Health, no less. But there's only a few left. I can put you in contact with the woman who runs the adoption program. She's Ukrainian, but speaks pretty good English."

"Oh, that would be great!" Marcus said in his dripping sycophantic voice.

"Wouldn't that be something?" Gloria said, "Our boys, growing up together. From the same nursery to the same high school. Wouldn't that be grand?"

This morning, on the phone, there was no excitement in Gloria Taggart's voice, no trace of joy. When Patricia called her from the clinic, the medical chart of the recently deceased Carson Taggart in her hands, Gloria only managed to blurt, "They killed my baby!" before letting out a plaintive wail.

"Gloria?" Patricia said as the woman sobbed on the other end of the line.

"They killed him, Patty. But they're going to pay. Duke will make them pay," Gloria said. "That Sheriff's deputy, believe me, he'll be the first to pay."

Patricia immediately knew which Sheriff's deputy she was referring to. She could see him in her mind's eye, carrying that rifle, walking solemnly on the lawn of South Lake High School.

After hanging up the phone, she resumed perusing Carson's file. He had been a healthy boy. Never hospitalized, no real concerns until just a few months ago when Gloria Taggart called her to say she had noted changes in his mood. The boy had more than one episode where he flew off the handle at the smallest slight. Duke had chalked it up to puberty. He even expressed a sense of pride that his son was exhibiting righteous anger triggered by what he perceived to be acts of injustice. Saw it as a sign that the boy would make an exceptional litigator one day, following in his father's footsteps. There certainly was no need for counseling as far as Duke was concerned. No need to get a shrink involved.

The temper outbursts made Patricia a little uneasy, but not enough to pursue the issue beyond asking Gloria to let her know if things got worse. The doctor was more puzzled by the matter of the curious patch of gray hair that had recently appeared on the side of the boy's head. Again, Patricia didn't think it was any cause for alarm but had started making arrangements for an evaluation by a dermatologist.

She flipped back to the very front of the chart, started reading the progress note for the very first office visit, unsure of what she was looking for. Had Carson really told Alex they were like brothers? What else did he tell her son? What did Carson know?

It started to seep in that what Patricia was searching for in her medical documentation, what she yearned for, was a sign, even the slightest indication that Alex and Carson were as different from each other as night and day. Whatever demons took hold of Carson Taggart, Patricia wanted to be sure they would not come to haunt Alex West.

* * *

Kyle Wagner parked his orange Ford Bronco at the far end of the clinic's lot, even though there were many spots available closer to the main entrance. He grabbed the stiff manila envelope from the passenger seat and hopped off the vehicle's step bar onto the blacktop. Patted his breast pocket to check for his badge, seeing as he was wearing street clothes, part of the deal for being assigned to administrative duties while the department conducted its internal investigation on the shooting. Today, his only assignment (it wasn't a punishment, his captain assured him) was to issue the subpoena and retrieve the medical records on the kid he had shot. Badge in pocket, warrant in hand, he walked across the dusty pavement toward the front door of the clinic.

A perky woman in a smart-looking pantsuit and flat-soled shoes accosted him just outside the entrance and said, "I'll show you mine if you show me yours."

Kyle stopped. He turned to look at her with a puzzled look. "Beg your pardon?"

She flashed him a badge. "Jamie Lee Foster, Austin PD homicide. Look, I know a cop when I see one, and you sure as hell fit the mold, even in a plaid Oxford and blue jeans."

Kyle Wagner pulled his badge out of his pocket, held it up, and said, "Kyle Wagner. Comal Sheriff's department."

"Looks like we're headed in the same building," Jamie Lee said.

"Looks that way."

"That envelope in your hand tells me you're on official business."

"I guess that's why you're a detective," Kyle said. Jamie Lee chuckled. "Question is," Kyle said, "why's Austin homicide here?"

Jamie Lee smiled. "Know the first thing I asked myself when I saw you jump out that old Bronco? Soon as I checked out your strut and took you for a cop?"

"What's that?"

"I asked myself, Jamie Lee, wouldn't it be something if you and him are working different angles of the same case?"

"I'd say that's unlikely," Kyle said.

"You know, I have this quirk. Coincidences bother the heck out of me. Don't they bother you? They just sit in my craw like a dry cracker."

Kyle asked, "Which doctor are you here to see this morning?"

"I don't know yet. What about you?"

"I'm just picking up some medical records."

"Sheriff's department picks up charts for medical litigation now?"

"The patient was involved in a school shooting," Kyle said.

"The South Lake shooting, I heard about that on the radio. There was another shooting at a high school in Portland, Oregon, just last week. Makes you glad summer's almost here."

Kyle said, "This one happened on the last day of school."

"Two school shootings in just a matter of days. Did I tell you how I feel about coincidences?"

"They stick in your craw," Kyle said.

"Like a dry cracker." Jamie Lee gave Kyle a look-over. "Wait a minute, you're standing here in street clothes. No service weapon far as I can see."

"Yeah."

"Holy crap! You're the one that fired the shot. Am I right? You take the kid down, and now they have you pick up his file? That's pretty cold."

"It's a small department," Kyle said. He reached for the handle of the front door.

"Hey Kyle," Jamie Lee said, "Tell you what. If it turns out we're meeting the same doctor, I'll buy you a cup of coffee."

At the medical office's front desk, Kyle Wagner pulled the subpoena out of the envelope, handed it to the receptionist along with his badge, Jamie Lee Foster standing behind him, peering over his shoulder.

"Dr. West has the chart in her office," the receptionist said. "I guess she was expecting you." She reached under her desk and buzzed open the door, which opened onto a brightly lit corridor. The receptionist walked Kyle up the hallway to an office near the rear exit of the clinic.

When he walked into the cramped office, Kyle Wagner did a double-take. He immediately recognized the doctor as the woman he saw at the school after the shooting. He introduced himself and reached out to shake the woman's hand. Dr. Patricia West crossed her arms, leaving the Sheriff's deputy with his arm stretched out over her desk.

"The Sheriff's department didn't have anyone else they could send?" Dr. West asked.

Kyle settled in an armchair without responding. Dr. West said, "You're the one that killed him."

Kyle avoided her gaze, turned his attention to a framed photograph of a younger-looking Dr. West holding an infant, standing on a vast outdoor sandstone stairway, a landmark that seemed oddly familiar.

* * *

"And how are you this morning? Jamie Lee said with a forced smile and a head tilt when the receptionist returned to the front desk. She casually flashed her badge. The receptionist looked from the detective badge to Jamie Lee's face with a puzzled look.

A minute later, Jamie Lee Foster was sitting in the office of Mrs. Myrna Zelinski, the clinic's office manager.

"All I need," Jamie Lee said, "is to find out who these phone calls were made to."

The office manager looked at the telephone company printout Jamie Lee handed her. She studied the time log of the highlighted calls.

"I wouldn't be able to say," Mrs. Zelinski said. "These calls were made Saturday morning. Our office is closed on Saturdays."

"Must be nice. What happens when a call comes in after-hours?" Jamie Lee asked.

"We use an automated answering system. The caller then has the option to page a nurse practitioner on call, in which case they're transferred to a live answering system, or they can choose to record a message on our voice-mail system."

"Do you keep a log of the calls handled by your answering service?"

"I can look it up on my computer," said Mrs. Zelinski. She swiveled in her chair and started typing on a computer keyboard with a clicking of manicured nails. Jamie Lee frowned and looked down at her own stubby fingers.

Mrs. Zelinski said, "It was this last Saturday, right?"

"That's right."

"It doesn't look like they took any calls that morning."

"Let's listen to the voice-mail then," Jamie Lee said.

The office manager turned to Jamie Lee with a horrified look. "Those calls contain protected confidential information."

"We can skip over the ones that don't matter till we get to the specific calls in question."

"You do have a subpoena," Mrs. Zelinski said.

Jamie Lee Foster pressed her lips together in a smile and nodded. She didn't want to debate Mrs. Zelinski on the necessity of a subpoena. "My partner, deputy Wagner showed the subpoena to

Sing the Rage

your receptionist. I believe he's talking to Dr. West right now. Go ahead, call your receptionist if you want."

"The office manager picked up the phone, tapped in a four-digit code. "Sally? Did deputy …"

"Wagner," Jamie Lee said. "Kyle Wagner."

"Did deputy Wagner show you a subpoena for medical records?" A pause. "Thank you, Sally." She hung up.

"We're all squared away?" Jamie Lee said with a grin.

Mrs. Zelinski put the phone on speaker and dialed in a code. After a few prompts, they were listening to recorded messages. When the first one started to play, Jamie Lee said, "Nope. Not that one." The office manager frantically pushed a button to skip over to the next recording to assure that the detective didn't overhear a request for a medication refill or other vitally sensitive information.

On the fifth recording, Jamie Lee said, "That's the one." She immediately recognized Miss Olga's voice.

"This message is for Dr. Patricia West," Olga Belenkova's recorded voice rang out. *For Dr. West, wouldn't you know?* Now, Jamie Lee would have to chase down that deputy. Buy him the cup of coffee she promised him and compare notes. "This is Mrs. Olga Belenkova. You remember me,

I'm sure, from the adoption agency," a slight chuckle, "so many years ago. Dr. West. Please, I must talk to you. It is very, very important. Please call me as soon as you can." Olga slowly recited a phone number, then repeated it, enunciating every digit with care. "Please, Dr. West. I wait for your call."

Jamie Lee said, "How do you feel about coincidences, Mrs. Zelinski?"

The office manager looked at Jamie Lee, dumbfounded.

"See, I don't like them either," Jamie Lee said. "They stick in my craw."

CHAPTER FIFTEEN

Detective Foster

Another cop walked into Patricia's office. A woman this time, with a cocky swagger and a self-assured smirk.

"My name's Jamie Lee Foster," the cop said. Patricia didn't bother to look at her badge and carried on with stuffing files she probably wouldn't even need in her leather briefcase.

"I already turned over the medical records to the other deputy," Patricia said.

"I'm not a Sheriff's deputy," Jamie Lee said. "I'm a detective."

Patricia's fingers tensed up. She didn't know whether she could keep her composure talking about Carson Taggart and the school shooting. This was the last thing she needed before getting in front of a crowd to give a speech.

"Can this wait for some other time? I'm in a hurry," Patricia said. "I'm scheduled to give a talk

119

at Austin Children's Hospital at noon."

"Austin? That's where I'm from," Jamie Lee
Foster said. "This won't take but a minute. Or I
can drive you up, and we can talk in the car."

Why would an Austin detective need to talk to
her? Patricia felt a guilty sense of relief. The
interrogation had nothing to do with the school
shooting. Feeling more confident, Patricia glanced
at her watch. "Just a minute, then."

Jamie Lee Foster nodded. She sat down, flipped
open a prim little notebook, and pulled a
disposable ballpoint pen from the inside pocket of
her jacket. Patricia frowned. It was going to be a
long minute, no doubt.

"Olga Belenkova," Jamie Lee said and just
waited.

Maybe this was about Carson, after all. Patricia
shrugged but said nothing.

"You know Olga Belenkova," the detective said.

"I know who she is."

"What's the nature of your relationship?"

Patricia shook her head. "There's really no
relationship to speak of. She organized some
international adoptions quite a few years ago, and
I was involved in the care of one or more of the
children."

"I didn't catch that, Dr. West. Did you say you
were involved with one or more than one
adoption?"

Patricia looked at her watch again. "If I don't

leave now, with traffic and all-"

"We're almost done," Jamie Lee Foster said. "I promise you. When's the last time you spoke to Miss Olga?"

Miss Olga? There was an unseemly familiarity in the way the detective referred to the woman.

Patricia sighed. "I imagine the last time we talked was about fourteen years ago."

Detective Foster looked up from her notebook. "Fourteen years? Are you quite sure of that?"

"Positive."

"I find that strange, seeing as last Saturday she left you a message on the clinic voicemail. A pretty frantic message at that, if you ask me. Said it was an urgent matter."

"Yeah, I only heard the message this morning when I got to the office. I was in Dallas for a conference earlier this week and I'm afraid I got behind on checking my messages. I tried calling her a couple of times. There was no answer. The last time we did speak was fourteen years ago."

Patricia wondered if she looked tense. Her voice was certainly strained. And she was choosing her words with deliberate care so as to tell the truth without revealing anything more than what was essential.

"What do you suppose could be so urgent now, after all these years?" Jamie Lee asked.

Patricia said, "I haven't the slightest idea. I don't mean to seem rude, detective, but I really do

121

have to get on the road."

Jamie Lee got to her feet. "Of course."

"Don't you find it strange?" the detective asked.

"Find what strange?" Patricia said.

"Don't you find it strange?" the detective repeated, "seeing as the two of you hadn't spoken in fourteen years, that the last three phone calls Miss Olga made before she died were to you?"

CHAPTER SIXTEEN
Comal

Jamie Lee Foster had always thought the
police headquarters in Austin was rather plain-
looking. Still, in comparison to the Comal County
Sheriff's department, her office building looked
like the new Scotland Yard. The Sheriff's
department office was a spartan one-story
concrete building that looked like it had been
drafted by a pre-pubescent boy with no tools other
than a number two pencil and a square ruler. The
whole structure was so devoid of curves, slopes,
or arcs that it could have easily been built entirely
of giant Lego blocks.

Jamie Lee found Kyle Wagner sitting at his
desk, pecking at a computer keyboard with his
two index fingers.

"Saw the orange Bronco in the parking lot,"
Jamie Lee said. "Knew you'd be here."

Kyle looked up from the keyboard without

saying anything. Jamie Lee sat down in the perp chair next to his desk.

"That thing sure stands out," Jamie Lee said. "Kinda cute, though. Is that a seventy-two? I almost bought a nineteen-seventy-two candy-apple-red El Camino once. But I noticed the seller kept parking it in a different spot, hoping I wouldn't catch sight of those little puddles of transmission fluid on the pavement. Too bad, though. I liked the way the engine made the cabin shake when I pushed hard on the gas pedal. Kind of tickled me in a naughty way."

"Seventy-five," Kyle said. "I'm guessing you met Dr. Patricia West."

Jamie Lee slapped her hand on the desk. "Now that's a mighty fine deduction, deputy. I knew you were as sharp as a dart. Ever consider being a detective?"

"And now you want to buy me a cup of coffee," Kyle said.

"Just look at you," Jamie Lee said. "You think I can't tell those little gears are spinning in your head? I know you've got about a million questions. Well, me too."

"I don't think I have any answers to your questions," Kyle said.

"It doesn't matter. More questions is always a good place to start."

Minutes later, they were driving down West San Antonio Street in Jamie Lee's Ford Taurus,

passing several Mexican joints before stopping at
a donut shop. There, they sat across from each
other at a booth whose hard plastic benches were
bolted to the cracked tile floor, and started sipping
coffee from Styrofoam cups.

"I'm investigating a murder," Jamie Lee said
after taking a sip. "The vic was an elderly Russian
woman."

"How was she killed?"

"Post-mortem is pending. Her pooch had its
throat slit ear to ear."

Kyle said, "Any suspects?"

"None so far."

"How does Dr. West fit in?"

"We checked the victim's phone log. The last
three phone calls she made are to the doctor's
clinic. So I come down here to chase down pretty
much the only lead we have, and I run into you."

"What did Dr. West have to say?" Kyle asked.

"She says she hasn't talked to the vic in fourteen
years."

"What about those phone calls?"

Jamie Lee said, "The calls were made Saturday
morning, while the clinic was closed."

"That around the time the murder happened?"

Jamie Lee nodded. "So the vic leaves a couple
of messages on the clinic voice mail. She says,
'Call me. It's very urgent.' That kind of stuff."

"Did Dr. West call her back?"

"Yeah, but it was too late. She got no answer.

Miss Olga was already dead by then."

Kyle took a sip of coffee. "How did Dr. West and this woman know each other?"

"The victim, an Olga Belenkova, worked for some kind of international adoption agency. Looks like Dr. West helped her with an adoption that took place many years back."

Kyle's eyes widened.

Jamie Lee said, "Look at you! I swear to God there's a little light bulb dangling over your head."

Kyle set his coffee cup down. "It doesn't make sense."

Jamie Lee tilted her head. "Are you going to tell me already, or do I have to pry open your mouth and jab a toothpick in your gums?"

Kyle shook his head. "That kid, the one I came to pick up the medical records for."

"The one that shot up the school," Jamie Lee said.

"I took a look inside his chart."

"Sneaky you!"

"He was adopted as an infant," Kyle said. "From Ukraine."

Jamie Lee furrowed her brow. "Assuming Miss Olga coordinated this kid's adoption, what are we saying? That she had information related to the school shooting? And then someone murders her to keep her quiet?"

"Doesn't make any sense," Kyle said.

"Especially since she called days before the school

shooting. Unless she was clairvoyant."

"Maybe she called because she knew her life was in danger, and Dr. West was the only one who could help her."

"Even though they hadn't talked to each other in fourteen years?"

"Perhaps, Dr. West isn't telling us everything she knows. Maybe, the good doctor lied to me." Jamie Lee took a sip of coffee. "What if it's Dr. West's life that's in danger? And Miss Olga was trying to warn her."

"You're reaching," Kyle said. "Sounds to me like you're trying to orchestrate a ruse to scare Dr. West in telling you something you presume she knows."

"It's not so far-fetched," Jamie Lee said. "Miss Olga feared for her life. That's why on the morning of her murder, she gave me a box of pictures for safe-keeping. She said she couldn't keep them because she was moving, but there were no moving boxes in her house when we found her body."

Kyle squinted. "Wait a minute. You spoke to the victim before she was murdered?"

Jamie Lee looked down at her hands. "She was my neighbor."

"You mean to tell me your department charged you with investigating the murder of your own neighbor?"

"I'm not assigned to the investigation in what

you might call an official capacity," Jamie Lee
said. "I'm assisting the lead detectives in an
advisory capacity."

Kyle asked, "Does your department even know
you're here?"

"They don't need to know," Jamie Lee said.
"I'm on vacation this week."

Kyle Wagner leaned back. He grasped his
forehead. "You're a real piece of work."

"So, I'm often told." Jamie Lee glanced at her
wristwatch. "How long do you figure a medical
talk lasts?"

Kyle shrugged. "An hour, maybe."

"Want to go for a drive to Austin? See if we
bump into Dr. West?"

"What for?" Kyle asked.

Jamie Lee started laughing. "What for? You
think I don't see that wicked little gleam in your
eye? Admit it, you got that itch, and you won't sit
easy til you scratch it. Kyle, you want answers as
badly as I do. Besides, neither one of us has
anything better to do today."

CHAPTER SEVENTEEN

Heading North

Jamie Lee and Kyle were heading north on
I-35, entering Austin city limits, Jamie Lee behind
the wheel of her beige Ford Taurus, when Kyle
asked her, "How am I getting back to New
Braunfels?"

"What's the hurry? I'm sure I have a spare
tooth brush in the guest bathroom. Might even be
able to find a clean pair of boxers that'll fit you."

"Sounds like you're in the habit of kidnapping
men," Kyle said.

Jamie Lee laughed. "Don't flatter yourself,
cowboy. If you're really aching to get back you
might be able to hitch a ride with Dr. West. Didn't
see a wedding band on her finger. She might
enjoy a little masculine company."

"And while I'm at it, I can interrogate her,"
Kyle said.

"Here's a little suggestion: don't use that word,

interrogate, with her. You look like a guy who knows how to be subtle."

Kyle rubbed his hands together. "I can't say I know much about how doctors think, but I'm guessing they don't take kindly to strangers who kill a patient they've been caring for fourteen years."

Jamie Lee shrugged her shoulders. "You were doing your job."

"Yeah, well, I think I might need that spare toothbrush. Unless I take a bus home."

"You don't need to play hard-to-get, Bubba," Jamie Lee said. "*Mi casa es su casa.*

Kyle looked out the side window at a guy cruising on a Harley, sporting a walrus mustache, a red bandana tied to his neck , denim vest with buttons straining to contain his barrel chest, a large sewn-on patch of a skull on his back. The throaty hum of the motorcycle's engine was oddly soothing, mesmerizing. So, Dr. West didn't wear a wedding band. And that framed portrait on her desk, the one of a younger Dr. West holding a baby (her son, no doubt) did not include a husband standing by her side. The good doctor wouldn't have picked that particular picture to decorate her office at random. There was clearly no man in Dr. West's life. Not that it mattered to Kyle. She was an attractive woman, successful, way out of his league. Still, there was something about that photograph that gnawed at him. It was bothering him now as it had it bothered him the moment he first saw it — that strange sense of familiarity.

The guy on the motorcycle signaled with two raised fingers and changed lanes, heading for an exit ramp. With the sound of the motorcycle engine receding, Kyle emerged from his reverie, and started feeling a growing tingling on the back of his neck. It was a feeling he was familiar with, one that would come on from time to time, like a warning light, to let him know of trouble brewing in his subconscious. It was that same feeling that kept him alive that February morning in 1991 outside Kuwait City International Airport, when when the Iraqi National Guard sniper spotted him. Kyle suddenly realized he was being watched. He rolled behind a concrete barrier just a fraction of a second before the round fired from the Dragunov sniper rifle slammed into the ground where he had been laying. But Kyle Wagner was not a superstitious man. There were no angels guarding his body and soul. On that occasion it had been the most subtle flicker of light, off in his peripheral visual field, which his subconscious correctly interpreted as the sunlight's reflection off of a sniper scope. Since then, he had come to rely on the knowledge that the sudden feeling of dread was the result of a deep implicit awareness: perception which had yet to percolate to his conscious mind.

What was eliciting the feeling now? The sound of the Harley? That patch with the skull? No. It was something he was thinking of just before that. Not the wedding band, or its absence on Dr. West's finger. The portrait. The damn portrait! How could he have missed it? He knew that place. And if Dr. West was standing there with her newborn son, it could only mean one thing.

Jamie Lee said, "You're awfully quiet."

It was too soon to share his insight. He had to think about it some more. "Just thinking."

"I can see that. I hear those little gears whirring inside your skull. Whatcha thinking?"

"You said we're going to approach Dr. West at the hospital when she finishes her talk," Kyle said. "And then what?"

"Then we try to solve a murder," Jamie Lee said.

"What exactly do you plan to ask her?"

"Don't worry. There's lots of time to think about that. First, I want to take you somewhere."

"Where are we going?" Kyle asked.

Jamie Lee grinned and said, "I'm taking you to church."

CHAPTER EIGHTEEN

Father Ambrus

St. John Chrysostom Orthodox church was a one-story building of almost apologetic modesty located just half a mile from Jamie Lee Foster's home. Its rounded roof and single gilded onion dome were the only architectural features that set it aside from the surrounding houses, but it was the presence of a parking lot and an adjoining vegetable garden that distinguished it from the squat lots of its neighbors. Over the past few years, Jamie Lee had come to know that Miss Olga was a devout believer. She had seen the elderly woman shuffle to evening prayers with a knitted shawl tossed over her shoulders and a silk scarf tied to her head. It had become clear to Jamie Lee that the old woman had selected her home in large part due to its proximity to the house of worship.

Jamie Lee, on the other hand, chose her home

133

purely based on economics and convenience. She
shunned all manner of ritual but insisted — on
those rare occasions when the subject was brought
up — that she wasn't opposed to religion per se; it
was *organized* religion that rubbed her the wrong
way. Organization gave spirituality its teeth, and
when those fangs showed through, they had quite
a chomp. The mystery to Jamie Lee was why Miss
Olga would have entrusted her, an outsider, with
what appeared to be valuable religious artifacts.
She was hoping the visit to St. Chrysostom might
shed some light on this.

Kyle and Jamie Lee walked toward the front of
the church, where a lanky man in a dark gray
frock was sweeping dry leaves from the front
steps with a besom.

"Excuse me," Jamie Lee said to the man.
"Know where we might find the priest?"

The man stopped sweeping. He looked up with
eyes that seemed overly exposed by the sagging of
his lower lids. "Father Ambrus is tending
tomatoes."

"Vegetable garden, huh?" Jamie Lee said. "You
expecting a good crop this year?"

The man said, "Who's asking? The IRS?" He
went back to his sweeping, turning a cold
shoulder to the intruders.

Jamie Lee looked at Kyle and raised an
eyebrow.

The two law enforcement officers headed

toward the garden. Jamie Lee had one of the painted icons in her hand, the box with the rest of the set stowed in the trunk of her car.

They found Father Ambrus kneeling in the garden, pulling weeds. He was a man in his early thirties garbed in somewhat eclectic attire: black sneakers, black sweat pants, and a gray apron over a collar-less tunic. His hair was tied up in a neat bun, and his black beard was carefully trimmed. With only minor adjustments to his wardrobe, he'd have quickly passed as a barista at a swank coffee shop. The priest looked up with a warm smile when Kyle and Jamie Lee approached him and said, "Glorious day, isn't it?"

"So tomatoes really do grow on plants," Jamie Lee said. "Only time I ever see them is in a bottle of ketchup."

Father Ambrus chuckled. "There's nothing like the flavor of a freshly picked tomato," he said. "Ask the raccoons. They always seem to get the pick of the crop. But I accept it as a form of tithing. Let them have their share. We're all God's creatures, after all." Turning more serious, Father Ambrus said, "But I imagine you're not here to talk only about my tomatoes."

"No, sir," Kyle said.

Father Ambrus shook his head. "Dreadful business. It's hard to imagine anyone would want to harm such a sweet lady." The priest got to his feet. "I'm sorry, I just assumed you were the police. Maybe I should have waited for you to introduce yourselves."

"I'm detective Foster, this is deputy Wagner."

The priest nodded. "I'm afraid I won't be of much help in your investigation. The incident has left me dumbfounded."

Kyle flashed a look at Jamie Lee as if to nudge her to cut the priest off. The last thing he wanted was to give the appearance that he was a party in some rogue interrogation regarding a murdered woman in a city where he had no jurisdiction. Not while he was already being investigated in another matter. This was Jamie Lee's turf, even if she was operating in an unofficial capacity.

"Did Miss Olga talk to you about anyone that might want to hurt her?"

"Yes, of course. Why, everyone was out to get her!" Father Ambrus said. "You have to understand that Olga had a bit of a paranoid personality, may she rest in peace. She had a nervous predisposition."

"Why do you think she was paranoid?" Jamie Lee asked.

"I'm not a psychologist, detective, but over the years, I've had quite a few parishioners who experienced life under the Soviet regime. A certain amount of residual diffidence is understandable when you've lived for years in fear that, on any given day, your neighbor, your coworker, your postman — dare I say your priest?

— may whisper in the ear of a commissar a morsel of compromising information that will land you on a midnight train to the gulag. Mrs. Belenkova had settled in a rather narrow and unyielding habit of thinking. Nonetheless, she was a very kind and devout woman."

"This paranoia," Jamie Lee said, "did it seem to get worse lately?"

"Not that I noticed," the priest said. "She attended the usual services, performed her typical functions."

Jamie Lee held out the painted icon she was holding for the cleric to see. "What do you make of this?"

The priest leaned in and smiled. "That is exquisite." He rubbed his hands on his sweatpants. "May I?" Jamie Lee handed the tiny painting to him. "This is Saint Theophan the Recluse. In some countries, icons such as this one are given as gifts to celebrate the birth of a child."

"Is it very old?" Jamie Lee asked.

"Not at all," Father Ambrus said. "This is painted by a contemporary master, Dr. Sergey Kovalenko."

"You seem very sure of yourself," Kyle asked, "How can you tell?"

"From the type of canvas used, the fine, delicate brush-strokes, the way light and shadow are handled in the background," Father Ambrus said, "but mostly from the fact his initials are painted in the lower right-hand corner." The priest held the painting up to show the other two."

Jamie Lee read aloud, "C.K."

"That C is an S in Russian," Father Ambrus said. "How did this gem fall in your hands?"

"Miss Olga gave it to me," Jamie Lee said. "Along with six more that look just like it."

"She gave them to you?" the priest said. "I don't understand."

"I'm a detective," Jamie Lee flashed her badge, "but I was also her neighbor. She brought them to me the morning of her murder."

The priest blinked his eyes. He looked at Kyle. Kyle placed his hands on his hips and looked down in embarrassment.

"Do you have any idea why she would give these to me?" Jamie Lee asked.

"What did she say to you when she gave them to you?" the priest asked.

"She said she hoped one day I would look at them in a different light."

Father Ambrus said, "She was a very devout woman, but it wouldn't be in her nature to try to convert you."

"What makes you say that?" Kyle asked.

"Our church does not proselytize," Father Ambrus said. A pained look emerged on the priest's face. "It is harrowing to consider the possibility that she knew that death was looming and that she placed the icons in your possession for a specific reason."

"And what might that reason be?" Jamie Lee asked.

"I don't know. Perhaps you can ask the artist."

"Say again," Kyle said.

"Dr. Kovalenko lives in Old West Austin, just a couple of miles from the University of Texas. That's why I'm familiar with his work; our church commissioned him for quite a few paintings, including one of St. Chrysostom, our patron saint."

"You have an address for this doctor?" Jamie Lee said.

"My address book is in the sacristy. I'd be happy to let you copy it."

Kyle asked, "What is Dr. Kovalenko's specialty?"

"Oh, I don't think he's a medical doctor," Father Ambrus said. "He taught at the university. He's retired now."

"He was a professor of art?" Kyle asked.

"No." The priest furrowed his brow. "Genetics, I think."

CHAPTER NINETEEN

At the Diner

Patricia West's lecture was extremely well received, perhaps in no small part thanks to Dr. Oliver Flynn's keen endorsement. After the talk, Dr. Flynn took her under his wing and introduced her to various department heads who gathered by the podium while the audience dispersed. There was one physician who stood to the side, his back straight, feet apart, arms behind him in a sort of military at-rest pose. He was a tall man in pressed scrubs who looked like he spent too much time for his own good curling dumbbells in front of a mirror. He winked when Patricia happened to look his way, then lingered quietly until only Patricia and Dr. Flynn were left at the front of the hall.

"Dr. West, let me introduce you to Dr. Benning," Oliver Flynn said with a nettled look, as though he had been trying to avoid having to

140

make the introduction, "Chief of emergency medicine."

Dr. Benning reached out and shook Patricia's hand, clung to it a tad longer than customary. "I didn't get any sleep last night, thanks to you," Dr. Benning said.

"I'm sorry?" Patricia said, retrieving her hand from his grip.

"Your book. I couldn't put it down."

Dr. Flynn flashed Patricia a sarcastic smile. "It seems there's always something or someone interfering with Dr. Benning's slumber. The sleep deprivation has a way of clouding his better judgment at times, but he is nonetheless a highly competent physician."

Dr. Benning took a step forward. "Your thesis makes some excellent points. I think the emergency room would be a natural laboratory to implement many of your suggestions. I hope we get a chance to work together when you join our faculty."

"Thank you, but I think we're getting a little ahead of ourselves," Patricia said.

Dr. Flynn said, "Dr. West has yet to sign a letter of commitment."

"Oliver, you'll have to be a lot more persuasive then," Dr. Benning said. "I would hate for her to get away." He handed Patricia a business card. "My door's always open, day or night," he said. He winked again and walked away.

Oliver Flynn waited until Dr. Benning was out of earshot before saying, "He comes on strong, but he's quite harmless. The boy is easily distracted, and he's savvy enough to know to move on when he discerns who's off-limits."

Patricia looked at the business card, turned it over. A phone number was scribbled on its back. It would have seemed crass for her to tear the card up in front of Oliver Flynn, so she slipped it in the pocket of her jacket just to free up her hands.

Dr. Flynn grasped Patricia's arm and began to lead her toward the auditorium's exit. "I hope you're not in too much of a hurry. I'd like to invite you to a little luncheon," Oliver Flynn said. "The faculty club has a surprisingly good buffet. I reeled the chef in myself from New Orleans just for her jambalaya."

Patricia stopped in her tracks. Standing by the doorway were detective Foster and that Sheriff's deputy who served her the subpoena earlier that morning. Seeing the two of them together struck a discordant note. Patricia struggled to make sense of why they would be together, and why on earth they would be here.

"I'm sorry, Dr. Flynn," Patricia said. "I'll have to take a rain check on lunch."

Oliver Flynn looked at the man and woman by the door who were eyeing Patricia. "Is everything all right?" he said.

Patricia smiled, "Absolutely. Thanks again for

inviting me, Dr. Flynn."

"Very well, then." Oliver Flynn clasped Patricia's hand, patted it softly. "We'll keep in touch."

No one moved or spoke until Dr. Flynn was out of the auditorium.

"How'd the talk go?" the detective said in her annoyingly perky voice.

"What the hell?" Patricia said unamused.

The Sheriff and detective exchanged glances. Detective Foster sighed and said, "Dr. West, we passed a swell-looking diner a half-mile up the road. Kyle's buying lunch." Patricia stared at her and didn't move. "Doc," Jamie Lee Foster said, her expression serious now, "we gotta talk."

Patricia looked at her wristwatch. She thought about it a moment. "Let me make a call first. I have to check on my son."

* * *

"None of what you're saying makes sense," Patricia said. She had hardly touched the club sandwich Jamie Lee had ordered for her. "Yes, Olga Belenkova coordinated Carson Taggart's adoption, but to suggest that her phone calls to me had anything to do with her murder, not to mention the shooting at South Lake High School seems... incoherent."

"I know this all sounds a little half-baked," Jamie Lee said, "but in the early stages of a case, I try to look for every connection I can find. I don't reject any notion, no matter how far-fetched it seems. Only later do I start pruning away what doesn't pan out. Don't you doctors think the same way? Kyle and I, we were just hoping you might help us shed some light on the Olga-Carson link. See if that connection means anything, or if it can be snipped in the bud."

"What information could I possibly have? I haven't talked to the woman in years."

Kyle Wagner cleared his throat. "Dr. West," he said. "Besides your dealings in the Carson Taggart adoption, did you have any other interaction with Mrs. Belenkova?"

"No," Patricia said.

"Are you sure of that?" Kyle said in a calm voice.

"Positive," Patricia said.

"Are you saying," Kyle persisted, "that Mrs. Belenkova didn't coordinate the adoption of your son?"

Patricia stared at Kyle with a dazed expression, then looked away, bringing her hands together on her lap. Jamie Lee turned her head to look at Kyle, her features expressing a mix of admiration and irritation.

Kyle said, "Did your son come from the same orphanage as the Taggart boy in Odessa?"

"How could you possibly know to ask me that?" Patricia said.

"One hundred and ninety-two steps of gray-green sandstone, a statue of the Duke of Richelieu perched way up at the top. I should have recognized it sooner," Kyle said.

Jamie Lee said, "You want to fill me in, partner?"

"There's a framed picture in Dr. West's office," Kyle said. He turned to address Patricia. "You're standing on some stairs, holding a baby - your son, I presume. The backdrop looked so darn familiar, but it was only as we were driving up here that I was able to place it." Kyle shook his head. "Odessa is not much of a tourist destination. Not even the Potemkin stairs draw much of a crowd. I should know - I've been there."

"Are we talking about Odessa, Texas?" Jamie Lee asked.

"Odessa, Ukraine," Patricia said. She pressed her lips together.

"I'm an old silent movie buff," Kyle said. "I thought I'd get a kick marching down the steps where they filmed The Battleship Potemkin. Try to find the exact spot where the baby carriage rolled down."

"Please, be quiet," Patricia said. "Just for a minute, stop talking."

A waitress came to the table with a pot of coffee, topped off everyone's cup. "Hope y'all saved a little room for a slice of pie," she said. "The banana cream is to die for."

Jamie Lee said, "Thank you kindly, but a girl's

gotta watch her figure."

The waitress pulled a bill from the pocket of her apron, placed it on the table. "I'll pick this up whenever you're ready."

Kyle Wagner took a sip of coffee. He glanced at Jamie Lee.

"I'm guessing he doesn't know," Jamie Lee said. "Your son, he doesn't know he was adopted?"

Patricia shook her head.

"Well, honey," Jamie Lee said. "Don't you fret now. No one here's going to tell him. Isn't that right, Kyle?"

Kyle said, "Can I have the car keys?"

Jamie Lee's eyes widened. "You ditching us, partner?"

"Getting something out of the trunk," Kyle said.

Jamie Lee handed him the keys. The detective didn't utter a word as the two women sat alone. She let out a soft sigh of relief when Kyle slipped back in the booth with one of Olga's religious icons in his hand.

"Dr. West," Kyle said. "You know how Detective Foster was talking about forming connections? Throwing things on the wall, so to speak. See what sticks. There's one other possible link to Mrs. Belenkova that might be important." He handed the painted icon to Patricia. "Does this mean anything to you?"

Patricia West studied it. "Where did you get

this?"

"It belonged to Mrs. Belenkova," Kyle said.

Jamie Lee said, "She gave me this, and six others like it, the morning she was murdered."

"Gave them to you?" Patricia said. "I don't understand. You met her before she was murdered?"

"She was my neighbor," Jamie Lee said. "The morning she was killed, Olga came over to my house, rings my doorbell and tells me she's moving. She said she couldn't take the pictures with her and wanted me to have them. I tried to tell her that of all the people in the world she could have picked, I was probably the worst choice when it comes to hanging saints on the walls of my house. But she said, 'You detective woman; one day you look at them under different light.' As if I'm going to see the light." Jamie Lee made a sound halfway between a snort and a scoff.

"So all this, what you're doing, it's not the actual official murder investigation," Patricia said.

Jamie Lee waited a moment. "I want to find out who murdered my neighbor," she said.

Patricia looked at Kyle. "And you? What are you hoping for, absolution?"

Kyle gritted his teeth together as if to ride out a spasm of pain. He exhaled slowly and said, "I'm just trying to get some answers, ma'am."

Patricia looked down at the icon in her hands.

"Does that icon mean anything to you?" Kyle asked.

"I'm not sure it does," Patricia said. "But I think I've seen it before."

Jamie Lee leaned forward. "You've seen it?"

"And a few more like it," Patricia said.

"Where was that?" Jamie Lee said. "In Miss Olga's home?"

"I've never been to Olga's house. No, I saw them in Odessa, in the ward of the orphanage where I met my son. Each crib had one. No, that's not entirely accurate. The empty cribs didn't."

Kyle turned to Jamie Lee and said, "Father Ambrus said icons like this were sometimes given as gifts to celebrate the birth of a child."

Jamie Lee leaned over the table. In as gentle a voice as the detective could muster, she said, "When you adopted your son..."

"Alexander," Patricia said.

"When you brought Alexander home," Jamie Lee said, "did the orphanage give you an icon as a sort of homecoming present?"

"No."

"So all the icons went to Miss Olga," Jamie Lee said, looking at Kyle. "Does that make any sense to you?"

"This may not be one of the actual icons from the orphanage," Patricia said. "I can't be sure that they're one and the same."

"You seemed pretty certain when you first saw

it," Kyle said.

"I could be mistaken," Patricia repeated.

"Well, there's only one way to find out," Jamie Lee said.

"How's that?" Patricia said.

"The artist that painted these lives in Austin, a hop, skip and a jump from here. He'll know for sure."

"Look, I have to get home." Patricia placed the icon on the table and reached for the check. Kyle snatched it away before she could get her hand on it.

"Lunch is on me, remember?" Kyle said.

Patricia reached for her purse.

"Dr. West," Kyle said. "I really think you should come to talk to this painter."

"Why should I?"

"I get this gut feeling sometimes; it's not based on emotion. It's more like the ghost of a thought, an idea that hasn't fully materialized. Does that make any sense?"

Patricia nodded. "In medicine, we call it tacit knowledge. It's a poorly understood cognitive phenomenon."

"I couldn't have come up with a better name for it in a million years," Kyle said. "This tacit knowledge has saved me from some pretty tight spots in the past. I get this... tingling. It's not a comfortable feeling."

Jamie Lee jabbed him with her elbow. "She's

not Dr. Phil, Kyle. If you've got a point to make, why don't you just hurry on up and spit it out?"

"I think your son may be in danger," Kyle said.

Patricia looked at his downcast eyes. She was embarrassed by the man's torment, so candidly revealed. She knew one thing: the man believed that what he was saying was true. And that terrified her.

"Come with us, doc," Jamie Lee said. "You've got questions too. I see it in your eyes. Maybe this doctor can give us some answers."

"Doctor? You mean painter," Patricia said.

"He's a retired professor," Jamie Lee said. "A doctor of genetics. Painting is his side-gig. Who knows? Maybe he's the one who can show me how to see these pictures in different light."

"Did you say, in different light?" Patricia said.

Jamie Lee said, "How's that?"

"In a different light," Patricia said, "or in different light? What exactly did Mrs. Belenkova say to you when she gave you the paintings?"

Jamie Lee leaned back and furrowed her brow. She seemed to consider the matter carefully for a few seconds. "In different light. Those were her exact words. But the woman talked funny. Does it matter?"

Patricia frowned. She reached in her purse for her cell phone, pulled a business card out of her jacket pocket, and started dialing. Dr. Benning, the Emergency Department head, answered after the third ring.

"Hello?"

"Dr. Benning? This is Dr. West. We met earlier today."

"Dr West." Benning chuckled. "I had a feeling you might call. Didn't expect it to be so soon."

"Are you in the emergency room by any chance?"

"In my private office. Just down the hall from the ER," Benning said.

"You mind if I drop by," Patricia said, "and borrow your Wood's lamp?"

CHAPTER TWENTY

Balakin

The stranger was kneeling quietly. His torso
was bent so low to the ground that when Father
Ambrus crossed over from the narthex into the
temple proper, he had not seen the supplicant. It
was only as he made his way toward the altar,
fumbling the keys to the sanctuary, that the cleric
caught sight of the kneeling man.

Father Ambrus stopped in his tracks, jolted not
by a pang of alarm, but by a sense of wonderment.
Under the dome depicting Christ Pantocrator,
showered by the jaundiced light streaming from
the stained glass window tucked deep in the nave,
the stranger was the picture of piety.

And how did this saint happen to fall from the sky?

The priest let out a soft cough. "Good
afternoon," he said.

The stranger shot to his feet, turned to face
Father Ambrus. He had piercing eyes, the eyes of

a soul who was no stranger to suffering. "I'm sorry, the door was open," the man said.

"As are our hearts," said Father Ambrus. "Welcome to St. Chrysostom."

The man approached the priest, knelt, and kissed the cleric's hand. "Bless me, father."

A Russian accent, Father Ambrus thought. "I bless you, my son. I'm sorry to have interrupted your prayers."

"Oh, not at all," the man said. "You are Father Ambrus, yes? I am here to see you, actually." The stranger let out a bashful chuckle. "I'm sorry. I'm not very exercised with this. He reached into his blazer pocket and pulled out a dog-eared business card. "My name is Balakin. Borya Balakin. I am deacon at Saint Spyridon Church in Ryazan. Near Moscow. You know?"

"You've come a very long way," Father Ambrus said.

"Ah! Airplane is very fast," Balakin said.

Father Ambrus smiled. From his closely cropped hair to his trim fingernails, the stranger was meticulously groomed, not with the flair of a dandy, but in the style of a man accustomed to a thoroughly disciplined regimen. "How can I help you, brother deacon?"

"I was admiring your beautiful painting of St. Chrysostom. Very, very nice."

"You have a good eye. It is my favorite piece of artwork in the temple."

"By Kovalenko, no?" the stranger said.

"You have an excellent eye, indeed!"

Balakin waved his hand back and forth in the air. "I am not an expert. But we had a very nice painting of Saint Spyridon, by Kovalenko, in our church. Before the fire."

"Fire? Oh, goodness!"

"Don't worry. Church is okay," Balakin said. "But the paintings, many of our icons . . ." He shook his head with a doleful smile.

"I'm so sorry to hear that."

"Yes," Balakin said and looked down at his hands.

"If there's any way I can help . . ."

"Thank you," Balakin said. "My church has already raised funds to commission Professor Kovalenko for a new painting of St. Spyridon. The only problem . . ."

"Yes?" the priest spurred him on.

"The only problem is I left my address book in the back seat of a taxi in Houston."

"I don't understand," Father Andrus said.

"Dr. Kovalenko's address was in that book," Balakin said. He raised his hands to his brow and shook his head. "I'm so clumsy sometimes. I came here, hoping you had his address. Not so many great masters in the city of Austin, I am guessing. I thought maybe your church must have some of his paintings."

"Well, your instincts were sound," Father

Andrus said. "I have Dr. Kovalenko's address at hand. You're not the first person today who has requested it." The priest made a gesture, and the two men started walking in the direction of the church office.

"Oh?" Balakin said.

"A couple of police officers stopped in this morning."

"Police?" Balakin blurted out in alarm.

Father Ambrus turned to face Balakin. "Nothing to worry about. They came to ask about a series of seven icons Dr. Kovalenko must have painted some time ago. Exquisite pieces. You would have fallen in love."

The two men started walking again. Balakin stroked his jaw with his fingers, just grazing the skin with his neatly trimmed fingernails. Looking down, as if deep in thought, his eyes no longer illuminated by the beam from the stained glass window, eyes that had all but lost their angelic glow, Balakin said, "Seven icons, you say."

CHAPTER TWENTY-ONE

Marcus

"I got better things to do than act as your personal chauffeur," Marcus West said, topping seventy-five on highway 123. He raced past a field of scorched corn, bugs the size of hummingbirds pinging off the front grill of his Cadillac CTS.

"I'm sorry," Alex said, "that being my father is such an inconvenience for you."

"Your mom's got you very well trained, doesn't she? Does she tell you the exact words to use to punish me?" Marcus shook his head. "She's the one who was supposed to drive you to your grandparents today in the first place. Always changing things to suit her whims."

The stench of dead skunk filled the cabin of the car.

"Jesus!" Marcus said. "How do people live out here?"

Alex opened the book that had been resting on

his lap and pretended to read.

In a mumbling voice, Marcus said, "She gets that job in Austin, she'll want to change the terms of the settlement. Well, it'll cost her. Plenty."

"Uh-huh," Alex said, without looking up from his book.

"Shouldn't read in the car," Marcus said. "You'll get motion sickness. Cost me hundred-twenty bucks to get the interior detailed. I don't need you to barf all over it."

"I'll barf out the window if I get the urge," Alex said.

Marcus sneered. "You were always barfing in the car as a kid. I'd drive you two miles to daycare, and I'd have to clean out vomit from the backseat."

"Don't forget. I quit Little League," Alex said.

"What does that have to do with anything?"

"I'm just trying to help you recount all the ways I disappointed you."

Marcus frowned. He looked up ahead at the two-lane highway where the heat made the blacktop look like puddles of water. After a minute, he said, "What are you reading, anyway?"

"Sun Tzu. *The Art of War.*"

"Again? What is it with you and that book?"

"There are some things I have to review," Alex said.

"What, you going to war?" Marcus said.

"Maybe."

"Look, Alex," Marcus West said in a softer tone, "What happened at school, that was horrible, okay? But it's done with. You're safe now. You don't need to worry."

"Uh-huh," Alex said.

"There's other books you should be reading. Books that will give you a leg up. Make you successful. You should check out *The 7 Habits of Highly Effective People*; Dale Carnegie's *How to Make Friends and Influence People*. Or how about Napoleon Hill, *Think and Grow Rich*? Those are some classics there."

"You know what other books are classics? The Iliad. Hamlet."

"You think I'm uneducated? Is that it? You think I never read Shakespeare? Have you ever read King Lear? You know what that's all about? Ungrateful children." Marcus rolled down the driver's side window, slowed the car, snorted something up and spit out the window. He rolled the window back up and pressed his foot down on the accelerator. "Maybe it's a good thing if your mom takes that job in Austin - put a little distance between us so we can all stop pretending."

Marcus gave the gas pedal a final thrust as if to drive home the point, then took his foot off and let the car coast to a stop at a red light. A stop that seemed completely superfluous for an intersection on this stretch of highway. He tried to get a glimpse of Alex from the corner of his eye. The boy had the book open on his lap but was staring out the windshield, focused, the way he would get when he was deep in thought. Marcus knew the kid was either thinking about a passage he had just read or was getting ready to let him have it. He tightened his grip on the steering wheel as if bracing for impact.

"Father," Alex said in a tender voice, "I'm truly sorry you couldn't live out your frustrated sports dreams vicariously through me."

Marcus didn't reply. *What kind of kid talked that way?* The light turned green. Marcus proceeded cautiously, his ears perked.

"Dad," Alex said, "Tell me the truth. What do you resent more, the fact that mom always earned more money than you, or that she never earned as much as you had hoped?"

CHAPTER TWENTY-TWO

Arkadi

The thing about unbaked Bavarian pretzel dough is that it's astonishingly hard, heavy, and sticky. Arkadi Volkov learned this years ago as a new hire at Dieter's Bakery and Cafe in the heart of New Braunfels. If you're not careful, you can break your knuckles if you punch a ball of it too hard. And shaping the dough by hand is a bit like bending rebar. Still, you've got to work fast when shaping pretzels, especially when you have to bake an order of five-hundred by noon.

Arkadi relished the challenge. After all, it was the acts of kneading and shaping (he had no doubt in his mind) that had brought his strength back, reviving the atrophied muscles in his hands, arms, shoulders, and back. Transforming them from gaunt sinews to chiseled brawn. Dieter would take on new apprentice bakers from time to time. Nearly all would quit after a brief spell, their spirits crushed by that obstinate, tenacious pretzel dough. Only Arkadi stayed on, year after passing year.

Arkadi liked Dieter. Or at least, he had found no reason to dislike him. The old Bavarian was discreet, didn't talk much, and was too busy running his shop to bother prodding into his employees' pasts. Only once did Dieter ask him a prying question. It came after a foiled robbery attempt. Arkadi had snapped the wrist of a drug-crazed thug who was threatening the cashier with a switch-blade. Then he bashed the would-be robber's forehead into the granite counter for good measure. After the police left with the perpetrator in handcuffs, Dieter asked Arkadi in a hushed voice, "Were you KGB?"

Arkadi chuckled. "KGB had guns," he said. And that was the end of that.

It was not the job at the bakery that tried Arkadi's soul. It was the utter loneliness of his existence. When he was not working, he spent most of his time dedicated to his mission. Armed with binoculars, night-vision goggles, and a Nikon camera with a 135 millimeter lens, he oversaw the mundane movements of a boy and his mother.

In truth, the camera was an unnecessary luxury. He picked it up for not too great of a bargain from a pawn shop off Walnut Avenue and justified the expense with the pretext that it might prove important to document the boy's growth and development with a photographic record. But soon, he found himself taking more pictures of Patricia West than her son. He was always discrete about it, considerate even. He limited his snapshots to public venues. Respecting her privacy was an utmost priority.

His favorite photograph of her was taken outside the medical office. She had stopped next to her car one evening after work to admire the setting sun, her profile accentuated by the crimson back-light in what appeared to be a rare moment of serenity for the harried doctor. That was the picture he kept on his bedroom dresser, next to a half-dozen photos of Alex at different ages. That blown-up snapshot, Arkadi knew, was the closest he'd ever get to her.

Now Arkadi was rolling a rope of dough on the maple worktable, leaning into it with his shoulders when Dieter poked his head into the kitchen. "Arkadi! Phone call."

"Phone call?" Arkadi said, quickly shaping the dough in the classic pretzel shape using the practiced technique Dieter had taught him.

"Man's voice. Sounds like a foreigner." The observation being uttered in a thick Bavarian accent that rendered the German barely intelligible when he spoke English.

Arkadi grabbed a towel, wiped his hands on it, and lay it on his shoulder as he walked to the front of the bakery.

"Hello?" Arkadi said, lifting the receiver of the wall-mounted telephone.

The man on the other end of the line said, "Austin American-Statesman. Section one, page three." Then in Russian, "We can no longer delude ourselves, dear comrade. The moment we feared is upon us."

Arkadi hung up without uttering another word. He shuffled past the server's station into the dining area where a crowd of regulars was sitting in linoleum booths, gorging on pancakes and buttered toast and sausage and eggs over-easy. Arkadi would never comprehend how American retirees could eat so much at breakfast, washing it all down with tumblers of dilute coffee. The Russian plodded along, his t-shirt and cotton skull cap growing damp with sweat. His apron was shedding clumps of flour, forming a narrow white trail on the floor, beckoning him to find his way back to the kitchen.

A young waitress, a needlessly sullen, pretty blonde who always blushed when Arkadi greeted her with a good-morning, stared at him wide-eyed. "Can I help you?" she stammered.

Arkadi ignored her. He walked past the waitress and headed to a mahogany shelf tucked in a corner past the cash register, newspapers piled on its three shelves. He found two copies of the Herald Zeitung, one San Antonio Express-

News, a Houston Chronicle, even an untouched print of the Wall Street Journal, but no Austin American-Statesman. Arkadi looked around the dining room. None of the customers seemed to pay him any heed. They weren't about to let an intruder spoil their breakfast ritual. They kept eating and chatting with the casual imperviousness that is the hallmark of the American morning diner. Arkadi walked down the aisle of booths, his eyes scanning the tables for newspapers. He saw one in the second booth and discerned by its size that it was a Herald Zeitung, New Braunfels' own daily publication.

He kept moving until he came to a booth where a portly gentleman sat alone, a newspaper folded neatly to the left of his plate of bacon and eggs. The man was bald and pale with stringy eyebrows that curved up at the sides, giving him the appearance of a pink, over-fed owl.

"Yes?" the man said, looking up from the newspaper to gaze at Arkadi towering over him.

"American-Statesman?" Arkadi asked, pointing at the newspaper on the table.

"Yes."

Arkadi grabbed the paper, flipped through the pages. The man said, "Excuse me. Can I help you?"

Why did people insist on using that expression, can I help you? Did it look like Arkadi needed help? It made no sense to him, this polite impoliteness. What was the proper reply to such stupidity? Arkadi didn't bother to offer a retort. He flipped the pages until he found section one, page three, and began to scan the headlines. There was an article about worsening traffic along the I-35 corridor. Another detailing how oil output from the wells in Midland-Odessa was below original projections. A third article had something to do with newly proposed changes to the admissions process at the University of Texas. Near the bottom of the page was the headline, Teenage Boaters Still Missing Off Galveston Island.

"This man just took my newspaper. Right out of my hands!" the bald man protested to a man sipping coffee in the adjoining booth.

Arkadi read the first line of the article about the missing teenagers. He pressed his lips together, paused a moment, then began tearing the piece out of the newspaper. That's when he noticed Dieter standing at his side.

"Arkadi," Dieter said. "What is the meaning of this?"

Arkadi turned the newspaper ninety degrees and made a final tear. He stuffed the article in his pocket, handed the rest of the journal back to the bald man. Only then did he turn to face Dieter square in the eyes. In a somber tone, Arkadi said, "I must go."

Dieter looked at him for a moment, too stunned

to say anything. He finally managed to say, "But the pretzels ..."

Arkadi shook his head. He repeated, "I must go."

Dieter put his hand on Arkadi's shoulder. "All these years, I never asked you about your business," he said.

"Thank you," Arkadi said. "Thank you for everything." He untied the bow of his apron, slipped it off, removed his skull cap, and handed the items to his employer. Then, without saying another word, he walked out the front door of Dieter's Bakery and Cafe for the last time.

CHAPTER TWENTY-THREE

Seven Icons

Patricia West walked into the heart of the
emergency room of Austin Children's Hospital,
flanked by Jamie Lee Foster and Kyle Wagner.
Jamie Lee was striding next to her in her usual
wide-arm swagger. Kyle proceeding in a more
cautious stride a few steps behind, carrying the
cardboard box containing the religious icons. Dr.
Benning, the ER chief met them in the hallway,
flashed Patricia a wistful smile, and said, "I was
hoping you were coming alone."

"Thanks for doing this, Dr. Benning," Patricia
said.

"What do you need a Wood's lamp for? Does
someone have a nasty case of ringworm?" Dr.
Benning said, turning his mocking gaze to Kyle,
studying him a moment. The ER doctor's
expression softened the instant he decided there
was nothing between this cowboy and the

beautiful Dr. West. She was way out of his league.

"We don't want to take any more of your time, Dr. Benning," Patricia said.

"It's in room twelve," Dr. Benning said. "My favorite room. No windows. Gets nice and dark in there."

Everything that came out the man's mouth seemed to have a creepy double entendre. Patricia had barely met the man, and he was already grating her nerves.

They entered the exam room without Dr. Benning following them in, thank God. The rectangular lamp with its purple fluorescent tube was laying on a counter next to a hand-washing sink. Patricia plugged the power cord in a wall outlet. At the same time, Kyle unpacked the religious icons from the box and set them one next to the other on the padded exam table.

"So, what's the deal with this lamp?" Jamie Lee asked.

"Basically, it's a black light," Patricia West said. "We use it to help us diagnose certain skin conditions."

"How's it going to help us?" Jame Lee said.

"I don't know that it will," Patricia said. "It's just a hunch. What that woman said to you ..."

"Miss Olga," Jamie Lee said.

"What she said to you about seeing the pictures under a different light," Patricia said. "I don't know. I might be grasping at straws here."

Kyle said, "There are some forms of invisible ink that are only visible in black light."

"Where did you learn that?" Jamie Lee said. "Special ops?"

Kyle shook his head. "There's a dance hall in Spring Branch we busted once for selling alcohol to minors. They used a black light ink-stamp to mark the hands of patrons at the front door."

Patricia flicked a toggle switch on the side of the lamp, keeping it pointed to the floor, and said, "When you're ready, we can turn off the overhead lights."

Jamie Lee flipped the overhead light switch to the off position.

Patricia began sweeping the lamp over the icons slowly, methodically. There were some flecks of material in the paint that stood out brightly white, but overall the effect was underwhelming.

"You see anything?" Kyle said.

"I hate to disappoint Miss Olga," Jamie Lee said, "but I'm just not getting a spiritual revelation here."

When Patricia finished scanning the face of the last icon, she said, "Let's try turning them over." She flipped over the first icon, brought the Wood's lamp over it, and her jaw dropped.

"Well, what do you know!" Jamie Lee said and slapped Kyle hard on the back of his shoulder.

On the wood backing of the frame, fluorescent green letters lit up. Patricia turned over another icon. It, too, had writing on its back.

"Can you read that?" Jamie Lee said.

"It's in Russian," Kyle said.

"I figured that much, hotshot," Jamie Lee said. "Is this where you tell me you also once busted up a Russian porn ring down there in Spring Ranch —"

"Branch," Kyle said.

"Whatever. Or maybe you took a crash course in Russian on your travels abroad?"

"No such luck. But, if we print out the Cyrillic alphabet from the internet, we might be able to decode some of this," said Kyle.

"Cyrillic?" Jamie Lee said.

"That's the name for the script most Slavic countries use," Kyle said.

Jamie Lee smirked, "Well, aren't you just the little know-it-all. In Wrangler jeans, no less."

Kyle rolled his eyes. "What does that have to do with anything?" he said.

"Makes a world of difference whether a man wears Levis or Wrangler. Don't bother trying to decode this. It's a waste of our time."

"Don't you want to know what this says?" Kyle said.

"Sure," Jamie Lee said. "But why go through all the trouble of decoding letter by letter when we can have our Russian painter friend just read it out to us. Maybe he can even tell us how they got on the back of his pictures in the first place."

Patricia said, "Is that your way of wheedling me to come with you?"

Jamie Lee chuckled. "I didn't know I had any wheedling left to do. I could have sworn, looking in your eyes, that I had you pretty well hooked back at the diner. You must be dying to know what this is all about."

"It would be beneficial if you came with us," Kyle said, in a more diplomatic tone.

Patricia took a deep breath. "All the same," she said, "we need to copy this down while we have the Wood's lamp. I'll go get a pen and some paper."

Jamie Lee pulled a tiny notepad from a pocket in her jacket. "No need." She whacked Kyle on the arm with the pad, handed him her ballpoint pen. "I'll let you do the honors, Mr. Cyrillic."

Kyle started copying the lettering from the first icon as Patricia held the black light over it.

"Look at the last two letters," Patricia said.

"T, X," Kyle said.

"Texas?" Jamie Lee said. "You think that's an address?"

"It's about the right number of words," Kyle said.

He turned over another icon. Patricia focused intensely as she studied the letters. The second word on the back of the painting made her heart skip a beat. "Oh shit," she said.

"What?" Jamie Lee said.

Patricia pointed at the word. The first letter looked like a capital B, the second a backward-facing E; the last two letters were a C and a T. "That's my last name in Russian, West. I remember that from the adoption documents. And that first word, that's Alexander; my son's name."

Kyle pointed at a number. "Four-five-two-one. Does that number mean anything to you?"

"It used to be my street address," Patricia heard herself say. For some reason, she didn't want to reveal that it was still her ex-husband's address. The house she had shelled out the down-payment for. The home Marcus' girlfriend had moved into three weeks after their divorce went through.

She flipped the icon over. "Can you turn the overhead lights back on?"

Patricia studied the painting. It depicted a saint with a long white beard, his haloed head covered by a blue hood that extended down past his shoulders.

"I know this painting," Patricia said. "That's St. Anthony of the Kiyv Caves. This was hanging on the wall over Alexander's crib in the nursery of the orphanage in Odessa."

"You seem pretty sure of that," Kyle said.

Patricia nodded. "Yeah, I'm sure." She walked to the wall behind her and flicked the overhead lights off again before a solitary tear escaped and rolled down her cheek.

CHAPTER TWENTY-FOUR

Wyatt

"Don't lose hope. There's still a slim chance he might grow into a man someday," Wyatt Holmes said. He rested his hand on his grandson's shoulder. The two looked on as Marcus West's white Cadillac moved up the desolate drive and finally turned onto the highway and raced out of sight.

"You really think so?" Alex West said.

Wyatt Holmes chuckled. "Miracles do happen sometimes." He bent down to pick up Alex's duffle bag and said, "Come on. Grandma's baking buttermilk biscuits."

"That's called alliteration," Alex said.

"Baking buttermilk biscuits? Yeah, it's a mouthful." He glanced at the book in Alex's hand. "What are you reading?"

"Sun Tzu. *The Art of War.*"

"Again?"

"It seems like a timely topic," Alex said.

"If the subject piques your interest, you might want to peruse Von Clausewitz someday. I think you can just about handle it now."

The smell of coffee and bacon and blueberry pancakes wafted through the living room when Wyatt Holmes and Alex West entered the home. The clacking of the front door closing behind them brought Betty Holmes scurrying into the living room from the kitchen.

"Oh, dear boy!" she said as she wrapped her arms around her grandson and planted a kiss on his forehead. "You had us so worried!"

"Good lord! Don't smother the boy," Wyatt Holmes said, plopping the duffle bag onto the floor. "Where are my biscuits and gravy?"

"Oh, shush, old man!" Betty cried out. She cradled Alex's face with her hands. "Tell me the truth. How are you, Alex?"

"I'm hungry," Alex said.

"Now that I can fix." Grandma Betty took Alex by the hand, pushed her husband out of the way, and marched her grandson toward the kitchen table.

Betty and Wyatt Holmes lived in a custom beach bungalow set on three acres just south of the Redfish Bay Causeway in Aransas Pass. Their sprawling back yard extended to a man-made boat canal, across which a new real estate development was taking shape. A fifty-foot boardwalk supported by round wood pilings ran along the waterfront leading to Wyatt's pride and joy: a two-slip boathouse complete with a bar, flat-screen TV, and outdoor grill.

The Holmes family had done well for itself. Betty had had a stellar thirty-year career as a patent attorney. Wyatt, a chemical engineer, managed to weather booms and busts in the oil industry and the maddening vicissitudes of the stock market to amass a considerable asset portfolio. Now the couple spent their days boating, fishing, volunteering at the local food pantry, and caring for three semi-domesticated tabby cats. It was as stress-free a life as they had known. And yet, like parents of adult children are apt to do, they often found themselves fretting over the welfare of their daughter. And of her adopted son.

Wyatt traced the disquiet back to Patricia's marriage. He had often voiced the opinion — to Betty's displeasure and despite her admonitions to keep his opinions to himself — that he had no use for Marcus West. Never had. Not that their eventual divorce brought him any sense of satisfaction or vindication.

After Alex finished polishing off his plate, Wyatt gulped down his second cup of coffee and said, "Come with me, son. I got something to show you."

Wyatt led his grandson into the backyard. They

walked down the stone-paved path that ran through the manicured lawn. Stepped onto the wooden boardwalk that stretched along the canal all the way to the boathouse.

Alex followed his grandfather eagerly. The boathouse was one of his favorite spots. In no small part, because it was off-limits to him, his entry allowed only in the presence of his grandfather. Of course, that also made it the perfect hiding place.

An antique cedar-hulled canoe bobbed in the water, moored in the first slip, it's line fastened to a stainless steel boat cleat on the boathouse dock. The other slip was empty.

"Where's *The Unthinkable*?" Alex asked.

Wyatt was fond of the clever name he had christened his fishing boat with. Betty, not so much.

"It *thunk*?" Alex said as though he had suddenly developed a lisp.

"No, *thilly*. It didn't *think*," Wyatt said, picking up on his grandson's jest. She's at Jake's marina getting a new power plant. Twin Evinrudes. Three-hundred horse-power each."

"Wasn't two-hundred horse-power enough?"

"Yeah," Wyatt said. "But, I wanted more than enough." Wyatt chuckled. "Don't worry. She'll be ready by the weekend. Then we can go down to Steadman's Reef. Or Ranson Island."

"Or Mustang Island," Alex said.

"Sure. Or South Padre, if you want. Why not?" Wyatt Holmes grabbed the rail of a metal spiral staircase which led to a second story, and started climbing up. "Are you coming?"

Alex looked around the boathouse. Every tool and gadget was in its proper place. Wooden oars were neatly tucked away in their paddle clips on the inside of the canoe. Fishing poles, arranged by ascending size, were stowed in a wall-mounted rack. Snorkels, flippers, and masks were stacked methodically in a large, rectangular, clear plastic bucket. A heavy boat anchor rested on the dock of the empty slip, its thick vinyl line coiled into a neat bundle. On the other side of the boathouse, the bar was spotlessly clean. Grandpa Wyatt could be compulsive to a near-neurotic level. It was the engineer in him.

Alex smirked. He pulled a fishing rod out of its holder and laid it on the dock. He stood up. Tilted his head to look at it. Bent down again and moved the handle of the rod slightly, cocking it at an odd angle. As he got back up, he had to press both hands to his mouth to suppress a giggle. Finally, he climbed up the stairs, trying to wipe the smile off his face.

"What took you so long?" Wyatt said when Alex's head came up over the floorboards of the loft.

Wyatt was crouching next to a wooden trunk on the far side of the loft. A blue tarpaulin was neatly

177

folded in the corner.

The loft was usually off-limits to Alex. It was what Wyatt Holmes referred to as the business part of the boathouse. The few times his grandfather had invited him upstairs, Alex had to feign a sense of wonderment so that the old man didn't catch on that this was where he always came to get away.

Still, the place was pretty amazing. Wyatt had personally designed the structure with the help of an architect friend. He had come up with the idea of installing two metal boat cranes onto steel beams that ran across the rafters. Each crane had its own electric winch. And just below, on the floor of the loft, were two wooden trap doors that opened directly over the boat slips. It was a setup that made lifting a heavy boat out of the water a cinch. But Betty Holmes had once forgotten that one of the trap doors had been left open when she was sweeping the floor upstairs. She was backing up distractedly and would have fallen right through that opening in the floor, plumb into the water down below if Wyatt hadn't pulled her to safety in the nick of time.

"What's in the trunk?" Alex asked, noticing the expectant grin on Wyatt's face.

"Why don't you come and open it and see?" Wyatt said.

Alex ambled next to his grandfather, squatted, and lifted the lid of the trunk. He looked inside.

Alex's first thought was that he had never seen such a beautiful object in his entire life. He turned his head to face his grandfather.

"Well?" Wyatt said. "What are you waiting for?"

Alex reached inside the trunk, grasped the object with both hands. Lifted it up to admire it. It was a sleek spear-fishing gun with a polished mahogany stock.

"It's beautiful," Alex said.

"That spool holds a sixty-foot line," Wyatt said. "And the barb on that arrow will hold onto a Mako shark, in case you happen to harpoon one."

"In case *I* happen to harpoon one?"

"It's yours, son."

Alex gently placed the speargun back inside the wooden trunk and wrapped his arms around his grandpa's neck.

Wyatt patted the boy's back. "Alright, alright, let's not make a big fuss, now," he said. Alex released his grip on the man. "Just one little thing, though. The reason I have it up here in the loft? Your grandmother's a little squeamish about these things. Best we keep it our little secret for now."

"Sure thing, Wyatt," Alex said.

The old man nodded. "You got a good look at it? Good. Let's go."

As they headed back down the spiral staircase, Alex remembered the little prank involving the fishing rod he had set up a few minutes earlier.

He couldn't help but feel a pang of guilt. Though he still thought it was hilarious.

Right on cue, when Wyatt got downstairs and saw the fishing rod on the floor, he put his hands on his hips and let out a, "What the ..."

Alex busted out laughing.

Wyatt turned, smiled at Alex, and said, "Why, you little weasel ..."

The old man let out a baritone chuckle, picked the fishing rod off the floor, and was about to put it back on its peg when Alex asked him, "Grandpa, do you remember the day I was born?"

Wyatt Holmes fell silent. He moved slowly, rotating the fishing rod slightly when it was already in its place on the rack.

"Do you remember what the weather was like?" Alex paused a moment. "Did you and Grandma Betty come to see me at the hospital?" Alex waited as his grandfather turned. The expression on the man's face was a mix of pain and embarrassment.

Wyatt walked to the empty boat slip, removed the flip-flops from his feet, set them down neatly, at a ninety-degree angle from the edge of the dock, and sat down with his feet dangling over the water. He said, "Come here, son."

Alex sat next to him. He looked on as Wyatt skimmed his toes over the surface of the water.

"That spear gun upstairs," Wyatt said. "That's our little secret, right?"

Alex nodded.

"Do you suppose," Wyatt said, "we can keep another secret between us? This one a tad bigger."

Alex put his hand on Wyatt's knee. "It's okay, Wyatt. You don't have to say anything. I already know."

CHAPTER TWENTY-FIVE

San Antonio

A Soviet Army captain had once told Borya
Balakin that America's empire would surely
crumble because its citizens are hypocrites to the
core. "For a handful of coins," the captain boasted,
"an American will sell his soul and still proclaim
his freedom." A year later, the Army officer was
court-martialed by a military tribunal. The official
line was that the captain had accepted a bribe
from an undercover KGB investigator posing as a
foreign agent. After a speedy trial, he was hanged
unceremoniously in the dark, windowless
courtyard of a government building. A few
months later, the Soviet Union collapsed.

Still, Borya Balakin thought there was a kernel
of truth to the captain's assertion, for fools and
madmen are known to speak the truth in rare
moments of lucidity. Borya Balakin often
wondered what lurked in the hearts of Americans.

But at the moment, he was more interested in indulging his curiosity on another issue: a matter that pressed on his soul. He knew better than to solicit evidence to validate his mission. After all, there is no need to gauge one's acts with the laws of man when executing the will of God. When charged with God's work, any demand for explanations is pure blasphemy. And yet he wanted to see something for himself, wanted to witness with his own two eyes the evil he had a hand in perpetrating and was now entrusted to destroy.

Borya Balakin knew that it was an unnecessary indulgence, but he had to satisfy this little curiosity of his. After some reflection, he decided this slight variation of his original plan was entirely acceptable seeing as it would still achieve its underlying purpose and remain within the boundaries of the overarching mission

He had studied the boy's movements for the last two days and had almost come to pity him. The boy seemed to have no friends, spent most of his time cooped up at home. Alone, on his computer, no doubt. Between two and three in the afternoon, the boy walked the distance of five blocks, crossing a small neighborhood market along the way, to reach a What-a-Burger where he ordered two Patty Melts, large fries, and sweet tea. He had eaten exactly the same meal two days in a row. That was a good sign. With any luck, the little monster was a creature of habit — a detail worth exploiting. It would have to be at the neighborhood market, which backed onto a hidden alley, where Balakin would set his bait.

At around one pm on the chosen day, standing next to a busy intersection a half-mile from the market, Balakin spotted a tall, lean black man holding a cardboard sign that read, "Hungry. Please help. God bless." The man wore a tattered coat, but his sneakers were in remarkably good shape, as though he were planning to join a pick-up game of basketball after filling his pockets with a good day's take.

Borya Balakin walked up to him, looked at his cardboard sign, and said, "Hunger is not your aunt. It will not bring you a pie."

The black man looked at him with a stunned expression and said, "Say what?"

"Old Russian saying," Balakin said.

"Yeah, well, here's an old American saying," the black man said. "Get the fuck out of my face before I hurt you."

"Aah! But that's exactly what I want." Balakin pulled two twenty dollar bills from his pocket. "I want you to hurt me a little."

"Hey, you freak. I ain't that way."

Balakin chuckled. "No, no. I'm not queer. No sex. I need you to act a little. It's a little joke on a friend. Takes five minutes; you make forty dollars."

"Make it sixty."

"I give you twenty now, forty later." Balakin handed him a twenty-dollar bill, stuffed the other one in his pocket. "Meet me at the Speedy-Mart in an hour."

An hour later, Borya Balakin was wearing the black man's tattered coat. His face smeared in grime. He pretended to drink from a brown paper bag as he pushed a shopping cart stuffed with plastic garbage bags. When the boy exited the What-a-Burger, Balakin raised the collar of his coat. It was the signal he had instructed the black man to watch for. He had urged the panhandler to make his playacting look convincing. To really go at it. Not to hold back. But would the guy follow through? Balakin was about to find out.

Sure enough, there he came. The black man walked over with a menacing stride, snatched the bottle from Balakin's hand. Smashed it on the ground. From the corner of his eye, Balakin could see that the sound of the bottle shattering had gotten his target's attention. So far, so good.

The man then kicked over the shopping cart. Balakin raised his arms in a display of submission.

Now was the critical moment. Borya Balakin hoped his accomplice would make it count.

The panhandler didn't let him down. He slammed his fist into Balakin's abdomen with unbridled enthusiasm. Balakin had been punched much harder in the past, but this would do quite well. He doubled over, crumpled to his knees.

Sure enough, the boy shouted, "Hey!"

Balakin raised his face just a little, put it in position.

The black man slapped him hard on the cheek.

Balakin had instructed his accomplice to slap rather than punch his face, not because he feared the pain, nor because he was particularly worried about maintaining the integrity of the panhandler's knuckles. Simply because Borya knew that there is something egregious, something undeniably inglorious and humiliating about an open hand landing on a man's cheek, which even a fist cannot evoke.

The boy yelled again. "Heeeey!"

Balakin's ears perked. There was no mistaking it. The boy's voice still echoed in his ears, mixed with the indifferent clamor of street traffic. In the boy's voice, Balakin could hear the desperate wail of indignity, a plaintive howl in the face of injustice. And he heard more. Balakin thought he heard the familiar notes of a primal shriek born of ancient battlefields — a sound only one emotion could bring forth: rage.

As instructed, his assailant reached inside the coat Balakin was wearing, pulled a package out from the inside pocket, and started running in the direction of the back alley. The boy ran up to Balakin, leaned down, and asked him, "Are you alright, mister?"

Clenching his abdomen, Balakin muttered, "My money bag."

Balakin had spent some time earlier that morning, considering his choice of words. "My wallet" would have sounded wrong. What kind of homeless man carries a wallet? "My purse" came off as too old-fashioned, too eccentric. No. Money bag was the right choice. Sure enough, the words catapulted the boy into a mad chase after the assailant.

Balakin gave the boy a twenty-yard head start, then started jogging after him. When he entered the alley, he was forced to quicken his pace. The black man had already tossed the package to the floor and was climbing a tall chain-link fence, but the boy gave no indication of abandoning his pursuit. He was already climbing the fence when Borya Balakin was able to grab his leg and say, "Thank you, thank you. I got it."

The boy would have kept going if Balakin had let go of his leg.

"Thank you," Balakin said. "I'm fine, I'm fine."

The boy released his grip of the fence and jumped down onto the pavement. For a moment, he stood there, fists clenched, his whole body shaking.

"It's okay now. Look," Balakin said, pointing at the floor. "My money bag."

The boy said, "I was gonna kill him."

"Yes, I know."

"What he did to you. That was wrong."

"But I'm okay now."

The boy leaned down to pick the money bag off the floor. Handed it to Balakin with a shaky hand. "You want to check that everything's there?"

"You have a patch of white hair," Balakin said. "Right there on your head."

The boy's eyes widened. He looked rattled. He raked his fingers through his hair and looked away.

"Let me see if everything is as it should be," Balakin said. "Ah, yes. Here it is." He pulled a screwdriver out of the money bag.

A common mistake among amateurs, when trying to stab someone in the heart with a shiv, is to try to deliver the blow straight through the chest, hoping they'll get lucky, and the blade will glide between the ribs somehow. That might do for a jail-house brawl, but when absolute certainty is required, when professionalism is at stake, a more fool-proof approach should be employed. Many years ago, a young Soviet doctor had been kind enough to teach Borya and his class-mates the proper procedure, which in medical circles was known as pericardiocentesis. The key was to penetrate the upper abdomen, just below the sternum, in an upward direction, pushing through the diaphragm and into the inferior wall of the right ventricle. The heart, the doctor reminded his students, was located more centrally than most people realized, so there was no need to aim the skewer toward the victim's left shoulder, an angle that would be impractical for most right-handers to achieve out in the field. Straight up would do.

Balakin happened to be left-handed, which was a blessing in this regard. In one fluid movement, he shoved the screwdriver in his victim's heart, feeling the differences in density and texture of the various tissue planes his weapon had traversed, cognizant of the fact that the boy would be dead in seconds. Borya Balakin would not have time to recite the entire Canon to the Most Holy Theotokos, the last rites practiced by his order.

Instead, he whispered, "On behalf of a man whose soul is departing, and who cannot speak, our Father, I commend to you his soul."

He gently lay the boy onto the pavement and traced the sign of the cross on the forehead of the lifeless body. Then he took the black leather wallet from the back pocket of the boy's jeans and walked away. Balakin pulled out all the money from the boy's wallet, twelve dollars in all, and pocketed it. He tossed the wallet into a dumpster at the entrance to the alley where the police were sure to find it.

They will say the boy died for a measly twelve dollars. What a pity!

CHAPTER TWENTY-SIX
Volya

Professor Sergey Kovalenko lived in a tidy
one-story red-brick house whose exterior was far
less presumptuous than the neighboring homes on
the quiet, tree-lined avenue, two blocks east of the
MoPac Expressway. In his teaching years, Dr.
Kovalenko was in the habit of riding to work on
his vintage Graziella folding bicycle. He'd pedal
down Windsor Road before heading east on West
24th Street for a mile or so until he reached the
Norman Hackerman Building, where his office
was tucked at the end of a narrow hallway
festooned with posters of scientific articles, high
up on the seventh floor.

When Patricia, Jamie Lee and Kyle reached the
house, it was Kyle who walked to the front door to
ring the doorbell, Patricia staying a couple of steps
behind him on the front porch, while Jamie Lee
snooped around on a walkway that encircled a

flower bed in front of the home.

"Looks like no one's home," Kyle said after a short wait.

"Try again," Jamie Lee said.

Kyle pushed down on the doorbell again. Patricia started having second thoughts about the company she was keeping, particularly when she noticed an emboldened Jamie Lee stepping off the walkway, into a bed of petunias and flowering cabbage, to peek through what would turn out to be the formal dining room window. Patricia folded her arms and pulled in her shoulders, feeling a bit like a turtle trying to hide in its shell, hoping to God no neighbors were watching. Right on cue, Jamie Lee's polished black boot snapped the head of a flower clear off its stem. And then Patricia's hopes of escaping notice were crushed by a strange yapping sound coming from behind her.

"Can I help you?" the tense voice of a young woman called out.

Patricia turned. A square-shouldered, brunette with a pink bandana tied around her neck, stood in the walkway, clenching the leash of a dog so tightly that Patricia thought she might choke the funny-looking mutt. The woman yanked back on the rope as though the creature she was handling were a wild beast that threatened to lunge at any moment. She kept her glaring eyes fixed on Jamie Lee Foster, who continued trouncing in the flower bed, unfazed. Jamie Lee moved deliberately as if to push home the point that she would not be intimidated by an ordinary civilian, even though her actions seemed to demand some sort of explanation, if not an outright apology.

The dog, which didn't appear to have a menacing bone in its body, was an odd-looking mongrel about the size of a Spaniel with a plush black and white coat, a pointed snout, floppy ears, and a white-tipped bushy tail which curved upward in a somewhat unnatural arc.

Something about the animal affected Patricia. Though it made no sense to her, the more she looked at the hound, the more she felt like she had seen it before. She unfolded her arms, wiped together her palms, which had grown moist. The sense that she had seen this dog before only grew stronger. She felt the skin on her forearms tighten into gooseflesh, and hen it came to her . . . The memory appeared in a flash, an incident from long ago, nearly forgotten — repressed perhaps. The teasing out of this memory, the act of bringing it into focus, did not bring the calming sense of discernment she had hoped for. It did nothing to grant her a reprieve from her distress: rather, it only heightened her anxiety. Her knees started to wobble. Patricia wanted to clear her mind, afraid that if she replayed the memory any longer, she might be overwhelmed by a swell of emotion she didn't even understand.

At last, Jamie Lee Foster put a merciful end to Patricia's reverie. The Austin homicide detective stepped out of the flower bed and ambled in the direction of the woman with the dog, leaving muddy footprints on the concrete walkway. There was an odd, shocked look in Jamie Lee's eyes.

"Is that your dog?" Jamie Lee said, stopping at a safe distance from the hound.

"You don't belong here," the woman replied.

"I asked you if that there's your dog," Jamie Lee said, raising her voice a notch.

"I'm calling the police," the young woman said, tugging the dog back as if Jamie Lee were preparing to snatch it.

"I *am* the police," Jamie Lee said, flashing her badge.

The woman looked peeved. "Well, why the hell didn't you say so?"

"You go to college here?" Jamie Lee said, with a nod in the general direction of the University of Texas campus. She asked the question in a strange tone as if she were trying a new tack, looking to sweet-talk the girl to gather intelligence. To Patricia, the effort seemed transparent.

"None of your damn business," the woman with the dog replied. This was going to be a tough nut to crack.

"What's your name?" Jamie Lee said.

"Brenda."

"Brenda," Jamie Lee said, "you on the softball

team or the rowing team?"

"Huh?" Brenda looked at Jamie Lee, her mouth agape.

"What is it? Your scholarship, softball, or rowing?"

"Rowing," Brenda said, her square shoulders sagging a bit.

"Figured as much," Jamie Lee said. "And with your build, I'm guessing you're not the coxswain." Because the other way to soften people to get information out of them, apparently, was to belt them with a tenderizer.

"Fuck you," Brenda said.

"That's the professor's dog, ain't it?" Jamie Lee said.

"None of your damn business."

"When do you expect him back?" Jamie Lee said.

The dog gave a little yelp and got up on its hind legs, its tail wagging fiercely. Brenda jerked the leash and the dog toppled on its side. It quickly got back up on its paws, panting loudly, its tail clenched between its legs.

At this point, Kyle Wagner walked past Patricia and stepped off the front porch. Brenda caught sight of him and said, "And who the fuck are you supposed to be? The good cop?" Kyle stopped in his tracks, settled in his usual wide stance, and slipped his hands in the front pockets of his jeans without replying.

Jamie Lee was getting ready to say something when Patricia cut her off.

"Brenda, my name is Dr. Patricia West." She stepped in front of Jamie Lee. "I'm a medical doctor, and I have to ask Professor Kovalenko some important questions . . . Very technical issues about his research. Things only he can answer."

"With cops in tow?" Brenda said. "Trampling his flower beds?"

"I'm sorry," Patricia said. "I think we might have gone about this the wrong way, but I'm certain Dr. Kovalenko is just as eager to talk to us as we are to talk to him."

Brenda looked in the direction of the trampled flowers.

"At what time do you expect him home?" Patricia said.

"He's out of town. I'm house-sitting for him," Brenda said.

"Until when?" Patricia asked.

"Tomorrow," Brenda said. "He should be back before noon."

"Thank you, Brenda," Patricia said. She started walking up the path in the direction of the curb where Jamie Lee had parked the car. She gave a sideways flick of her head to prompt Kyle and Jamie Lee to follow her.

"That dog have a name?" Jamie Lee said as she walked around Brenda, giving her and the beast a wide berth.

The young woman let out a spiteful laugh. "See, you're not as smart as you think you are, policewoman."

"Because I don't know the mutt's name?"

"Because you haven't even figured out it's not a dog." The woman paused for effect. "Volya's a fox. A Siberian silver fox."

Kyle stepped between Jamie Lee and the creature and said, "Doesn't look like any fox I've ever seen."

"Of course not," Brenda said. "It's one of the professor's foxes."

"You mean he's got more of these?" Kyle said.

"No, Sherlock," the young woman said with a smug look on her face. "I mean one of the professor's foxes. The ones he created. You guys are really thick! Okay, genius, try to follow." Brenda began speaking in a condescending slow clip. "Volya is one specimen of the breed of foxes the professor genetically engineered."

CHAPTER TWENTY-SEVEN
Dr. Robinson

"Dr. Kovalenko genetically engineered foxes?" Patricia asked Brenda as she studied the animal that the young woman held tightly on its leash.

"How is that even allowed?" Jamie Lee said.

"Who would stop him?" Brenda said.

"I don't know. I imagine there's got to be some government agency." Jamie Lee said.

"Which government?" Brenda said with a laugh. "You really don't know the first thing about the professor, do you? What are you going to grill him about, anyway?"

"That's none of your beeswax," Jamie Lee said.

"Official police business," Kyle said in a more conciliatory tone.

"I haven't seen *your* badge, hotshot," Brenda said. "Or are you pretending *you're* a doctor too? I take that back. You do look like a cop, don't you?"

197

"Brenda," Patricia said, walking back up the walkway, "tell me more about the foxes."

Brenda shrugged. "What's there to say? They're Siberian silver foxes genetically engineered to be docile. This old boy's name is Volya. Want to pet him? He won't bite."

Patricia kneeled, put her hand out hesitantly. The animal sniffed her fingers, started licking them with delight, and worked itself in a frenzy of excitement. Brenda yanked back on the leash.

"What more can you tell us about the foxes?" Patricia asked.

"What you're really asking me is, what more can I tell you about the professor," Brenda said. "You'll have to wait and ask him. But if you want to know my opinion, I don't think he should talk to you at all."

No one said a word as they drove off. Jamie Lee took a left on West 24th Street, and within a couple of blocks, the traffic in front of them congealed, bringing them to a stop. The Austin homicide detective turned up the fan of the AC. "Damn construction," she muttered. She waited another minute before pulling off an illegal u-turn.

Jamie Lee said, "I think we could all use a drink. I know a place on Pearl Street, serves the best iced-lattes in the galaxy."

A few minutes later, they were sitting in the shade of a wisteria-draped pergola, Jamie Lee and Patricia sipping iced coffee. Kyle surprised them all by ordering an Aperol with a twist of lemon.

"That looks like cough medicine," Jamie Lee said. "Smells like it too."

Kyle smiled. He took a sip of the red liquid and said, "Why did you react like that? When you first saw the fox?"

"Thought I saw a ghost," Jamie Lee said. "Miss Olga, my neighbor, had the same exact kind of pooch. I'm guessing the professor must have given it to her." She frowned. "I could have sworn it was him, but it couldn't have been the same animal. Course not. Miss Olga's dog—"

"Fox," Kyle corrected.

"Fox . . . had its throat slit," Jamie Lee finished. "That was the first hint at the crime scene that Olga's death was not natural."

"That's horrible," Patricia said.

"Actually, Detective Foster," Kyle said, "My question wasn't directed at you."

The sheriff deputy's gaze was fixed on Patricia now.

Patricia sipped on her coffee and did a double-take. She swallowed hard and said, "Who me?" I don't know. I just . . . I don't particularly like dogs. Or foxes that look like dogs, I suppose."

"Got bit as a kid, I bet," Jamie Lee said. "It never leaves you, that fear, when you get bit as a kid, does it?"

Patricia smiled. "I wouldn't know. I don't recall ever getting bit."

"Course you're the doctor," Jamie Lee said. "I don't need to be telling you what you already know."

"I thought I saw a look of recognition in your eyes," Kyle said.

Since the statement wasn't formulated in the form of a sentence, Patricia didn't feel compelled to provide a rebuttal. She looked at her watch.

"I should probably start heading home," Patricia said.

"You pulling my leg?" Jamie Lee said with a grin.

"It's getting late," Patricia said. "I'd like to get out of Austin before rush hour."

"Come on, you two aren't going nowhere tonight. You heard Brenda the body-builder. The professor's coming back tomorrow, before noon," Jamie Lee said. "Oh, don't even pretend you're not dying to talk to him."

Patricia said, "I kind of had other plans."

"So we got two connections now, between Miss Olga and this professor. First, we have the little paintings. Second, we have these foxes. And you know what they say: all good things come in threes. So what's the third link?"

"Orphans," Kyle said.

Patricia bristled at the word.

"I should have printed that damn Russian alphabet," Kyle said. "I could be deciphering those inscriptions on the back of the icons already."

"Don't beat yourself up about it, sport," Jamie Lee said. "The professor ain't the only Russian in town, I'm sure."

"I was able to make out another name from that list," Kyle said. He pulled out the paper with the Russian cipher from his wallet, smoothed it out on the center of the table. He pointed at two words written in Russian characters. "See that? It's Carson Taggart. Those letters that look like right angles had me stumped for a minute. And the 'R' looks like a 'P.' But after you look at it a while, the name sort of pops out at you."

Jamie Lee said, "That's the kid from the school shooting."

"Dr. West's former patient," Kyle said.

"The one you shot," Patricia said.

"Dr. West," Jamie Lee said. "Look, it can get rough out there, honey."

"I'm supposed to meet my son in Aransas Pass tomorrow," Patricia said.

"Your son Alex," Jamie Lee said. "The one whose name was written with invisible ink in Russian behind a painting that belonged to a murdered woman, a painting painted by some sort of crazy scientist that creates stupid-looking mutant foxes just for laughs. Yeah, I understand your complete lack of interest in the case."

Kyle Wagner cleared his throat but said nothing.

Jamie Lee sighed. "Look, Dr. West, I have no idea where this is all going, or if it's going anywhere at all. Earlier today, Kyle said he thought your son might be in danger. I'd hate to think he's right. We could use your help sorting this all out. Somehow, you, or your son, might be the linchpin that holds this all together, see? And Lord knows you've got a way different skillset from Sheriff Woody here and me." She turned to Kyle. "That was a compliment, by the way. I loved Toy Story. You're still in, right?"

Kyle's lips stretched into an expression that seemed to be half-way between a smile and a grimace. He said, "I'm not going anywhere."

"There you go, soldier boy," Jamie Lee said, slapping him on the knee. "Y'all can stay over at my house tonight. Got plenty of room. Kyle, you don't mind crashing on the couch. I only have the one guest bedroom. Hell, it'll be fun! Like a goddam slumber party."

After finishing their refreshments, Patricia, Kyle, and Jamie got in the car and headed north. Jamie Lee made a right turn onto West 24th and proceeded quietly until the red-tiled roof of the University Methodist Church came into view up on the left. The Texas Tower, the infamous landmark of the University of Texas at Austin, stood looming farther in the distance on the right.

"Where are we going?" Patricia asked as Jamie

Lee drove onto the bustling university campus.

"Professor Kovalenko taught here, didn't he?" Jamie Lee said. "There's gotta be some old some co-workers that could tell us exactly what kind of work he did."

"It's a huge university," Patricia said. "You going to just walk up to the first person you see on the quad and ask them, 'Excuse me, do you happen to know a Professor Kovalenko?'"

Jamie Lee chuckled. "More or less." She glanced over at Patricia. "Don't worry, I'm a detective, remember? That's what I do, I detect. Got a knack for it. Wanna know the hardest part? The hardest part of every case I've ever worked on is finding parking. But I got that covered too." She popped open the glove compartment and pulled out a placard that said City of Austin Police — Official Business.

Some forty minutes later, Patricia, Jamie Lee, and Kyle settled into surprisingly comfortable swiveling office chairs in a conference room on the seventh floor of the Norman Hackerman Building. There, they were welcomed by an exuberantly helpful secretary of the Department of Genetics and Molecular Biology who assured them they'd soon be received by Dr. Roger Robinson. In addition to being one of the most senior faculty members of the department, Dr. Robinson also happened to be Sergey Kovalenko's weekly adversary on the chessboard.

Jamie Lee tapped her wristwatch with a gloating smile. "Not bad, eh?" she said.

Dr. Robinson lumbered into the room, all six-foot-four of him. He bubbled with good cheer as he introduced himself to the three-some, as though he were meeting a fresh batch of freshman students. When he sat down, he folded his legs, clasped his hands together, interlocking his remarkably long fingers, and narrowed his eyes as if he were settling deep in thought.

"We were wondering," Patricia said, "If you could tell us a little about the type of research Dr. Kovalenko was involved in while here at UT."

"Oh, that's easy," Dr. Robinson said. "I can answer that in one word: none."

"None?" Jamie Lee said.

"None at all," Robinson said. "He was strictly a lecturer. Taught the introductory Molecular Biology course and a few graduate seminars. Took great pride in it too. But he had no lab. He conducted no research to speak of during his entire stint here."

"Isn't that a little unusual?" Patricia said.

Dr. Roger Robinson let out a guffaw. "Well, yes. But Sergey is an unusual fellow."

Jamie Lee said, "So as far as you know, Dr. Kovalenko has never done any research?"

"Oh, I didn't say that. Sergey was a brilliant scientist in his field. Legendary one might say, first at Oxford, then in the former Soviet Union."

"Can you tell us what kind of research he was involved in?" Patricia said.

Dr. Robinson tilted his head to the side. "Does the name Lysenko mean anything to you?" He directed the question directly at Patricia West.

She shook her head.

"Trofim Lysenko," Dr. Robinson said in a near growl. "A name that will forever live in infamy in the annals of science."

"Who was he?" Kyle Wagner asked.

"He was a rather obscure Soviet agronomist in the early part of the twentieth century, who rose to prominence under Stalin after making some bold, scientifically unfounded claims on how he could dramatically increase crop yields. One can only hope the man was suffering some form of self-induced delusion, that he wasn't driven by darker motives. Because his theories plunged the country into a dark period of pseudo-science and probably contributed to the starvation of thousands upon thousands of peasants when his disastrous schemes failed to pan out. His next great act was to reject Mendelian genetics in favor of a new Soviet biology."

"Didn't anyone question him? Try to stop him?" Patricia asked.

"Sure," Dr. Robinson said. "There were a few brave souls who tried to stand up to him. But he was a ruthless man, and, being a favorite protege of Joseph Stalin, he was able to wield enormous power. He quashed those who opposed his theories by labeling them enemies of the state, getting them sent to prison camps. The man showed no mercy. Many prominent Soviet scientists of the day were executed under his watch. By mid-century, Lysenko had single-handedly ravaged the scientific fields of agriculture, biology, and genetics, not only in the Soviet Union but in all Soviet-bloc countries."

"That's amazing," Kyle said.

"How does our good friend, Dr. Kovalenko, tie into all this?" Jamie Lee asked.

"In 1953, Joseph Stalin dies. Lysenko's power is no more, and, slowly, the biological sciences are resurrected. In the field of genetics, two men come together to bring light to the darkness. The first was a man by the name of Dmitri Belyaev; the other—"

"Sergey Kovalenko," Patricia said.

"That's right," Dr. Robinson said. "None other than my dear friend and chess foe."

Kyle asked, "What did they do?"

Dr. Robinson unfolded his legs and smiled. "Well, the first thing Belyaev did was get demoted for opposing Lysenko. Luckily for him, and for humanity, he wasn't executed on the spot but simply shipped off to Siberia with a weighty demotion, and the tawdry assignment of helping workers in the fur industry find a more effective way of handling the prized Siberian silver fox. Dr.

Belyaev was trained as a zoologist, after all. Now these silver foxes are wild animals. When held in captivity, as you might imagine, they can act downright ornery, particularly when confined to small metal cages, which they always were on these fur farms. Belyaev thought there might be a way to domesticate them, somehow. He had nursed a hunch for some time, that dogs had descended from wolves. In some unknown way, he figured, over a long period of time, wolves had been bred to be tame. Belyaev wondered if the same could be done with foxes. So he selected out the most docile foxes among the bunch, those that didn't immediately bite a gloved hand introduced in their cages — how would you like that job? Sticking your hand in a wild fox's cage? — and bred the most timid foxes with other timid foxes. Well, within just a few generations, he had tame little things that wagged their tails and licked their caretakers' hands."

"Well, I could have told you that," Jamie Lee said. "My grand-pop did the same thing with billy goats. So did his pop before him."

"Yes, but then something truly remarkable happened," Dr. Robinson said.

"The foxes started looking like dogs," Kyle broke in.

"That's right," Dr. Robinson said. "Surprisingly, they developed floppy ears, curly tails, spotted fur. They even started barking …

207

sort of. They made a yapping sound. But wait, how did you know?"

"We met Volya," Patricia said.

"So, you already met with Sergey?" Roger Robinson said.

"We met his dog-walker. Fox-walker," Jamie Lee corrected herself. "Old Sergey's out of town."

Patricia asked, "Was Dr. Kovalenko an associate of Dr. Belyaev?"

"Not at the beginning. Belyaev was thrilled by his results and correctly inferred that, in the fox genome, whatever genes are responsible for docility must necessarily be located in the vicinity of those genes responsible for curly tails, floppy ears, and spotted coats. He understood that the genes coding for these traits, as a result of their proximity on the genome, managed to travel together through multiple generations in his experiment. It was the same process that must have occurred in the evolution of wolf to dog. The only problem was he didn't know what the genes in question were. Nor did he have the ability or the know-how to identify them."

"So that's when he turned to Sergey Kovalenko," Patricia said.

"On a trip to Moscow, Dmitri Belyaev meets a hot-shot post-doc at the university."

"Dr. Kovalenko," Kyle said.

Roger Robinson nodded. "Belyaev is able to convince Sergey to apply for a position as a junior faculty member at the prestigious Oxford University so that he can master the latest techniques in molecular biology developed in the West. He even takes the trouble to pen a glowing letter of recommendation for the lad and mails it directly to the department head at Oxford. Well, a letter of recommendation from Dr. Dmitri Belyaev, by now a legend in the field of genetics, gets noticed. And how! Sergey goes to Oxford where he becomes a rising star. A few years later — and Belyaev is in his twilight years by now — Professor Sergey Kovalenko takes a midnight train from Moscow to Siberia. The wagon he's riding in is overflowing with wooden crates packed with state-of-the-art laboratory equipment. The day he arrives, he holds a private meeting with Dr. Belyaev. The next morning he rolls up his sleeves and gets to work on the fox genome project."

"I'm guessing he was successful in his efforts," Patricia said.

Roger Robinson smiled. "What's most remarkable is that he was in completely uncharted waters. He had to develop new techniques, which were used again many years later in the mapping of the human genome."

"Well, this makes no sense then," Patricia said. Robinson tilted his head. "I mean, if he was such a pioneer in laboratory techniques, how is it that he didn't do any research while here at UT?"

Dr. Robinson chuckled. He leaned forward. "Let me tell you a little story. One afternoon, Sergey and I are playing chess in the faculty club. I have the first move and I decide to start with a rather conventional opening. The old goat counters with his knight — not his typical move, mind you. So I make my next move and he quickly counters by moving a pawn in a very dangerous position, leaving his other knight completely exposed. By now, I'm quite sure I've got the best of him. Then, just a few moves later my king is pinned. Checkmate! I lose. It took me two weeks to figure out that what he had managed to pull off was the Flick-Knife attack." Robinson shook his head and laughed.

"I'm sure there's a point to this story," Jamie Lee said.

Professor Robinson leaned forward again. "Sergey Kovalenko is the most eccentric, whimsical, unpredictable man I've ever met. He always keeps you guessing. One day he discovers a new technique to unlock the genetic code,   the next he decides he wants to spend the rest of his life painting religious figurines. A brilliant man, no doubt, but don't try to understand his motivations. It'll drive you crazy."

"What was the control group?" Patricia said. The question seemed to come out of the blue. Kyle narrowed his eyes, as though he were trying to understand why Patricia had asked the question.

Roger Robinson's smile faded. His mouth fell open, his eyelids fluttered. "The control group?" he finally managed to utter.

"Surely, the genetic material of the tame foxes was compared to that of controls," Patricia said. "What did Dr. Kovalenko use as a control group?"

"Well . . ." Roger Robinson said. "Other foxes, of course."

"Just any other fox?" Patricia said.

Roger Robinson shook his head. He hesitated, seemed reluctant to respond. "In addition to breeding docile foxes, Belyaev bred hyper-aggressive foxes, specifically for this purpose, to serve as his control group."

Patricia West crossed her hands and looked down. When she looked up again, her eyes locked onto those of Kyle Wagner. He offered her a wistful smile, a smile that left Patricia feeling exposed. As a way of explaining away her sudden sullenness, to let Kyle know that whatever thought was going through his head, he should rid his mind of it, she said, "Poor creatures."

CHAPTER TWENTY-EIGHT
Deacon Balakin

"So what do y'all make of that?" Jamie Lee Foster said as they exited the Genetics and Microbiology building.

Kyle said, "Still trying to sort it out."

"I think I should be heading home," said Patricia West. "If you don't mind driving me back to the Children's Hospital, my car is still parked in the guest lot."

"Seriously?" Jamie Lee said. "You're telling me you're not the least bit curious to chat with this Kovalenko character."

"You heard what Dr. Robinson said. Kovalenko's research was all about foxes. There's nothing to chat about."

Kyle Wagner said, "You don't want to ask him why your son's name was written in invisible ink on the back of an icon he painted?"

"Maybe he doesn't even know," Patricia said.

"Maybe those names were etched in by someone else, long after he painted them."

"The orphanage was half-way across the world, but judging from the addresses on the back of the icons, every single kid ended up in Texas," Kyle said.

"Ain't that something?" Jamie Lee said.

Patricia said, "Well, if Olga Belenkova, the person arranging the adoptions, lived in Austin, wouldn't it make sense that the prospective parents she could most easily reach were all in Texas?"

"And Dr. Sergey Kovalenko also lived in Texas," Kyle said. "In the same city as Olga Belenkova."

"Ain't that something!" Jamie Lee said.

They were walking down University Way, toward a small parking lot across the street from the UT Turtle Pond.

"So?" Patricia said.

"And don't forget, they both owned mutant foxes," Jamie Lee said.

"Genetically engineered," Patricia said. "So they knew each other. What does that have to do with me?"

"Why would they arrange to have all the adoptees stay in Texas?" Kyle said. It sounded like Kyle was setting up Jamie Lee. As if the two of them were in cahoots all of a sudden.

"To keep an eye on these kids," Jamie Lee said

as they reached her car. "Why else? Keep them close." She pulled her car keys out of her purse but didn't press the button on the fob to unlock the car, keeping Kyle and Patricia holding onto the door handles. "Now, why would they want to keep an eye on these kids?"

Patricia pulled up on the handle of the passenger side door, yanked it hard when it didn't budge.

"And who murdered Olga Belenkova?" Kyle said. "What could have been the motive?"

"Open the door," Patricia said.

"Olga gave me those paintings the day she was murdered," Jamie Lee said. "For safekeeping. She knew someone was out to kill her. Those paintings are linked to her murder."

Patricia shouted, "Will you just open the goddam door?"

Jamie Lee and Kyle looked at her in silence. Patricia brought her palm up to her mouth. She squeezed her eyes shut. "I have to get to my son," she said.

Jamie Lee walked around the front of the car, stopped just short of Patricia West.

"I have to go to my son," Patricia repeated, looking at Jamie Lee with teary eyes.

Jamie Lee took a tentative step forward and wrapped her arms around Patricia in an awkward embrace. Patricia's shoulders tightened but she didn't recoil. Slowly, she relaxed, letting her body sag against the frame of the detective, leaning against her until she felt the hardness of Jamie Lee's holstered gun pressing against her hip.

"We won't let anything happen to your son," Jamie Lee said. "Everything's going to be alright."

Patricia wished she could believe her. She straightened, withdrew from the embrace, and wiped her face with the back of her hand.

"So, what's next?" Patricia said. "What do you have in mind now?"

"I'd like to go back to church," Jamie Lee said.

Father Ambrus was bidding farewell to a group of parishioners on the front steps of St. Chrysostom church after evening service when Jamie Lee steered her car into the church parking lot. The cleric was wearing a black cassock and what looked like a brimless stovepipe hat. A large silver crucifix dangled from his neck.

"Wonder if he's still wearing sneakers under that bathrobe," Jamie Lee said as they approached the priest.

Father Ambrus waved at them and flashed a smile that might have been sparked from a sense of surprise rather than delight.

"You are back," he said. "With a new friend. Welcome." He approached the trio with long strides and extended his hand to Patricia West. "My name is Ambrus."

Patricia shook his hand. "Patricia West."

"Policewoman?" Ambrus said.

"She's a doctor," Jamie Lee broke in.

Father Ambrus opened his mouth in a quizzical expression.

"Believe me, Padre, I'm as confused as you are," Patricia said.

"We're all confused," Jamie Lee said. "But, we thought you might be able to help us straighten something out."

"I'd be happy to help any way I can," the priest said.

"Do you speak Russian?" Kyle asked.

"I studied it in college," Father Ambrus said. "But I'm certainly not fluent. It's an astonishingly complicated language."

"You still remember your Russian A, B, C?" Jamie Lee said.

"I know the alphabet, sure," Father Ambrus said.

"Good enough," Jamie Lee said. "We need you to translate something for us." She handed him the paper on which Kyle had transcribed the writing from the back of the painted icons.

"These are names and addresses," Father Ambrus said, looking at the sheet of paper.

"All we need is for you to write them down in English," Jamie Lee said.

"If it's not too much trouble," Patricia added.

"I'd be happy to do it, Dr. West," Father Ambrus said.

As they walked to the church office, Father Ambrus asked Patricia, "What branch of medicine do you practice?"

"I'm a pediatrician."

"Lovely," Father Ambrus said. "How are you related to this investigation?"

"This isn't part of any official investigation," Jamie Lee said. "We just need a favor is all."

"I see," said Father Ambrus.

"My son's name is on that list," Patricia said.

The priest held up the paper, pointed at the second entry. "Alexander West," he said. "I guess I don't have to translate that one for you."

It might have taken the priest not more than a minute to translate the entire document if he didn't find it necessary to chat after every entry completed, as though he needed a brief mental respite with each effort. "May I ask where this list came from?" Father Ambrus said.

"You've been very helpful," Jamie Lee said in a vague tone. "We don't want to trouble you any more than we already have."

"Did you get a chance to speak to Professor Kovalenko?"

"Not yet," Kyle said.

"What a strange coincidence! Another man came looking for him today," Father Ambrus said.

"Another man?" Jamie Lee said.

"A Russian gentleman."

"A Russian?" Kyle said. "What did he look

like?"

Father Ambrus chuckled. "When I first saw him, I have to confess, I thought I was in the presence of a saint. His demeanor was so pious, so humble, so serene."

"I can't say I've ever seen a saint," Jamie Lee said. "Plenty of devils but not a single saint. Not sure I'd be able to pick one out of a lineup. Can you give us something more along the lines of a physical description?"

"He was quite tall, with dark hair, intense dark eyes, angular facial features. There was something tortured in his expression."

"A tortured saint," Kyle said. "Like Saint Sebastian."

"Precisely," said Father Ambrus.

"What else did he say to you?" Kyle asked.

"We had a rather pleasant chat on the philosophy of St. John Chrysostom, our patron. Are you familiar with his aphorisms? They are sublime. Earned him the moniker of Golden Mouth. I joked with Mr. Balakin that my favorite quip of the Golden Mouth is, 'The road to Hell is paved with the bones of priests and monks, and the skulls of bishops are the lamp posts that light the path.'" Father Ambrus chuckled. "He found it humorous I should pick that passage. Well, it's a reminder that there's a lot more to being a good Christian than growing a long beard and wearing fashionable black clothing."

"You said his name is Balakin?" Jamie Lee said, without a smile.

"Oh, I should have mentioned that sooner," Father Ambrus said. "His name is Borya Balakin. He's a deacon at St. Spyridon Church — I forget the name of the city, it'll come to me in a moment — outside of Moscow."

"What's a Russian deacon doing in Austin, Texas.?" Kyle Wagner asked.

Father Ambrus snapped his fingers. "Ryazan!" He exclaimed. "That's the name of the city. It was on the tip of my tongue. St. Spyridon in Ryazan. He came here to commission Professor Kovalenko to paint a portrait of their patron saint."

"Huh! You'd figure there might be one or two unemployed painters that can draw a picture of a saint over in Russia. You shouldn't need to fly all the way to Texas to look for one," Jamie Lee said.

"They had a church fire that destroyed some of their artwork," Father Ambrus said. "Dr. Kovalenko had painted the original. Apparently, they want to replace it with an exact likeness."

"You're right," Jamie Lee said. "This *is* a strange coincidence. Tell me again why he came to your church."

Father Ambrus said, "For the same reason you came here earlier today. He needed the address for Dr. Kovalenko."

"You're telling me this guy makes the trek all the way from outside of Moscow to commission a painting, but he doesn't have the address for the painter?"

"He lost his address book in a cab in Houston," Father Ambrus said, confused by the tone of the questioning.

Jamie Lee thrust her hands on her hips and looked at Kyle with a raised eyebrow.

"Perhaps we should finish the translation," Kyle said in an even tone. "If you don't mind, father."

Father Ambrus nodded. He looked at the sheet of paper and read, "Carson Taggart."

The sound of the name read out loud unsettled Patricia.

"We don't need that address, father," Kyle said. "Do you mind writing down the rest of the names?"

A short while later, the priest had transcribed the entire list of names and addresses. He accompanied his visitors to the church's exit, shook their hands, and made the sign of the cross. "May God Almighty guide you and protect you," he said. He watched as Patricia, Jamie Lee, and Kyle walked toward the parking lot.

Patricia stopped, turned, and asked Father Ambrus from afar, "What was *his* favorite quote?"

"I'm sorry?" Father Ambrus said.

"This man, Mr. Balakin," Patricia said, "Did he mention what his favorite quote by St. John Chrysostom was?"

CHAPTER TWENTY-NINE

Mayor Tully

Father Ambrus said, "He said his favorite
quote by Saint John the Golden Mouth was, 'For
Christians, above all men, are forbidden to correct
the stumblings of sinners by force.'"

Jamie Lee nodded. "Damn right. That's what
cops are for," she said, patting the gun holstered
under her blazer.

"Being a police officer does not preclude one
from being a Christian," Father Ambrus said.
"Our doors are always open, detective."

Patricia pressed her lips together and nodded.
"Thank you, father," she said, and walked quietly
to the car, Kyle and Jamie Lee trailing her.

"Bet you've seen your share of stumbling
sinners," Jamie Lee said, eyeing Kyle in the rear-
view mirror as she pulled out of the church
parking lot.

"Every time I look in the mirror," Kyle said.

Jamie Lee scoffed. "Come on, cowboy. You're no sinner," she said. "Sinners are the life of the party. No offense but you're not part of that club."

For the next two blocks, the only sound was the whining of the car engine.

"Jesus!" Jamie Lee finally said. "What we need is pizza."

"Pizza?" Kyle said.

"The perfect brain food," Jamie Lee said. "And that's a scientific fact. It'll help us go over what we got, work out some of the connections."

"And I bet you know the perfect place," Kyle said.

Jamie Lee smiled. "This is my town, cowboy."

Jamie Lee ordered a large pepperoni and jalapeno deep-dish along with a pitcher of beer. She waited for the beer to be poured before saying, "Okay, let's go through the list."

Kyle said, "Well, we have Alexander West, and Carson Taggart, but we knew that already. Then we have the one without a last name or address, Mikhail."

"Why do you think that is? Why doesn't this kid have a last name and address?" Jamie Lee asked.

"Maybe he didn't get adopted," Kyle said.

"Or maybe he didn't survive," Patricia said. Kyle and Jamie Lee looked at her. "It happens. The facilities in Odessa were not exactly state of the art. With the exception of the adoption ward, the hospital was pretty . . . substandard."

"Yeah. That's definitely a possibility," Kyle said. "Let's skip Mikhail for now. Here's one with an Austin address: Thomas Roberts."

Jamie Lee almost spit out a mouthful of beer. "Say that name again."

"Thomas Roberts," Kyle said. "Ring a bell?"

"Everybody just hold on a second," Jamie Lee said. She pulled out her cell phone and started dialing. A moment later she called out, "Hey, Finnigan! It's Foster." A pause. "Yeah, I'm having a hell of a vacation. I'm at the beach over here in St. Tropez, don't you know. Doing the whole topless thing and all ... Yeah, I bet you'd like to see that. Listen up, you old lecher. That kid, you know, the one that tried to kill the owner of the Greek restaurant, what was his name again?"

Jamie Lee tapped a button to engage the speaker function and held the phone out for the others to listen in..

Kyle and Patricia leaned in as the voice on the other end of the line said, "That would have been Florakis. Mr. Florakis of Aesop's Tables."

"No, not the Greek," Jamie Lee said. "What was the kid's name?"

"The kid?" Finnigan said. "Roberts. Tommy Roberts."

"Did Tommy Roberts reside on Arcadia Avenue?" Jamie Lee said.

There was a pause. "I'm very disappointed," Finnigan said.

Detective Espericueta's voice could be heard in the background muttering, "Crushed."

"Doesn't sound like you're on vacation in St. Tropez," Finnigan said. "To think that for a moment Detective Espericueta and I were sporting the blush of youth, thinking you were talking to us in just a bikini bottom, your bosom *au naturel*. Sounds to me like you haven't detached your little duchess nose from the grindstone, detective."

"Don't know what you're talking about. Okay, so maybe I still got all my clothes on, but I'm just sitting back, having a few beers with some friends. Arcadia Avenue, right?"

"That would be correct," Finnigan said. "You got something you want to share with us?"

"Nah. That's already a closed case," Jamie Lee said. "Ain't it?"

"That would be correct," Finnigan said.

"Thanks, Finnigan," Jamie Lee said. "I'll send y'all a postcard." She hung up and put her phone away.

Kyle downed his mug of beer and said, "Tell us about Tommy Roberts."

Jamie Lee shot a look at Patricia. "Tommy's this kid, an honor student at McCallum High School, lives with his mom, a hairdresser. Mom has an affair with the owner of a Greek restaurant. Then one day the guy roughs her up pretty good. Tommy comes unhinged. He goes to the restaurant and starts stabbing the guy in the chest with a kitchen knife. Jesus! The whole thing was caught on security footage. The kid looked like he was jazzed on drugs or something."

"So Tommy Roberts killed this guy Florakis?" Kyle said.

"Almost killed him," Jamie Lee said. "Would have killed him if Florakis's wife hadn't come out with a handgun and shot the kid dead."

Patricia said, "That's just horrible."

"Tox screen on the kid?" Kyle said.

"Negative," Jamie Lee said. "Apparently the kid had been struggling with anger issues. Outbursts of rage and such."

"Like Carson," Patricia said.

Jamie Lee and Kyle turned to look at her.

"Carson Taggart started having temper outbursts a few months ago," Patricia said. "His mother came by my office a couple of times to seek my advice. I never thought he'd—"

"You couldn't have," Kyle said.

A waitress came plodding to the table, pizza tray in one hand, an over-sized spatula in the other. Jamie Lee pushed back her chair and shot to her feet. She said, "I don't believe it!"

The waitress froze and in a meek voice said, "Pepperoni and jalapeno?"

Jamie Lee sprinted to the far end of the

restaurant, barked at a waiter behind the bar to crank up the volume on a wall-mounted television. On the screen, a somber anchorman said, "In a press conference earlier this afternoon, Galveston mayor Andrew Tully made an impassioned plea to the island's citizens."

The shot changed to the exterior of Galveston city hall, where an impeccably dressed man spoke in a bank of microphones. "On behalf of my family, I urge the good citizens of Galveston ..." He paused to swallow. "I implore you, if you have any information whatsoever relating to the whereabouts of my son, James Preston Tully, or his friend, Aubrey Hurst, please call the hotline set up through the Galveston Police Department."

The camera shot cut to a field reporter who said, "Jason Preston Tully and Aubrey Hurst were reported missing three days ago when they didn't return from a fishing trip on Mayor Tully's motor boat in Galveston Bay. The coast guard has been combing the waters around the island but so far the search has been fruitless. Foul play has not been ruled out."

Kyle Wagner tapped Patricia on the forearm. He pointed to the last entry on the list flattened out on the table top. It read, James Preston Tully, with an address on East Seaside Drive, Galveston. Patricia looked searchingly into Kyle's eyes. Their eyes stayed locked until Kyle shook his head slightly.

Jamie Lee staggered back to the table and slumped in her chair. She said, "What the hell is going on?" and guzzled her beer in one long drag.

"We have to check on all the others," Kyle said. "See what their status is."

"Seven kids," Jamie Lee said. "Two dead, one gone missing just in the last week."

"That leaves four kids," Kyle said. "But we can skip over Mikhail, for now. The kid with no last name and no address."

"Wanna bet that kid's dead too?" Jamie Lee said.

"And then there's Alex West," Kyle said.

"But he has nothing to do with this," Patricia said.

"I was just about to make the point that we don't have to look him up," Kyle said. "We already know he's safe and sound."

Jamie Lee said, "That leaves only two kids. She reached for the list, scrolled down the paper with her finger. "Jonathan Muller in Dallas, and Boris O'Keefe in San Antonio."

"Those names sound familiar at all?" Kyle asked Patricia.

She shook her head.

Jamie Lee was already back on her cell phone. "Finnigan? Me again. Can you run a couple of names for me?" She paused. "I can't access the database from St. Tropez, or I'd do it myself." She gave Finnigan the names of the two boys. There

227

was another pause. "Arrest records, warrants, death certificates, whatever you can find."

Patricia leaned back in her chair and exhaled.

"These are minors," Jamie Lee said. "Both born in nineteen ..." she turned to Patricia and jutted her chin at her.

"Ninety-one," Patricia whispered.

"All born in 1991," Jamie Lee said into the phone.

"There's one more name," Kyle said.

"Hang on, Finnigan," Jamie Lee said. She looked at Kyle.

"Have him check out Borya Balakin," Kyle said.

Jamie Lee nodded. "One more. This last one's not a minor, Finn. The name's Borya Balakin." Jamie Lee raised her eyebrows, looked at Kyle for help.

"B-O-R-Y-A," Kyle said.

Jamie Lee spelled out the rest of the name with Kyle's prompting. "The guy's a Russian national. A deacon of some sort with the Eastern Orthodox Church. See what you and Espericueta can dig up on him."

When Jamie Lee hung up, Patricia said, "Now what?"

"Now we eat pizza," Jamie Lee said. "Then we go to my house, wait for Finnigan's call and crash. We have a long day tomorrow."

"What do you make of this Tully kid missing?"

Kyle said.

"Do you *really* want to know my opinion?" Jamie Lee said. "I'm a murder detective. I only know how to carry but one tune."

CHAPTER THIRTY
Diplomat Balakin

An hour earlier, Patricia West typed the name Sergey Kovalenko in the search bar of PubMed: a massive collection of medical and scientific articles maintained by the U.S. National Library of Medicine and the National Institutes of Health. Now, she was still sifting through the abstracts of a couple dozen articles that listed him as an author.

Jamie Lee plopped a cup of coffee on the desk in front of Patricia and placed a hand on her shoulder. "Can you make out what that says, Doc?"

"Not really," Patricia said. "These papers all deal with laboratory techniques in genetics. I'm way out of my depth."

"Nothing about mutant Russian foxes, huh?"

"Thanks for the coffee," Patricia said. She took a sip. "The problem is I don't really know what

I'm looking for."

"Maybe it's time for a break, then," Jamie Lee said.

As if on cue, Jamie Lee's cell phone rang. She looked at her phone. "It's Finnigan," she said. "Gather round y'all." She lifted the phone to her ear. "What have you got for me, Finn?" She pressed the speaker-enable button and held the phone up for all to hear.

"What time is it in St. Tropez?" Finnigan asked.

"I don't know. My watch stopped."

"Well, I hope I didn't wake you," Finnigan said.

"Can't sleep," Jamie Lee said. "I think I'm jet-lagged. What have you got for us?"

"I don't know. This thing's got Espericueta and me befuddled," Finnigan said.

"Dumbfounded," Espericueta's voice came over the speaker.

"Those two kids you told us to look into? Kid number one, Jonathan Muller of Dallas, Texas, is currently in juvenile detention for aggravated assault and battery."

"What did he do?" Jamie Lee said.

"Used a tire iron to rearrange the kneecaps on his girlfriend's father after the old man kicked her dog. The kid's getting counseling for anger management. Should be released in six months unless he goes bat-shit crazy again."

"What about kid number two?" Jamie Lee said.

"Boris O'Keefe? His funeral's the day after tomorrow," Finnigan said. "Service at ten in the morning, Holy Trinity Catholic Church in San Antonio."

"What the hell are you talking about?" Jamie Lee shouted.

"He was found dead in an alleyway a few blocks from his home," Finnigan said. "Stabbed in the heart with a screwdriver. SAPD says it looks like a mugging gone bad."

Jamie Lee exchanged wide-eyed glances with Patricia and Kyle.

Finnigan said, "Want to hear about your Russian fella, this Borya Balakin?"

"If you tell me he's dead too, I'm gonna shit a brick," Jamie Lee said.

"Well, detective, there's no need for you to increase your dietary fiber just yet. As far as we can tell, Mr. Balakin's body has yet to reach room temperature."

"So, who is he?" Jamie Lee said.

"A Russian diplomat," Finnigan said.

"You sure about this?"

"He passed customs at Houston Intercontinental Airport last week," Finnigan said. "State Department has no record of him ever traveling to the United States before, at least not under this name. Which is a bit odd for a diplomat, if you ask me. But there's something even more perplexing: his Russian passport was issued in Moscow just ten days ago."

"Maybe he's a rookie," Jamie Lee said.

"A late bloomer, I'd say. Seeing as he's forty-two years and eight months old according to his passport," Finnigan said.

"Did you try contacting the Russian embassy?"

"Sure," Finnigan said. "They hung up on us. Twice."

"You only called them twice?" Jamie Lee said.

Finnigan chuckled on the other end of the line. "Espericueta and I have other news for you, but first you have to tell me which one of our cases you're investigating without departmental authority: the Tommy Roberts case, the Olga Belenkova case, or both?"

"Don't know what you're talking about," Jamie Lee said with a slight laugh. "I'm on—"

"Yeah, yeah. You're on vacation," Finnigan said. "Meanwhile, Espericueta and I are losing our marbles trying to figure out the connection between these kids, a Russian diplomat, and Miss Belenkova."

"What makes you think there's a connection?" Jamie Lee asked.

"You," Finnigan said. "Seeing as you're snooping into all three. You're the connection. So are you going to open the door and let us in? If we stand here on your front porch any longer, a neighbor's liable to call the cops."

CHAPTER THIRTY-ONE

Finn

"Better let me do the talking," Jamie Lee said, before opening the front door.

Kyle asked, "You gonna hold out on your partners?"

"Technically, they're not my partners," Jamie Lee said in hushed tones. "Just co-workers. Nosy ones. Look, you don't know these guys. Finnigan and Espericueta are ... different. Kind of kooky. But strictly by the book. If they get too involved, they'll just gum up everything and slow us down."

Jamie Lee opened the front door, and the two detectives walked into the living room, nodding their good-evenings. Finnigan eyed Kyle and Patricia.

"Had I known you had company," Finnigan said, "I'd have brought a box of bonbons."

Jamie Lee said, "Kyle Wagner, Patricia West,

meet Finnigan and Espericueta."

"Enchanted," Espericueta said.

"Any friend of detective Foster …" Finnigan's voice trailed off. He turned to Jamie Lee. "That's funny. I didn't think you had friends, I mean, outside of the station. Never considered the possibility."

"I'd offer you a beer, but it looks like you boys are working," Jamie Lee said.

Finnigan said, "We just went off duty."

"I'll take a cold one," Espericueta said.

"Make that two," Finnigan said as he settled on the sofa.

"Anyone else?" Jamie Lee said.

"I'm fine," Patricia said.

Kyle shook his head.

Jamie Lee turned on her heels and headed for the kitchen. Came back with two bottles of beer. She handed the bottles to the two Austin homicide detectives, their caps still on.

"You're an excellent host," Finnigan said.

Espericueta grabbed his bottle of beer, thrust its cap into the fleshy part of his forearm, gave the bottle a twist popping the cap off. He raised the bottle and said, "Prost!" before taking a long drag. Finnigan placed his beer on an end table, unopened.

"Tell us about these kids," Finnigan said.

"Which kids?" Jamie Lee said in a coy voice.

"Well, let's see. There's Tommy Roberts of

Austin, deceased; Boris O'Keefe of San Antonio, deceased; and Jonathan Muller of Dallas, incarcerated. What, are there others?"

"You seem to know more about it than I do," Jamie Lee said.

Finnigan chuckled. "Funny, because you're the one who gave us their names to check out." The veteran detective grabbed the beer bottle, twisted the cap off. He looked at Kyle and said, "You look like law enforcement. But I'm guessing you're not Austin PD. What are you, a constable?"

"Sheriff's deputy," Kyle said.

"Travis County?" Finnigan asked.

"Comal," Kyle replied.

"Comal? You don't say." Finnigan swallowed a sip of beer. "What brings you up in these parts?"

Kyle looked over at Jamie Lee.

"I found him on one of those internet dating sites," Jamie Lee said. "Ain't he a doll?"

Finnigan moved his gaze to Patricia. "Then I'm afraid you're the third wheel. Unless this is a ..." Finnigan made circles in the air with his index finger.

"Menage-a-trois," Espericueta blurted out.

"Well, this was a swell visit, boys," Jamie Lee said. "We should do it again someday. Time to drink up your beers and shove out."

Ignoring her comment, Finnigan said, "So at the center of it all we have a dead Russian woman."

"Ukrainian," Jamie Lee corrected. "If you're talking about Miss Olga."

"And this other character, the diplomat, Borya Balakin — he's Russian too."

"They look like completely different matters from where I'm standing," Jamie Lee said.

"How'd you get his name?" Finnigan asked.

"I'm telling you, there's no connection."

Finnigan ignored her again. "And then you've got these kids. We're having a hell of a time discerning how they fit into all of this." Finnigan put his beer down and rubbed his palms together. "We just about split our noggins trying to figure that one out. Far as we can tell, there's no relation, blood or otherwise, between your late neighbor, Olga Belenkova, and the dead kids."

"We already established they're not all dead," Jamie Lee said.

"Only thing we were able to come up with," Finnigan said. "Is that Miss Belenkova worked as an adoption counselor. Specialized in international adoptions as a matter of fact. So we went to visit her old employer earlier this evening, an outfit called City of Hope. Fortunately for us, they have this fancy computerized database. They've got records for every adoption they handled going way back to when they opened their doors for business in 1987."

"Really?" Jamie Lee said, in an impassive tone.

"But get this," Finnigan said. "They have no

record of a Tommy Roberts. Or a Brian O'Keefe. Or a Jonathan Muller."

"Looks like you were wrong then," Jamie Lee said.

"Unless," Finnigan said, "Unless Olga Belenkova was doing a bit of freelancing on the side. What do you know about it?"

Jamie Lee shrugged her shoulders. "How would I know?"

Finnigan paused a moment, then shrugged. "Oh well," he said as he reached for his beer. "Guess we'll just have to wait till the morning and ask Miss Candy Benson. You know, Tommy Robert's grieving mother."

"That's probably not such a good idea," Jamie Lee said. "Not right now. I mean, after everything that woman's gone through. Just to chase a wild hare of a hunch."

"It breaks my heart to do it," Finnigan said.

"Mortifying," Espericueta said.

Finnigan looked at Kyle and, in a more authoritative tone, said, "What's your connection to the case?"

"Another kid," Kyle said before Jamie Lee could stop him.

Finnigan raised his eyebrows. "And what is the status of this other kid?"

"He's dead," Kyle said.

"May I inquire as to the manner of death?" Espericueta asked.

"I shot him," Kyle said.

"You — shot — him?" Finnigan said, pronouncing each word with deliberate care.

Jamie Lee exhaled. "You heard about the school shooting out in Canyon Lake?" she said.

"Sure," Finnigan said. He studied Kyle Wagner. "Ah. So, your kid was the shooter." He turned to Patricia. "I'm sorry. I'm almost afraid to ask. What was your relation to that boy?"

"I was his doctor," Patricia said.

"Psychiatrist?" Espericueta asked.

"Pediatrician," Patricia said.

Espericueta and Finnigan exchanged dumbfounded looks. Finnigan said, "I may need another beer."

Jamie Lee said, "Sorry. All out."

"What, in heaven's name, is going on here?" Finnigan said. "What's the common denominator?"

For a minute, no one spoke.

The common denominator, Patricia knew, was that all the children came from the same orphanage. And that Olga Belenkova organized each adoption. It was a thought that sent a shiver up her spine even though she couldn't make sense of it. She looked at Jamie Lee. The detective had insisted on doing all the talking. Maybe she had good reason not to fully trust these two odd characters. Or perhaps she had more personal motives. She glanced over at Kyle to see if he was about to say anything. Kyle sat quietly, his eyes downcast.

Finnigan broke the silence. "If this partnership is going to work-"

"What partnership?" Jamie Lee said.

"We'll have to share intelligence with each other," Finnigan managed to finish his sentence.

"I scratch your back. Vice versa," Espericueta said.

"Clearly, you have been less than forthcoming," Finnigan said.

"I don't know how many times I got to tell you …" Jamie Lee said.

"Did I mention that we got the autopsy report on your neighbor, Miss Olga?" Finnigan said. "The cause of death was … Well, I think this will blow your socks off."

"I'm listening," Jamie Lee said.

Finnigan shook his head. "It's gotta be a two-way street," he said. "You go first."

"You bastards," Jamie Lee said. "How many times do I have to tell you that's all we know?"

Kyle cleared his voice. Everyone turned their gaze toward him. "Belenkova handled the adoptions. All of them."

"Holy Joseph and Mary!" Finnigan said. "What about your shooter?"

"Him too," Kyle said.

Jamie Lee crossed her arms and scowled. She kept her eyes fixed on Kyle and started cranking her head side to side as though she were trying to work a crick out of her neck.

"I'm baffled," Finnigan said. "I mean, what are the odds?"

"Infinitesimal," Espericueta said.

"Precisely," Finnigan said. "But what's the common thread? I'm stumped here. If I were superstitious, I'd say this was some kind of curse."

"But you're not," Espericueta said and made the sign of the cross.

"But I'm not superstitious," Finnigan said. "So what else can you tell me, sheriff?"

"We told you what we know," Jamie Lee said. "Now, how about you tell us about that autopsy report."

Kyle said, "The boys all came from the same orphanage, around the same time."

"How do you know?" Finnigan said.

Kyle glanced at Jamie Lee. He said, "We came across a list."

Patricia started to wonder if this is how law enforcement routinely went about their business. Furtiveness, vague answers, withholding critical information, it was a miracle that crimes were solved at all.

"Are there more boys on that list?"

Patricia decided it was time to speak up. She said, "My son's on that list." She turned to her side just in time to catch Jamie Lee rolling her eyes.

Finnigan sat back on the sofa as if a weight was pushing on his chest. In a cautious tone, he said, "And your son, ma'am, if you don't mind me asking, what is his current state of being?"

"He's fine," Patricia said. "He's with my parents. Yeah, he's fine." She looked at each person in the room, nodding as if she were searching for some sort of affirmation.

"I'm glad your son is safe," Finnigan said, leaning forward. "What is his name?"

"Alex," Patricia responded. "Alexander West."

"I can't perceive how he could be in any imminent danger," Finnigan said. "Nonetheless, his continued safety has to be the primary objective of our investigation."

"Agreed," Espericueta said.

"Thank you," Patricia said.

"The autopsy report," Jamie Lee said.

Finnigan hesitated. From his pained expression, it seemed his intent was not to add unnecessary suspense to the situation but to evoke, out of respect for the victim, a sense of solemnity. Finally, he said, "Poisoning."

"Poisoning? Of course! What did the tox screen show?" Jamie Lee asked.

"The routine toxicology screen was negative," Finnigan said.

Jamie Lee said, "I don't understand."

"Luckily, the medical examiner who did the post-mortem is an old goat who's seen everything under the sun, and then some. Well, this reminded him of a case he had back in the seventies over in Arkansas. So he ran some a few more tests, and his suspicions proved right. Olga Belenkova was poisoned with hemlock."

"Hemlock?" Patricia said.

"That's a plant, right? Some kind of ancient poison," Jamie Lee said. "Now, of all the ways to kill someone, what kind of sicko would choose hemlock?"

"Hard to detect. Impossible to trace." Finnigan said. "The plant grows in the wild like a weed. And it's not like we can pull up pharmacy sales and find our perp that way."

"Okay, but why not just stab her with a kitchen knife?" Jamie Lee said. "With the same knife he used to kill her dog."

Jamie Lee said, "dog" when she knew that Olga's pet was, in reality, a fox. Patricia thought it was a careful choice of wording on her part. The detective was still intent on keeping information close to the vest.

"Maybe it was meant to be symbolic," Kyle said.

"Like he was sending a message to someone?" Finnigan asked.

"Hemlock was used to poison Socrates," Kyle said. "His death was a sort of honor suicide after he refused to renounce his teachings."

Finnigan said, "We had the dregs of Olga's

teacup tested. Chock-full of hemlock."

"She had to know her killer," Jamie Lee said.

Espericueta said, "That's what the crime scene suggests."

"Which is why we're going to her funeral," Finnigan said. "Maybe the killer gets a little sloppy, decides to pay his last respects."

"Jesus! I forgot about that," Jamie Lee said. "When is it?"

"Tomorrow morning," Espericueta said. "Interment at Oakwood cemetery."

"Better bring an extra Thermos of coffee tomorrow, partner," Finnigan said. "I have a feeling we'll have a few guests joining us."

CHAPTER THIRTY-TWO
Jack Daniels

After closing the front door behind the Austin detectives, Jamie Lee turned to Kyle and Patricia and said, "Good thing I told you to let me do all the talking."

"Don't make this about you," Kyle said. "Those two detectives could be really helpful."

"Or they can report me to my lieutenant for running an unauthorized investigation and shut us down." Jamie Lee scoffed. "Oh, hell! Who could use a little pick-me-up?" She didn't wait for an answer. She turned on her her heels and headed for the kitchen. From there, she called out, "At least you didn't tell them about the doctor."

"Which doctor?" Kyle said. He looked at Patricia. "Dr. West?"

"No, dummy," Jamie Lee said, returning to the living room with a bottle of Jack Daniels and three shot glasses. "The Russian professor. The geneticist."

Maybe it was the sight of the bottle of whiskey.
Or perhaps it was something in Jamie Lee's tone
of voice, but the words made Patricia woozy.

Kyle sat down on a recliner. "You realize he
could be a suspect," Kyle said. "He knew Olga.
His knowledge of medicine is highly
sophisticated. I wouldn't doubt that he knows a
thing or two about horticulture too. And he
happens to be out of town right after her death."

Jamie Lee said, "You think he was busy
manufacturing an alibi?" She placed the shot
glasses on the coffee table and filled them.

"If I were a homicide detective, the first thing
I'd ask him is where he was on the day in
question," Kyle said.

"His paintings," Jamie Lee said, setting the
bottle down. "Olga gave them to me for safe-
keeping. He knew she had them, and maybe he
wanted them back. Felt like they belonged to him,
perhaps. Olga wouldn't give them up for some
reason, so he poisons her."

Patricia said, "Why would Olga give the
paintings to you but not to him?"

"Because they have the names of the boys
written on them," Kyle said. "She was trying to
protect their identity."

Jamie Lee downed her shot of Jack Daniels,
screwed up her face as if she'd bitten into a lemon.
"That's it. That's got to be it," she said, still

squinting.

Patricia looked on as Kyle reached for his whiskey, gulped it down in one swig.

"I don't know," Patricia said.

Jamie Lee chuckled. "You think doctors aren't capable of committing murder? I've got news for you, doc."

"It's not that," Patricia said. "It's the fox."

"What about it?" Jamie Lee said.

"The animal was brutalized," Patricia said. "I don't think he would do that to one of his foxes."

"It wasn't *his* fox. It was Olga's."

Kyle said. "Yeah, but he created the damn breed. Patricia's got a point there."

Up until now, Kyle had always referred to her as Dr. West. Patricia wasn't sure if this was a slip or if Kyle had unilaterally decided to abandon this point of deference. She found herself not minding. So few men called her by her first name that she found it oddly rejuvenating. Not that she was about to encourage the sheriff's deputy to get all chummy with her now. But she couldn't deny that all in all, Kyle Wagner had behaved pretty gallantly throughout the day.

"Yeah. I guess you're right," Jamie Lee said. "Didn't look at it from that angle. So, Patricia," Jamie Lee shot her a smirk, "you're not going to wimp out on us now, are you?"

Patricia said, "I'm here. Aren't I?"

"I was talking about the whiskey," Jamie Lee

said.

Patricia looked at the single shot glass sitting on the coffee table that was still full. She reached for it with both hands to steady that damn intention tremor, brought the glass to her lips and guzzled it in one gulp.

* * *

Patricia lay in bed, staring at the ceiling fan, which hummed a rhythmic tune as it wobbled on its downrod. Jamie Lee had been kind enough to let her borrow a t-shirt and pair of shorts — police academy issue which reminded Patricia of her old high school gym clothes. She tried closing her eyes though she felt wide awake.

It was too late an hour to check in on Alex again. Earlier, when Patricia spoke to him on the phone, there was no indication of anything being amiss. It was another *Good even, Audrey* in a steady tone. When Wyatt got on the horn and Patricia asked him how Alex was holding up, her father replied, "He's always great when he's with us." For Wyatt, Alex's only problem had always ever been Marcus.

From the time Alex had started taking his first steps, Marcus had begun to pester her. "There's something wrong with him," he'd say. "He's not like the other boys." That was the phrase that really got to her, the one that pricked her pride. *He's not like the other boys.*

There was no denying that Alex had developed

248

at his own pace. He was a late talker, but when he did begin to formulate his first words, his enunciation was impeccable. And soon, he was constructing remarkably sophisticated phrases, surpassing his peers, as though the initial delay was simply for lack of something to say.

"There is a wide range of normal when it comes to development," Patricia would tell Marcus in response to his provocations. It was one of her pet expressions, a quip she had grown accustomed to reciting with equanimity to so many anxious parents in the examining rooms of her general pediatric practice over the years. But in addressing her headstrong husband in the privacy of their bedroom, the same remark took on a defensive note.

"I'm just saying," Marcus would rebut. "He's not like the other kids."

After Alex's fifth birthday, Patricia asked a colleague to evaluate him for Asperger's syndrome. She never told Marcus about it. Not even after the behavioral specialist reassured Patricia that the child did not meet the diagnostic criteria. "Not by a long shot," the doctor said to Patricia's relief.

And yet, Patricia could not deny that she too had had misgivings. Alex could be so warm and tender towards her, but by the age of seven had developed an unmasked disdain for his father, which he could scarcely conceal. The young boy showed intense empathy for all living creatures, which could bring him to tears, but his thought process on almost all matters was cold and rigidly analytical.

There was no denying that Alex provided the jolt that rattled Patricia and Marcus's already rickety marriage and finally brought it tumbling down. Despite their efforts, the couple bungled the vain attempt to conceal this fact from their adopted son. But it didn't seem to bother Alex.

The evening of the day the divorce was finalized, Patricia was standing by the kitchen sink washing carrots in preparation for dinner. Nine-year-old Alex walked next to her, put his hand on her elbow, and muttered in a calm, unapologetic tone, "*Good even, Audrey,*" the greeting from *As You Like It* that meant everything was well. "Don't worry, mom. We're better off without him."

Alex was right, of course.

Still, in the ensuing years, from time to time, Marcus's voice seemed to echo in Patricia's mind: *He's not like other boys.* Now, Patricia worried, she might find out more about her son than she bargained for.

If she could talk to Alex now, what would she say? Would she dare to say, "*Peace be to France,*" the secret code that meant that something's wrong?

She rolled onto her side, tried to reshape the

overstuffed pillow with her fist.

How stupid could she be! Alex was her son. No one knew him as well as she did. Whatever untold secrets existed about his biological parents and his early infancy were utterly irrelevant. How could any of it alter the bond between a mother and her son?

So there were other boys from the same orphanage who had somehow run into some form of misfortune or other. What could this possibly have to do with Alex?

She opened her eyes and looked out at the darkness. Her pulse was pounding in her ears, a jabbing pain was building behind her left eye. It felt as though a pick were being hammered into her skull to the cadence of her heartbeat.

Patricia rolled out of bed. She headed to the kitchen for a glass of water. In the living room, Kyle was sprawled on the sofa, snoring softly. Patricia tried not to wake him. She didn't even turn the light on in the kitchen, feeling her way along the kitchen counter. After filling a plastic tumbler with tap water twice, emptying it in slow, steady gulps each time, Patricia headed back toward the guest bedroom but stopped when the glow of Jamie Lee's computer screen caught her eye.

She sat down behind the desk, rolled the mouse across the screen, and in the internet search box typed in the name "Sergey Kovalenko." This time she would not be hunting for academic papers but for the man himself. Dozens of links appeared. Since earlier that day, when they had tried calling at the professor's home, a question had begun to nag at Patricia.

She decided to try to answer it by trying to find a photograph of the professor. Finally, after going to several fruitless links, she managed to find a headshot of Sergey Kovalenko. She studied his features carefully, focusing on the eyes. Eyes don't change as you age. It didn't take long for her to be quite sure that the man was a complete stranger to her. Or at least, he wasn't who she feared he might be.

She took a deep breath, exhaled slowly. Feeling more relaxed, she decided to try to scan a few more scientific articles penned by the professor. None of the papers she managed to find were recent. Not a single one published in the last couple of decades. The ones she was able to access dealt with molecular biology laboratory techniques. Very dry technical stuff. Like she had done earlier, Patricia tried to scan the introductory sections, not knowing what she was looking for. Her headache, fortunately was subsiding. Twenty minutes later, her eyes were growing heavy.

She covered her mouth to stifle a yawn when she heard a groaning sound coming from behind her. She turned quietly. Kyle lay stiffly on the sofa, his eyes closed, his neck stretched and taut in a posture resembling opisthotonos. He seemed to be mumbling through clenched teeth.

Patricia approached him slowly.

Kyle's restlessness grew. His lips moved, his voice swelled in incoherent grumbles. His brow crumpled in deep furrows. Patricia could see that his eyes were darting under his eyelids. He was deep in REM sleep: the stage of sleep when dreams take flight.

She leaned over to place her hand on his cheek, not wanting to wake him but hoping to redirect his dreams to more serene landscapes.

Kyle began to quiver. He let out a stifled wail, then began sobbing.

"Kyle," Patricia whispered. She sat down on the couch, next to him. Caressed his cheek. "Kyle. Wake up," she uttered a little more loudly.

Kyle lurched. His eyes flew open. For a few moments, he stared at Patricia with glassy eyes, his chest heaving. Gradually, as he regained his bearings, his breathing slowed.

"You were dreaming," Patricia said, her hand still on his cheek.

Kyle drew a hand over his right eye. He muttered, "Jesus!"

"Bad dream?"

"Sorry. Was I loud?"

"You're okay." Patricia let her hand linger on his cheek, lightly drew her fingers across the stubble that covered his jaw as she pulled her hand away.

"Oh, shit! I'm sorry," Kyle said. "Did I wake you?"

Patricia shook her head. "I was up. I couldn't sleep."

Kyle pulled himself up to rest his shoulders on the sofa's arm.

"What time is it?" Kyle said.

"Who knows?" Patricia said. "Can I get you something?"

Kyle looked at her. He was studying her expression as if he were trying to read her.

After a pause, he said, "Desert Shield. First Gulf War."

"What?" Patricia said.

Kyle didn't immediately reply. As if he couldn't get himself to repeat what he had just disclosed. Then he said, "I was a sniper in the 2nd Marine Division."

Patricia crossed her hands in her lap. "It must have been rough."

"I'm sorry I shot Carson Taggart," Kyle said.

Patricia clenched her teeth. She waited a moment before saying, "Did you have a choice?"

"I've been wondering how things might have turned out had I waited. I keep playing it over in my head."

"And?"

"It always ends badly," Kyle said.

Patricia sighed. Her shoulders slumped. "I

guess you didn't have a choice. I'm the one who should apologize. I was hard on you. I shudder at the thought but … you probably saved my son's life that day."

Kyle shook his head. "Carson wasn't after your son. I don't know why, but I have a feeling that he wasn't going to hurt Alex."

Patricia fixed her eyes on Kyle's. "That's what Alex said."

Kyle looked away. He directed his gaze to the computer on the corner table. "I've been doing a lot of thinking these last couple of days. Thinking it was fate that put me at the high school with a hunting rifle. It was up to me, and me alone to pull that trigger. It was my burden to shoulder."

"Why do you say that?"

"What I've done in my life, hell, I'm already irredeemable. No need to stain another man's soul."

Patricia reached over to him and squeezed his hand. Then timidly pulled away and lay her hand back in her lap.

"Kyle, you're in law enforcement, and you were a soldier once. What do you think is going on?"

"Nothing makes much sense yet. And maybe it never will. I've got more questions than answers to tell you the truth."

Patricia said, "What kind of questions?"

Kyle looked at Patricia as if he were trying to size her up again. "Why'd you react the way you did when you saw the professor's fox?"

Patricia's head started pounding again. She looked down and closed her eyes.

"Sorry," Kyle said. "Didn't mean to put you on the spot. But I don't believe it's because you're scared of dogs."

"I saw that thing before," Patricia said. "At least I thought I did."

"What, the fox?" Kyle said.

"Exactly," Patricia said with a smile. "What the fox!"

Kyle smiled. He glanced in the direction of Jamie Lee's bedroom to make sure they weren't talking too loudly. "When? Where?"

"I had almost forgotten the incident," Patricia said. "Alex must have been six or seven at the time. We had this routine of going to Landa Park to feed the ducks. I'd bring a book sometimes to read while he played on the lawn. And then this creepy guy started coming to the park with this funny looking dog. He'd just sit on a park bench, with these giant pretzels and feed the squirrels. Never talked to anyone. Just ripped up those pretzels with his hands, tossed the pieces at the squirrels like he was trying to hit them."

"Who do you think he was?"

"For a second, tonight, I wondered if it might have been Professor Kovalenko. But it wasn't. I found a photograph of the professor on the internet. Couldn't have been him. The guy in the park was a lot younger. Very different facial features."

"What did he look like?" Kyle asked.

"Tall, dark. I'd even say handsome if he wasn't so intimidating."

"Intimidating?" Kyle said.

"Well, maybe that's just how I remember him now because of what happened next. Sometimes, Alex would venture close to the guy's bench to see his dog. I always kept an eye on him. But one day I got distracted reading a novel. When I looked up, Alex was kneeling next to the guy, petting his dog. And the man was caressing Alex's hair. That expression on the man's face, the way he was looking at my son — it freaked me out. I just about blew a gasket."

"What did you do?"

"I jumped up, shouted something."

Kyle said, "What did the guy do?"

"He got to his feet. Started walking away slowly. I thought, this guy's a predator. That's what he looked like. A child predator. As for the dog, well, that's the oldest ruse in the world to attract little kids. So I started following him. I remember the guy looked back at me, quickened his pace. I started running, chasing him. And the guy jogs past Comal Spring, slips into Panther Canyon, and just vanishes."

"Did you report the incident to the police?" Kyle said.

"I talked to an officer. Nothing ever came of it. And Alex and I stopped going to the park."

"You never saw him again?"

"No."

"But now you think that dog was actually Kovalenko's fox?" Kyle said.

"I'm almost sure they're one and the same. How long do foxes live, anyway?"

Kyle shrugged, "About as long dogs, I suppose."

"Let's assume it was the professor's fox. What can we surmise from that?"

"I don't know. Olga, the adoption lady, she had one of those foxes too. And maybe there are others."

Patricia said, "This is too much of a coincidence."

"So, what do you make of it?"

"I'm starting to think this man in the park was keeping an eye on my son," Patricia said.

"For what reason?"

There was the sound of a door opening and footsteps down the hall. Jamie Lee entered the living room wearing a silk robe, cut mid-thigh. She said, "Look at the two of you, snuggled together. You look so sweet you're making my teeth hurt."

"Didn't mean to wake you," Kyle said.

"I'm sure you didn't," Jamie Lee said with a grin.

"We were talking about those foxes," Patricia said.

Jamie Lee sat on a couch across from them, crossed her legs, letting the hem of her robe ride high on her thigh. She said, "What about them?"

"I think we decided we don't much care for them," Kyle said.

"I can't stand them," Jamie Lee said. "But we're going to have to suck it up. We're paying a visit to Professor Kovalenko in the morning. And his stupid fox."

CHAPTER THIRTY-THREE

Kovalenko

"That's him," Patricia said. "I recognize him from his photograph on the internet."

Patricia, Kyle, and Jamie Lee had been waiting in Jamie Lee's Ford Taurus for the better part of an hour, parked in the shade of a large Magnolia tree half a block away from the home of Professor Sergey Kovalenko. As Jamie Lee wondered aloud whether the retired doctor was ever going to come home, an older make Volvo turned onto the street and pulled up to the curb. A gray-haired man of slight build got out of the car, pulled a leather duffel bag out of the hatchback compartment, and made his way up the walkway to the front door with a sprightly gait which seemed discordant with the rather pronounced hunch of his shoulders. The professor had an aquiline nose and pointy overgrown ears. His skin was of a tawny complexion which, along with the sharp angles of his facial features, lent him a vaguely exotic bearing. As the trio looked on from inside Jamie Lee's Ford Taurus, Kovalenko unlocked the front door and entered his home. A minute later, Brenda, the house-sitter, walked out, hauling a bicycle, and casually pedaled away.

"Didn't park his car in the garage," Jamie Lee said. "Think he's heading out again?"

"Maybe," Kyle said. "Or maybe his garage is full of junk, like half the garages in America."

"Well, I don't want to give him the chance to give us the slip," Jamie Lee said. "Let's go on in and pay him a visit."

The professor had a befuddled look when he opened the door, and Jamie Lee flashed her detective's badge with a brief introduction. To add to the confusion, Volya, the fox began scurrying around the atrium yapping, more than once driving its little head against the professor's shins. After a moment's hesitation, Kovalenko said, "Come in, come in. Don't worry about Volya. He's harmless."

"Yeah, we know," Jamie Lee said as she crossed the threshold of Kovalenko's home.

The professor ushered them into a well-lit living room adorned with countless religious paintings. He invited his visitors to sit but remained in a standing position himself. "Can I interest you in a cup of tea?" he asked. "I'm afraid I don't keep coffee."

"That won't be necessary," Jamie Lee said.

Kyle said, "Thank you. We're fine."

"Did you paint these all yourself?" Patricia asked the professor as she inspected a gilded image of Virgin and Child painted on a wooden tablet.

"Almost all of them," Kovalenko said, a bashful note in his voice. "Those two over there are ..." The professor's expression changed as his voice trailed. "How did you know I paint?"

"We met Father Ambrus," Jamie Lee said before Patricia had a chance to reply.

"I see," Kovalenko said. "I imagine you're investigating the death of my cousin."

"Your cousin?" Jamie Lee said.

"You're here to ask me about Olga, no?" Kovalenko said.

"Of course," Jamie Lee said, shooting Kyle and Patricia a conspiratorial look.

"I'll be happy to answer your questions, but I really don't think I'll be able to shed any light on this ghastly affair."

"Were you close to your cousin?" Kyle asked.

"We got along quite well, yes," Kovalenko said. "We had our share of squabbles when we were younger, of course. But when you get to a certain age, that age when all your friends and relatives start to die one by one, then, and regrettably only then, you start to gain a new appreciation for your own blood. And you begin to show more kindness and consideration for those few family members that remain as your bloodline approaches an inexorable dead end. Olga was the last of my kin."

"Doesn't sound like such a warm relationship," Jamie Lee said.

"Dear detective, if you think I had anything to do with her murder, you can let that albatross of a thought fly out of your head," Kovalenko said.

"How do you know she was murdered?' Jamie Lee asked.

The professor frowned. "I hope you haven't come here to waste an old man's time. So, tell me, has the medical examiner determined the cause of death?"

"She was poisoned," Kyle said. Jamie Lee gave Kyle a surreptitious kick in the ankle.

The professor said, "Hmm, what was the poison?"

"Hemlock," Patricia answered. Jamie Lee glared at her.

The professor muttered something incoherently but maintained an unfazed demeanor, entirely void of emotion. He looked down and stroked his lips with his finger, deep in thought.

"Virtually untraceable," Kyle said, apparently trying to spur him on to talk.

"You can't just pick up a vial at your corner drugstore, if that's what you mean," the professor said. "Of course hemlock is a hardy plant. Just a weed, really, and a very adaptable one at that. It can grow in the wild in all sorts of climates and environments. Central Texas weather is particularly favorable for its growth. It's not terribly hard to spot an odd shrub of wild hemlock hidden in the brush if you know what you're looking for."

"Can you think of anyone who would have wanted to hurt your cousin?" Kyle asked.

The professor didn't answer. He kept stroking his lip, a vacant look in his eyes. He appeared to be in a sort of trance. Kyle and Patricia exchanged puzzled glances.

"Professor Kovalenko," Jamie Lee said. "Do you know anyone who might have had a grudge with your cousin?"

The professor shook his head. "Olga was a simple woman. She kept to herself. She had no enemies."

"And yet she was murdered," Jamie Lee said.

"Like I told you," Kovalenko said. "I'm afraid I won't be able to shed any light on—"

"Where were you on the morning of her killing?" Jamie Lee asked.

Professor Kovalenko sighed. "You can't be serious, detective. Look at me. I'm an old man. How could I do such a thing?"

"You seem to know a good deal about hemlock," Jamie Lee said. "And you didn't bat an eye when we disclosed the manner of death to you."

The professor brought his hands to his temples and shook his head. "You'd best leave now. I must get ready for Olga's funeral. Please, leave."

"Do you think whoever killed her was after the paintings?" Kyle said.

"What paintings?" the professor asked.

"Miss Olga gave me a set of seven paintings," Jamie Lee said. "For safekeeping. I think she knew her life was in danger."

"What? Why would she give them to you?"

"I was her neighbor," Jamie Lee said.

"Tell us about the paintings," Kyle said.

"How should I know?" the professor said. "We're Ukrainian." He let out a hollow chuckle. "So, we love our religious icons!"

"These were unusual paintings," Kyle said. "Each with a name on the back, written in ink only visible with ultraviolet light."

"And how would I know anything about that?"

"You painted them," Jamie Lee said.

"I paint a lot of paintings," the professor said, raising his voice, motioning with his arm to the stash of artwork in his living room.

"Did you etch those names on the back of the paintings?" Jamie Lee said.

"I don't know anything about it." The professor was becoming increasingly agitated. His face reddened.

"Professor Kovalenko," Patricia said in a gentle tone. "My name is Dr. West. I'm a pediatrician in

New Braunfels. One of those names, on the back of a painting, was that of one of my patients. A child who was recently killed during a school shooting."

The color seemed to drain from Sergey Kovalenko's face. He reached out with his arm to lean against a wall.

Patricia continued in a steady voice. "Other children, whose names are on those paintings, also recently died in unusual, violent circumstances."

The professor shuffled to an armchair and slumped into it.

Patricia waited for a beat before resuming. "One painting had the name of —"

"I know, I know," the professor said. He brought his hands together and interlaced his fingers. "How is little Sasha?"

Patricia closed her eyes a moment, took a deep, composing breath. She said, "He's well."

Jamie Lee said, "Sasha? Who's Sasha?"

"My son," Patricia said. "Sasha is the Russian nickname for Alexander."

Kyle got to his feet, cleared his throat to get Jamie Lee's attention. "Let's step outside for a moment."

Jamie Lee gave him a dirty look. "What, are you kidding me?"

"I think they need to talk," Kyle said. "Come on."

Jamie Lee frowned but quickly got to her feet

and headed toward the foyer. Kyle followed her out of the front entrance and shut the front door behind him.

Patricia and Professor Kovalenko exchanged glances. Patricia leaned forward. She said, "Dr. Kovalenko, do I need to worry about my son?"

In a monotone, Kovalenko said, "Your son is not like the other boys."

If the utterance was meant to reassure Patricia, it landed off the mark. How many times had she heard Marcus repeat the exact same phrase? *He's not like the other boys.* Now the words took on an entirely different meaning, and Patricia wanted desperately to believe what she was hearing.

"How is he different? What do you know about this?"

"Where is he?" the professor asked.

"What?"

"Where is Alex?" there was an urgency in the old man's voice. "Is he here?"

Patricia shook her head. "He's with family." Oddly, it was as though the professor were the one in need of reassurance now.

Kovalenko offered a heartening smile, apparently sensing Patricia's growing apprehension. He waited as if he were anticipating Patricia to say something more, holding her gaze with his pale blue eyes. Finally, he said, "Yes, well, I'm sure he's safe then."

"Obviously, you know I adopted Alex from an

orphanage in Odessa," Patricia said.

The professor nodded.

"Like all the boys linked to the paintings your cousin gave to detective Foster."

"Yes," the professor said.

"What do you know about these boys?"

Professor Kovalenko let out a long sigh. He glanced at his watch. "I really do need to get ready for my cousin's interment," he said. "Perhaps, if you come back after the service we can talk some more. I would like very much for you to tell me about your son."

"I need to go to him," Patricia said. "I was supposed to meet him yesterday."

"What a pity!" Sergey Kovalenko said, ignoring her last statement. He smiled wistfully. "Did you know? I was there when he was born."

CHAPTER THIRTY-FOUR
The Funeral

The three of them trudged along a gravel path
between weathered granite headstones, Patricia
West, Kyle Wagner, with Jamie Lee Foster in tow,
to join Finnigan and Espericueta. The two Austin
detectives were standing on a trampled patch of
grass a respectful distance from the gathered
mourners. Standing amongst the grievers was
Father Ambrus, clothed in a drab black cassock
with a velvet skufia covering his head. He was
reciting the graveside service mixing English with
a language Patricia could not discern. Behind him,
Professor Kovalenko stood with hands clasped in
prayer, swaying, as if he were being battered by
raging gusts of wind.

Detective Finnigan turned in the direction of
the threesome to nod a solemn greeting. He said,
"The good padre is just about to wrap it up. Pity
you're late. You missed a helluva service. The

269

priest has a way with words."

"Poetic," Espericueta added.

"Never mind the poetry," Jamie Lee said. "You notice anything?"

Finnigan said, "A professor Kovalenko, the cousin of the deceased, delivered the eulogy."

"Never mind him," Jamie Lee said. "We already talked to the professor. He doesn't know diddly."

"Does he have an alibi?" Finnigan asked.

"Airtight," Jamie Lee said.

Kyle Wagner glanced at Patricia, poker-faced. Patricia managed to pull off a barely detectable shrug.

As if to change the subject, Jamie Lee said, "What did you find out about this Russian guy? The diplomat."

Finnigan slipped his hands in his trouser pockets, leaned his shoulders back, and said, "Borya Balakin. Russian national. Forty-two years old. Entered the United States on May thirteenth at Houston Bush Intercontinental Airport on a diplomatic visa." Finnigan stopped abruptly.

"Keep going," Jamie Lee said.

Finnigan and Espericueta exchanged glances. "That's all," Espericueta said.

"What do you mean, that's all?" Jamie Lee asked.

"I'm afraid that's all the information we're going to get on comrade Balakin," Finnigan said.

"Says who?" Jamie Lee said.

"Says the State Department of the United States of America," Finnigan said. He turned to look at the mourners, took his hands out of his pockets, and made the sign of the cross. By the open grave, a man in an ill-fitting dark suit began operating a mechanical device that slowly lowered Olga Belenkova's casket into the ground. Father Ambrus held his hands together in prayer while a young acolyte in an ankle-length white frock swung a brass thurible by its chains.

Finnigan said, "It's over. We'll position ourselves by the parking lot. Get a better look at the mourners as they file out. The three of you can stay here if you like." He motioned to Espericueta, and the two detectives walked away.

Jamie Lee bit her lip as the casket sunk in the earth. She looked on as Professor Kovalenko approached the grave, grasped a handful of dirt from a stainless steel bucket and tossed it into the grave.

Jamie Lee said, "I thought this Balakin guy was supposed to be a deacon. Why would he be traveling with a diplomatic visa?"

Kyle cleared his voice and said, "Immunity."

"Immunity?" Jamie Lee said.

"Diplomatic immunity," Kyle said.

"You think the deacon doesn't want to pay for parking tickets?" Jamie Lee said.

"Something like that," Kyle said.

Jamie Lee turned to face him. "He would need friends in very high places to get that sort of immunity," she said.

"Upper echelon," Kyle said. "I'm not exactly sure how that works, but it's safe to say that the Russian authorities don't hand out those visas like Christmas candy. Do you think we can get a passport photo of him, at least?" Kyle said.

"What's going through your mind, sheriff?" Patricia asked.

He looked up at the cloudless sky. "I don't know," he said. "I really don't know."

The graveside service came to an end. A few mourners gathered around Professor Kovalenko, who was flanked by Father Ambrus, to offer their condolences. Meanwhile, others shuffled down a gravel path toward the parking lot.

"How the hell does a deacon get diplomatic immunity?" Jamie Lee said.

"We don't really know that he's a deacon," Patricia said. "He just said he was."

"But we do know he was looking for Dr. Kovalenko," Kyle said. His eyes focused on the professor.

Patricia followed Kyle's gaze. The mourners were dispersing now. She looked on as Professor Kovalenko, and Father Ambrus exchanged words, their hands clasped together.

"They could be talking about him right now," Jamie Lee said.

An inexplicable sense of guilt started gnawing at Patricia. She felt like a voyeur, brazenly intruding on the professor's grief. The sentiment was quickly eclipsed by a more ominous thought.

"What if he's in danger," Patricia said.

"Who, the professor?" Jamie Lee asked.

"We don't know who Balakin is," Patricia said. "All we know is that he was asking Father Ambrus how to find the professor. If that man had anything to do with Olga's death ..."

"The professor was out of town till this morning," Kyle said. "And now he's in a public place. If Balakin had nefarious motives, he wouldn't have had a chance to seek him out even if he'd have wanted to."

"You think we should get some eyes on professor Kovalenko?" Jamie Lee said.

"I think we should warn him," Kyle said. "At least ask him if he knows who this Balakin character is."

"I don't think this is the right place or the right time," Patricia said.

"You said he wanted to talk to you some more," Jamie Lee said. "About your son and all. You can discreetly bring up the subject of Balakin. For all we know, the guy really is a deacon wanting to commission some artwork, and we're just barking up the wrong tree, wasting our time."

What Patricia really wanted to do was get in her car and head for the Gulf Coast. She wanted to see Alex. Assure herself that he was alright, and keep watch over him, making sure nothing would harm him. But the professor had said something she could not let go of.

I was there when he was born.

Was Kovalenko there when the other boys were born as well? Patricia wondered. If there was anyone who might have any insight on the fate of these orphans, anyone who might be able to shed light on their ghastly misfortunes, it had to be Professor Sergey Kovalenko.

"Let's go," Patricia said.

"Now?" Jamie Lee said.

Kyle nodded. "Let's go."

Sitting in the front seat of Jamie's car Patricia said nothing. Years ago, she had lost her way, and had become mired in an inescapable fog of guilt and impotence. As much as she wanted the fog to lift, Patricia was terrified of what she might find once the landscape laid bare.

Patricia could no longer deny there was some truth to what Marcus had repeatedly told her. It was not just his way of skirting his responsibility as a father. Anyone could see that Alex was not like other boys.

He was undeniably different. He had a peculiar temperament: coldly logical, detached, rigidly precise. From a young age, he appeared to be excessively introspective as if he were always trying to make sense of his surroundings, seemingly incapable of comprehending the behavior of others but desperately trying to find a way to fit in. Alex understood he was different, and he seemed intent, in his cold, logical way, on trying to discover the root cause of his idiosyncrasies. It was a heart-wrenching quest for a mother to witness.

Patricia needed to be with him. Just be with him. Be there to listen, to understand him, and to let him know she would always be there for him. There were no grand mysteries to solve, no conspiracy theories surrounding his birth that needed unraveling. The only thing that mattered was love. Her love. A mother's unwavering love for her son.

Patricia latched her seat belt and looked out the passenger side window as the car started to roll. She was feeling charged, energized by her new sense of resolve when her gaze was pulled to the figure of a man in a worn leather jacket standing in the shade of an oak tree.

Her first thought, *who the hell wears a leather jacket in Texas this time of the year.* There was something alluringly exotic about the man's features: the deep, narrow eyes, the high cheekbones, the full lips. And yet, despite its foreignness, that face looked oddly familiar. The man in the leather jacket looked back at her across the expanse of the parking lot, holding her gaze. He smiled slightly and gave a timid nod, as though he too had recognized her.

Jamie Lee turned the car south towards the East 14th Street exit. There was a delay of a few seconds, a brief refractory period as the various stimuli traveled the circuits of Patricia's brain, as chemical transmitters swam the treacherous gulfs of dormant synapses. When the realization finally washed over Patricia, it hit her with the force of a tidal wave.

Patricia shouted, "Holy shit! That's the guy!"

"What guy?" Jamie Lee said.

Patricia turned to face Kyle in the back seat. "The guy I told you about last night. The guy at the park with the fox. The one that touched my son."

Jamie Lee said, "What the hell? A guy with a fox touched your son? You didn't tell me that."

"Where is he?" Kyle asked.

"Stop the car!" Patricia shouted.

Jamie Lee stepped on the brake making the car lurch to a stop with a shrieking of tires. Patricia turned toward the oak tree. The man was still standing there. She pointed in his direction. "There he is."

"That guy? Let's mosey on over and have a little chat with him," Jamie Lee said, cranking the steering wheel all the way to the left to make a U-turn. As the car came around, the guy bolted across the cemetery.

"Looks like we got a runner," Kyle said.

"Sweet!" Jamie Lee said.

"That could be our Russian diplomat," Kyle said.

"Don't fret now. I'm not gonna run him over," Jamie Lee said. "I just want to body-slam his ass to the ground before he can pull out his credentials. Hold on now!"

Jamie Lee gunned the engine, and the car sped through the parking lot heading for its far end where the lot ended on a shallow embankment that led to a sprawling lawn. Patricia held onto the dashboard as the front end of the car pitched up and lunged over the embankment. The car skidded across the grass, leaving deep marks in the turf.

"This guy's a rabbit. He sure can move for a big boy," Jamie Lee said as they gained on him.

The man in the leather jacket made a sudden cut to the left, accelerated off the lawn, running between granite headstones.

"I hope those boots of yours have non-skid soles, cowboy," Jamie Lee said as she slammed on the brakes.

Kyle jumped out of the back seat and started chasing the runner. Jamie Lee told Patricia, "You better stay here," before she hopped out of the car and started her pursuit.

"The hell I will," Patricia muttered. She got out of the car, started jogging. Stopped to take off her shoes, and began running barefoot on the grass,

managing to just keep up with Jamie Lee. This
spook had slipped away from her once before,
years ago, when she had chased him in a blinding
rage. She would have gouged his eyes out had she
caught up with him that day. Now, all she wanted
was answers.

Who are you? What do you want from my son?

The runner was heading for a tall chain-link
fence, but Kyle was gaining on him. Jamie Lee, on
the other hand, was falling behind.

A few moments later, the guy in the leather
jacket sprung onto the fence and was climbing
fiercely, but before he was able to clear the top,
Kyle grabbed one of his ankles and tried to pull
him back down. It seemed the two were at an
impasse: the man no longer able to scale the fence,
Kyle unable to pull him down.

Suddenly, the man in the leather jacket released
his grip, pushed back hard from the fence, made a
sort of backward somersault, twisting in mid-air,
landing cleanly on the palms of his hands before
catapulting to his feet. The move took Kyle by
surprise. The mid-air twist forced Kyle to release
his grip on the man's leg. Before the deputy was
able to regain his bearings, the runner pulled a
judo foot-sweep move, and Kyle landed hard on
the pavement. The runner was scaling the fence
again while Kyle remained sprawled on his back,
the wind knocked out of him.

The stranger hurdled over the top of the barrier

and landed heavily in a tripod stance on the sidewalk of the street side of the fence. He stopped, brushed off his hands, flashed Kyle a smug smile, and then darted across the avenue into a residential neighborhood.

By now, Jamie Lee reached the fence. She unholstered her gun.

Scrambling to his feet, Kyle shouted, "Are you out of your mind? Put your gun away!"

"Tell you what, that's no church deacon," Jamie Lee said, trying to catch her breath.

"You think?" Kyle said in a sarcastic tone. "The way he moves, that guy had to have special forces training."

"He got you pretty good, didn't he?" Jamie Lee said, slipping the gun back in its holster. "You okay?"

Kyle nodded. "Only thing hurt is my pride."

"Come on," Jamie Lee said. "We can still catch him."

"Not this guy," Kyle said. "Not unless he wants to be caught."

CHAPTER THIRTY-FIVE
The Rostov Conjecture

Finnigan and Espericueta were leaning on
Jamie Lee's car when Kyle, Patricia, and Jamie
Lee got back to the cemetery lawn where they had
ditched the vehicle. Finnigan's jowls were beet
red.

He said, "Tell me you didn't almost shoot a
foreign dignitary."

Jamie Lee said, "Never even took the safety
off."

"Christ, Foster!" Finnigan shouted. "I don't
want to finish my career as the whipping boy for
an international incident."

"Relax, Finn," Jamie Lee said. "We don't even
know if that was our guy."

"Then why'd you pursue him?" Espericueta
asked.

"Because he ran," Jamie Lee said. "You know
the drill."

"He ran before you started chasing him?" Finnigan said.

"We were approaching him, and he ran," Jamie Lee said.

Finnigan crossed his arms and said, "Why were you approaching him?"

"Wanted to ask him a few questions," Jamie Lee said.

"About what?" Finn asked.

"Well, it might interest you that this guy was seen with the same kind of dog Miss Olga owned," Jamie Lee said. "A dead ringer for the pooch, in fact."

"Judas priest!" Finnegan said through clenched teeth. "Good thing Miss Olga didn't own a Labrador Retriever, or you'd be chasing down half the citizens of Austin."

"I'm sorry. Did I say, dog?" Jamie Lee said. "I meant to say fox."

Finnigan faced Espericueta. "You getting any of this, partner?"

"Clear as mud," Espericueta said.

"I can explain," Patricia said. "That man, I recognized him from an incident a long time ago. He was … inappropriate with my son. In a park in New Braunfels."

"You have his name?" Finnigan asked.

"No. I don't know who he is," Patricia said.

"Did you file a police report at the time?" Espericueta asked.

"I notified them," Patricia said. "I don't remember filling out an official complaint."

"Excuse me, doctor. A man fondles your son in a park, and you don't fill out a police report?" Finnigan said.

"It wasn't like that," Patricia said. "He was talking to my son in what I thought was an overly impassioned way. He caressed his hair."

"Did you confront him?" Espericueta said.

"I tried," Patricia said. "But he ran off into a canyon. Disappeared."

"When did this happen?" Finnigan asked.

Patricia shook her head slightly. "About eight years ago."

Finnigan and Espericueta exchanged quizzical looks.

"Foster, you mentioned something about a fox," Finnigan said in a calmer voice.

"The freak at the park had a fox on a leash," Jamie Lee said. "Like the one we found dead in Miss Olga's kitchen. Like the one Professor Kovalenko has."

"Kovalenko owns a fox too?" Espericueta said.

"He used to breed them in Russia," Jamie Lee said. Her statement was close enough to the truth, Patricia thought, without bringing up the disturbing subject of genetic engineering.

Finnigan rubbed his jaw. The ruddiness was starting to dissipate from his face.

"Simplest explanation," Finnigan said, "is that

Miss Olga and Kovalenko both owned foxes as pets, which is not terribly bizarre, seeing as they were cousins. You say Kovalenko used to breed them. He probably gave a pup to Miss Olga as a gift some time back. Chances are your runner is also a friend or family member who came to pay his last respects. Maybe he got a pup from Kovalenko too. Unless the fox he was walking in the park happened to belong to Miss Olga or Kovalenko. I mean, how many people have domesticated foxes as pets in this neck of the woods?"

Espericueta said, "What was he doing in a park in New Braunfels?"

"Good question," Finnigan said. He looked at Patricia. "Dr. West, do you have any connection with the deceased that you can think of?"

"Yes," Patricia whispered. "She coordinated the adoption of my son."

Finnigan opened his mouth to speak but seemed to hesitate. "If you don't mind my asking, was it an international adoption?"

Patricia looked off in the distance and nodded. "My son was born in the former Soviet Union, in what is now Ukraine."

"Like Tommy Roberts," Espericueta said.

Finnigan raised his hand to cut his partner off.

"Dr. West," Finnigan said, "this may seem like an odd question. Does your son have a white patch of hair on his head?"

283

Patricia felt as though a jolt of electricity had
buzzed through her body. She looked at Kyle
Wagner and tried to study his expression. The
sheriff deputy looked as though he were working
hard to remain impassive, but there was a slight
narrowing of his eyes, as though cogs were
turning in his head.

"No," Patricia said. "He doesn't."

"Why'd you ask?" Jamie Lee said.

"Well, it's the oddest thing," Finnigan said.
"This morning, we went back to interview
Tommy Robert's mom. Like we told you, we
would. Tried to get a better sense of the boy's state
of mind in the days leading up to the tragedy. The
woman's a wreck, God bless her. The strangest
thing is that she's become … What's the word for
it?"

"Obsessed," Espericueta said.

"That's it," Finnigan said. "Obsessed with an
idea. She blames the whole thing — get this! — on
a patch of white hair. Right here." Finnigan
tapped his head. "A white tuft of hair on the boy's
head. First reaction, Espericueta, and I thought
this was a classic case of …" He snapped his
fingers, trying to search for the right words.

"Disordered thinking of bereavement,"
Espericueta said.

Finnigan gave his partner a nod of
acknowledgment. "Lord knows, we've all
witnessed it before. But she kept at it, that the boy

had never shown a temper until this white patch of hair sprung up on his head some six months ago. She was insistent."

"Unrelenting," Espericueta said.

"So we wrap up the interview and drive off thinking it was a complete wash," Finnigan said. "Until we get a call from our contact over at the San Antonio Police Department. Says the post-mortem on Boris O'Keefe was finished and a preliminary report drafted and did we want it. I says, 'Sure we want it. Send us a fax.' So we get back to headquarters, pick up the fax and start skimming through the autopsy report when a little detail catches our eye."

As if they had rehearsed the routine, Espericueta chimed in. "White patch of hair over the left temporal area."

"Just like Tommy Roberts," Finnigan said. "We read it twice. Three times. I mean, what are the odds, right?"

"Infinitesimal," Espericueta said.

"So we get the idea to call out the juvenile detention center over in Dallas where that other kid, Jonathan Muller, is locked up," Finnigan said. "And guess what?"

"White patch of hair behind the right ear," Espericueta said.

"So it got us wondering," Finnigan continued, "about your patient, the school shooter."

There were a few moments of tense silence.

Finally, Kyle Wagner said, "He had it. A tuft of white hair on the crown of his head. I saw it."

"He was your patient, doctor," Finnigan said.

"Patricia nodded. "It grew out a few months ago."

"What does that mean, medically?" Espericueta asked.

"White patches of hair can be seen in some genetic syndromes," Patricia said. "Like Waardenburg syndrome, where it's associated with hearing loss. There's also a condition called piebaldism, an autosomal dominant disorder, where you can have white patches of hair along with hypo-pigmentation of the skin. But that's typically evident at birth. In Carson's case, my impression was that this was an isolated minor anomaly. Merely a cosmetic issue. A dermatologist I referred him to agreed with my assessment."

"So, what should we make of this improbable coincidence?" Finnigan said.

"Did I ever mention that the second toe of my foot is bigger than my big toe?" Jamie Lee said, without letting Finnigan's question linger. "Makes it hard to find comfortable shoes."

The others exchanged dumbfounded looks.

"Your point being . . ." Kyle said.

"Most people's big toe is longer. Turns out, my pappy had the same toes as me. So did his brother, my uncle. So did most of my cousins and at least three second-cousins that I know of."

"Are you saying you think these kids are related?" Kyle said.

"Why not?" Jamie Lee said. "They could be brothers for all we know."

"Unlikely," Kyle said. "For starters, they're all nearly exactly the same age."

"Okay. Cousins, maybe. Or they're all from the same village. Some backwoods place where there's lots of inbreeding."

"I don't know," Kyle said. "They're all too close in age."

Jamie Lee scoffed. "I grew up in the South," she said. "Let me tell you, it happens all the time. In some of those little towns out in the sticks, it's matter-of-course. Especially nine months after a major power outage."

"My son doesn't have white hair," Patricia said. "Professor Kovalenko told me he's not like the other boys."

"He said that, did he?" Jamie Lee said.

"He made it a point to tell me," Patricia said.

Finnigan took a deep breath. "How would he know?"

Espericueta said, "Miss Olga was his cousin. She's the one who organized the adoptions. So she knew where these boys came from and passed on the information to the professor."

"So maybe they all came from the same litter," Finnigan said. "So to speak," he added in an apologetic tone, directing his gaze towards Patricia. "Dr. West's son, on the other hand, is the only one that's unrelated. Miss Olga knew it, and that's how the professor knows it too."

Jamie Lee said, "You know, the two of you together almost count as one whole brain. How do you guys tie your shoelaces when you're apart?"

"Loafers," Espericueta said.

"You knew Carson Taggart intimately," Kyle said, looking at Patricia. "Did he bear a resemblance to your son?"

"None," Patricia said. "Not in appearance. Not in temperament, even." Her voice trailed off.

"But there *was* something," Jamie Lee said, trying to spur her on.

"Well, there was a strange bond that formed between them," Patricia said. "I wouldn't say they were best of friends, but Carson had quite a growth spurt this year, Alex trailed behind, and Carson became somewhat of a big brother figure for my son. He started looking after Alex. But not in a particularly warm or friendly way."

Finnigan asked, "Does Alex know he was adopted?"

Patricia shook her head. "We never told him."

"You think he suspects he was?" Finnigan said.

Patricia looked up, trying to replay a recent conversation with her son. "I never thought he did," she said. But he made a strange comment the morning of the shooting, just before I dropped him off at school."

"What did he say?" Kyle asked.

"It wasn't so much of a comment," Patricia said. "It was more in the form of a question. He asked me if I remembered what the weather was like on the day he was born. I felt like he was testing me."

"He knows," Jamie Lee said, tossing her hands up. "Smart kid to put it to you that way."

"Marcus and I never told him," Patricia said. "Unless Marcus—"

"I don't think your ex told him," Jamie Lee said. "I think the kid figured it out."

"Or Carson Taggart figured it out," Kyle said. "And told Alex."

"Carson knew he was adopted," Patricia said.

"You think that's why his behavior changed?" Jamie Lee asked. "Started acting out when he found out those weren't his biological parents?"

"Oh no," Patricia said. "He's known for years. It was never a secret. His father insisted he should know."

Kyle said, "So there's a good chance Carson found out Alex was adopted too. From his parents. Maybe they let it slip that the two of them came from the same orphanage. Which explains why he acted like a big brother towards him. And finally, one day, he let Alex in on the secret." Kyle rubbed the nape of his neck. As if he were thinking aloud, he said, "I had an odd feeling, that day at the school, that Carson had no intention of hurting Alex."

"You mentioned it. But how does whether or not my son know he was adopted have any relevance on what's going on?" Patricia said, in exasperation.

"We're just looking at this puzzle from all angles," Jamie Lee said. "See if any new clues stand out."

"Any way you look at it," Finnigan said, "kids adopted from the same orphanage dying of different, seemingly random causes in a short period of time makes no sense at all."

"They're not really so random," Kyle said. "They were all violent deaths."

Patricia looked at Kyle. He was looking deep in her eyes, sizing her up again, his eyes focused, probing. And as they're eyes remained locked, Patricia realized that with his gaze, Kyle was seeking Patricia's consent to further his argument."

"Rage," Patricia said. She watched for Kyle's reaction. Kyle looked away.

"Rage?" Jamie Lee said.

"Uncontrolled rage is the common denominator," Patricia said. "Carson acted in a fit of rage. So did that boy at the Greek restaurant, Tommy Roberts. And the kid in Dallas who's locked up for assault, we can presume he acted in a moment of rage as well."

"What about Boris O'Keefe?" Finnigan said.

"He got a screwdriver in the heart in a mugging gone bad."

"Or so we think," Espericueta said.

"Maybe you can interview his parents," Kyle said. "Ask them if he had any recent behavioral changes, outbursts of anger."

Finnigan looked at his partner. "We have to call our buddy in San Antonio, stat."

Espericueta nodded.

"And *we* better pay Kovalenko another visit," Kyle said. He opened the front door of Jamie Lee's car for Patricia. She quickly slipped in. Finnigan and Espericueta started walking away as Jamie Lee went around the front of her car.

Finnigan turned, "By the way. Where did you get the name of Borya Balakin?"

"Never mind him," said Jamie Lee. "Call me if you find out anything about this, Boris kid."

She slammed her door shut, started the ignition, and drove off.

CHAPTER THIRTY-SIX
Professor Kovalenko

Professor Kovalenko's Volvo was parked in
the driveway when they arrived at his house.
They made their way up the walkway to the front
door when Patricia stopped and said, 'This time,
you better let *me* do the talking."

Jamie Lee looked at her with raised eyebrows.

"There are some medical issues I want to
discuss," Patricia said. "Highly technical, scientific
points."

"Well, look at *you*, doctor," Jamie Lee said.
"Jumping in the driver's seat, just like that. Okay,
honey. You go right ahead." Jamie Lee hooked
her thumbs on her belt, letting the fingers of her
right-hand slide onto her holstered sidearm. "Of
course, we're always here to back you up, should
you get in over your head."

Jamie Lee stepped onto the shallow front porch
and rang the doorbell.

"I was expecting you," Sergey Kovalenko said as he opened the front door. "Come in. I have a kettle of black tea steeping."

Jamie Lee strode into the foyer, followed by Kyle and Patricia. She stopped suddenly when Kovalenko's fox bounded in front of her, sliding on the smooth parquet floor, yapping with delight.

"That thing ever bite?" Jamie Lee asked.

Kovalenko chuckled. "He was bred for docility. Please, make yourselves comfortable. You know your way to the living room."

They ambled down the sunlit corridor as Kovalenko slipped through a side door to the kitchen. Patricia and Jamie Lee sat down on opposite sides of a sofa while Kyle paced around the room, inspecting the various paintings and religious icons. He stopped to study a painted wooden tablet displayed in a locked glass cabinet.

Kovalenko entered the room, carrying a tray of piping cups of tea. He set the tray down on the coffee table, walked up behind Kyle, and said, "You have a good eye, deputy."

"I don't know about that, but I can tell this one's different from the others," Kyle said. "Really stunning."

"Alas! Not one of mine. It's an original Andrei Rublev. Fifteenth-century. Priceless."

"Priceless?" Jamie Lee said. "And you have it hanging in your parlor?"

"It was a gift." Changing the subject, the

professor said. "I saw you at the interment today. Thank you for attending. Olga would have been gratified by the presence of her neighbor."

Patricia wondered if he had seen them chasing that man, the man who once stalked her son.

As if she had read Patricia's mind, Jamie Lee said. "Wouldn't have missed it for the world. By the way, who was that man?"

"Which man?" Kovalenko said.

"Big fella," Jamie Lee said. "Ruggedly handsome. The one that knocked deputy Wagner flat on his backside."

"I'm afraid I don't know what you're referring to," the professor said in a smooth voice.

"You couldn't miss him. The boy stuck out like a pickle in a box of donuts. Tough guy. Leather jacket. But skittish as an alley cat. Took off running when we approached him and jumped over a fence."

Kovalenko shook his head. "I haven't the faintest idea. I left almost as soon as the service was over."

"That's alright," Jamie Lee said. "We'll just have to ask Father Ambrus. I'm sure *he* saw him."

Patricia tried to redirect the conversation. "I had some questions about your work, professor. I read some of your papers, but I couldn't find any published articles that described your experiments with Siberian silver foxes."

Kovalenko walked up to Patricia, picked up a

cup of tea along with its saucer, and handed it to her.

"I was not allowed to publish that work," Kovalenko said.

"You were blocked from publishing?" Patricia said.

"By the Soviet Ministry of Foreign Trade. You see, fox furs were a lucrative export commodity for the Soviet Union. All activity related to the industry was considered a state secret. I was given wide latitude in conducting my research, but I could not share my findings with the scientific community. It was frustrating."

"I can imagine," Patricia said. She sipped her tea, took a moment to gather her thoughts. "I was wondering about the control group."

"Control group?" Kovalenko said.

"In addition to raising docile foxes, Professor Belyaev bred hyper-aggressive specimens. Your former colleague Dr. Robinson told us as much."

"That is correct. Belyaev created a line of particularly aggressive foxes."

"I imagine that in your genetic studies, you were able to identify the gene responsible for that behavior."

"It was the key to our understanding," Kovalenko said in a reluctant tone.

"But again, you weren't allowed to share that knowledge with the scientific world," Patricia said.

"It was out of the question," Sergey Kovalenko said.

"Because the Ministry of Foreign Trade would not have allowed it," Patricia said.

Kovalenko paused. "When I identified the gene involved, I suddenly found myself under the purview of a different government agency: the Ministry of Defense."

"The Ministry of Defense?" Patricia said.

Kovalenko slumped into an armchair, rubbed his brow. "A particularly nasty little man came in on an overnight flight from Moscow. He walked into my office, ordered my staff to leave, and told me my work was being reclassified. It now fell within the auspices of national security. He said I should speak to no one except him about my findings and that my work with foxes was to cease until further notice."

Patricia leaned forward. "Professor Kovalenko, what gene did you isolate?"

Sergey Kovalenko furrowed his brow. "It was a newly discovered permutation of the Mono-Amine Oxidase A gene."

"Say again," Jamie Lee said.

"Mono-Amine Oxidase A, or MAO-A for short, is an enzyme involved in the metabolism of a variety of brain neurotransmitters," Kovalenko said. "Dopamine, Serotonin, Epinephrine, Norepinephrine — they're all in the same metabolic pathway."

Patricia asked, "Is this what's known as the warrior gene?"

Sergey Kovalenko unexpectedly raised his voice. "I told them there was no such thing! It's a gross over-simplification to attribute the complexity of human behavior to a mutation in a single gene."

"You told who?" Kyle asked.

"Those army generals!" Kovalenko said. "Four months later, I was reassigned. I was shipped out to a military hospital installation in Odessa."

"I don't understand," Kyle said. "Why did the army get involved?" Kyle said.

"In February of 1989, Colonel-General Boris Gromov completed the withdrawal of Soviet forces from Afghanistan. It was a complete humiliation for our military. There was panic throughout the ranks as the root causes for the disaster were being investigated. Many officers were severely punished. And then, to the relief of all but a few of us, a nascent theory took flight: the Rostov conjecture."

"I've never heard of it," Kyle said.

"How could you have? It is still classified intelligence in Moscow. What I am about to tell you is a state secret." Kovalenko took a sip of tea and swallowed it with an expression of pain in his features. "Major General Vladislav Rostov offered a simple observation. The Soviet Army was armed with weapons that were far superior to anything the Afghanis had in their possession. The weapons were superior because they were specifically designed for that end. The problem in the Afghanistan debacle was not an inferior arsenal but an issue of personnel, of troop morale. The Afghanis were the better warriors: ruthless, determined, unflinching. Rostov's conjecture was that the Soviet military would forever remain hampered until the Soviet soldier, like the weapons at his disposal, could be deliberately designed to confer an advantage."

"Genetically engineered fighting men," Patricia said.

"As a youth, Rostov had enjoyed the benefits of a classical education. He was well versed in Homer, of course. There was one passage in particular from the Iliad that seems to have made an indelible impression on the pre-pubescent Rostov: the story of Diomedes. Do you know it?

"Diomedes was a Greek warrior, an Achaean, to be precise. After being wounded in battle, he prays to Athena to grant him the power to exact his revenge. She imbues him with superhuman strength but, if that weren't enough, she also fills him with what the ancient Greeks referred to as noble anger. Diomedes returns to the battlefield, a man possessed, and slaughters every Trojan who has the misfortune to cross his path."

Kovalenko rubbed his hands together, took a deep breath before continuing. "Rostov got it in

his head that the ingredient missing in the Soviet
Army was soldiers gripped by noble anger,
brimming with a focused rage which would make
them virtually invincible.

"He concocted a thesis which was
enthusiastically endorsed by his superiors. What
the Soviet Army urgently needed was an elite
corps of super-warriors, armed with the noble
rage of Diomedes. Such an elite corps would be
enough to tip the scales in our favor in any
conflict. When Rostov happened to learn of the
work I was engaged in, he could hardly contain
his excitement. He saw my discovery as the means
to his ends: genetically enhanced soldiers imbued
with focused rage."

"Things didn't end up too well for Diomedes, I
seem to recall," said Kyle.

"Indeed," Kovalenko said. "Athena had warned
Diomedes not to turn his wrath against the Gods.
But when the goddess Aphrodite appeared on the
battlefield to give aid to her own son who had
been wounded by Diomedes' sword, Diomedes
attacked her too. Things really turned sour then."

Kyle said, "It's a recurring theme, isn't it?
Things going south when the affairs of gods
become entangled with the affairs of mere
mortals."

"A lesson Rostov never learned," Kovalenko
said.

Patricia asked, "What happened next?"

"Major General Rostov was consumed by his idea. He became my direct superior and ordered me to do with men what Belyaev had done with foxes, but quickly, using the molecular tools I had developed. I tried to explain to him it couldn't be done."

"Or it shouldn't be done," Kyle said.

"Of course," Kovalenko said. "The ethical implications were unthinkable. Rostov remained undaunted. He told me it was not my job to worry about ethics: the project had already been approved at the highest levels of leadership. And if I didn't think a single gene alteration could create the desired outcome that I should introduce multiple genes — whichever ones might provide the desired result. He had already assembled a group of elite men: proven warriors, with remarkable physical prowess, fearlessness, and field-tested fighting abilities. These men would provide the genetic material which I was to genetically enhance, and which then would be introduced by in-vitro fertilization into a group of young women who had undergone a careful and thorough medical evaluation."

"Tell me about the hair," Patricia said. "The white patches in the hair of the boys."

"Dr. West, I must reiterate, Alex is not like the other boys."

"The white hair," Patricia repeated.

Volya, the fox curled its body at Kovalenko's

feet, plopping its drowsy head on the professor's shoe.

"I decided the best approach was to create an inducible gene."

"What's that?" Jamie Lee said.

In a slightly annoyed voice, Patricia said, "A constitutive gene is one that is continually being transcribed at a relatively constant rate. An inducible gene is only expressed in response to a cellular need, some environmental change, or a trigger."

"Like a switch," Kyle said."

"More or less," Kovalenko said. "Like a switch."

"What change makes your gene switch on?" Kyle asked.

"Puberty," Patricia said before Kovalenko had a chance to reply.

"That is correct," Kovalenko said. "A surge in testosterone to be precise."

"And the patch of white hair?" Jamie Lee asked.

Kovalenko reached down and petted the fox. "We had learned from Belyaev's original experiments with foxes that genes which are in close proximity tend to travel together. So that as foxes became more docile through generations of selective breeding they unexpectedly also developed physical characteristics that we tend to associate with domesticated dogs: curly tails, floppy ears, particular patterns in fur color. It gave me an idea. I wanted to have an easy way to ascertain whether the genes I had implanted had turned on."

"So you spliced a gene for white hair on the tail end of the nucleotide segment you created," Patricia said.

"Precisely," Kovalenko said.

"And it worked," Jamie Lee said.

"Yes," the professor said. "I have to admit, I'm a little embarrassed by how well it all worked."

"So, the boys from that orphanage were test subjects," Kyle said. "Why were they given up for adoption in the United States?"

"The parents of the children were made to sign away all parental claims when they were enrolled. At gunpoint if need be. The babies were to be the exclusive property of the Soviet Union. But then, during the period of gestation, the Soviet Union collapsed. Ukraine asserted its independence. In the confusion that ensued the project was abandoned. And I suddenly became the parent of seven infant boys. I knew I had to get the children to safety, before the Russian authorities got a chance to stake a legal claim on them. I had a cousin living in Texas."

"Miss Olga," Jamie Lee said.

"She worked for an adoption agency," Sergey Kovalenko said. "Knew the process of international adoptions intimately. She worked day and night to find good families for all those boys."

"Except for one," Patricia corrected.

Kovalenko exhaled and shook his head. "Ah, poor Misha. What a tragedy!"

"Who's Misha?" Jamie Lee asked.

"Mikhail," Patricia replied. "The boy with no last name."

"Only one in ten thousand children are ever born with anencephaly. Misha, unfortunately, was one of them. He was a severe case, literally born without a brain."

Jamie Lee said, "So, he died?"

"His father, that is to say, the donor of half the boy's genetic material, was an Army officer — the highest ranking participant in the experiment. The man was crushed by the news of the boy's condition. He looked for solace in religion, and became convinced that Misha's impairment was a punishment from God. When his grief turned to madness, he killed his own son."

Jamie Lee was growing restless. "Who the hell is Borya Balakin?"

The professor looked at her with a defeated look on his features.

Jamie Lee persisted. "You know the name? Balakin?"

Kovalenko nodded.

"So, what is he?" Jamie Lee said. "A deacon or a diplomat?"

"He is neither," Kovalenko said. "And he is

both."

Jamie Lee shot Kyle a quizzical look. He ignored her.

"Okay then," Jamie Lee said. "Let's break this down, one at a time. Is Balakin a deacon?"

"He is a holy man of sorts," Kovalenko said.

"Is he a diplomat?" Jamie Lee asked.

Kovalenko took a moment to reply. "He works for the Russian government when it suits them."

"Who does he answer to?" Jamie Lee said.

Kyle ventured a guess. "Major General Vladislav Rostov. Right?"

"He's no longer a Major General," Sergey Kovalenko said. "Rostov is a rogue player now. Protected by a shadow wing of the government's central hierarchy."

"Borya Balakin is Misha's father," Patricia said.

Kovalenko nodded. "The Ukrainian authorities locked him up in a jail in the Crimea when he killed the boy. A few weeks later, in a daring raid on the prison, Rostov's men freed him, but Balakin had become so unstable by then, even the Major General had come to fear him. So he confined him to a monastery outside of Moscow, where he could be kept in check."

"Balakin is here," Kyle said.

Kovalenko nodded. "Father Ambrus told me as much."

Kyle said, "Professor Kovalenko, we have reason to believe your life may be in danger."

Kovalenko laughed. "My life is in danger? You don't say! Dear deputy, I know very well my life is in danger. I was diagnosed with pancreatic cancer five months ago. The amazing thing is that I don't feel at all like I'm dying. Even the doctors agree that I check out wonderfully for a man my age. Except for my metastatic cancer, which continues to eat away at my body, undaunted by the futile remedies of modern medicine."

"I'm so sorry," Patricia said.

"I was in Houston at MD Anderson Cancer Center the day Olga died. My doctor sent me for a second opinion. The specialists there told me what I already knew: I don't have much time. They suggested I get my affairs in order. This is why I'm so pleased to have been able to talk to you, Dr. West. I owed you that much."

"What should I expect with my son?" Patricia asked.

Kovalenko leaned forward. "Where is Alex?"

"He's with my parents," Patricia said. Kyle shot her a reprimanding look. "What will happen to my son?"

In an even voice, Kovalenko said, "Alex was not a test subject."

"Not a test subject?" Jamie Lee said.

"There were unanticipated circumstances," Kovalenko said, pausing mid-sentence, "which prevented me from altering his genetic material."

"But he came from the same orphanage,"

Patricia said.

"Yes. And for that reason, we had to get him to safety," Kovalenko said. "Lest someone come to an unfortunate conclusion. All you need to do with Alex is love him. And protect him."

"Protect him," Kyle echoed. "Lest someone like Balakin comes to the wrong conclusion too."

Kovalenko reached for his teacup. Took a sip and winced. "Getting cold, already."

"Why are these boys all dying, professor?" Jamie Lee said with a sharp edge in her voice.

"Rage is the mother of violence," Kovalenko said. "And violence begets more violence."

Patricia sprung to her feet. "I have to get to my son," she said.

Kyle stood up and said, "Let's go."

Jamie Lee followed suit. The three bid the professor farewell, walked to the foyer, and out the front door. When they were halfway down the walkway, Sergey Kovalenko called out, "Alex will be fine, Patricia. Trust me."

* * *

Sergey Kovalenko pulled the curtains back and peered out the front window, looking on as Jamie Lee Foster's car pulled away from the curb with its passengers. He waited until the vehicle was out of view before shuffling back to the living room, picking up a phone from a walnut credenza, and dialing a number.

He heard two ring tones before a man answered

on the other end. "Hello?"

In Russian, Kovalenko said, "They just left."

"How did she take it?"

"It hardly seems to matter now. The boy is with his grandparents. They're on their way there. You better get there quickly."

The person on the other end of the line didn't bother to reply. He simply hung up.

CHAPTER THIRTY-SEVEN
Marcus West

Borya Balakin sat at a long wooden picnic table in the vast dining room of a road-side self-serve restaurant on the north side of San Antonio. He gnawed half-heartedly on a fried chicken leg with his gaze fixed on a fat woman who was ordering her dinner, her hands planted on the counter by the cash register, no doubt to ease the weight of her massive frame. The girth of her thighs was astonishing to the Russian.

Americans were a different breed, Balakin thought. And not just in terms of size. The fact had become quite apparent to Balakin through the every-day interactions he had had in just the few days since landing in Houston. Americans possessed a whole-sale naivete, girded by irrational hope and excessive enthusiasm, which propelled them to trust others without question, to take everyone at their word. He might have found

308

such an attitude endearing, even mildly refreshing, if it weren't so foolish and dangerous, a stance which left those who practiced it utterly vulnerable.

Russians, on the other hand, were afflicted by a deep sense of skepticism, if not outright distrust. They are by nature tight-lipped with anyone outside their guarded circle of family and friends. He had heard it said that this was the logical legacy of communist rule. It was how they managed to survive The Terror of the 1930s, and the Thaw of the 1950s: eras during which today's acquaintance, coworker, or neighbor, could become tomorrow's accuser. Through it all, modern Russia's network of interpersonal relationships evolved into a segmented web of discrete underground communities, each pursuing its own interests.

Luckily for Balakin, that was not the case in the cozy neighborhood Professor Sergey Kovalenko had chosen to settle down in and create his new life. Kovalenko's neighbor, a Mrs. Angeline Whitman, a tall woman whose lips were thickly coated with a glossy lipstick the color of Turkish cherries, was all too happy to have a friendly chat with him, to tell him that the professor was out of town for a few days. "He's gone down to MD Anderson Cancer Center in Houston, don't you know. What a pity! And such a kindly old gentleman."

It had forced Balakin to alter his plans a bit. Obliging him take an unexpected detour, south into San Antonio to take care of Boris O'Keefe before he'd have the pleasure of confronting the professor. He told himself it didn't matter. In fact, it would be better this way. Kovalenko would be back in Austin soon enough. And what greater satisfaction than to see the pained expression on the old man's face, to witness the unmitigated suffering when told that all his little monsters, his seven deadly sins, were now dead?

The woman with the elephant thighs sat down at the other end of the table, shifting the bench Balakin was sitting on with her weight. She leaned in his direction and said, "You using that hot sauce, honey?"

Balakin looked at her, and in the best Texas accent, he could muster replied, "Not a'tall."

"Would you be a dear?"

Balakin got to his feet and carried the bottle of hot sauce to the end of the table.

"Oh, you're a real sweetheart, you are," the fat woman said.

Balakin smiled warmly, made a gesture as if he were tipping his hat, and said, "My pleasure, ma'am."

He returned to his side of the table, sat down, and popped a cold french fry in his mouth.

A different breed. No doubt about it.

He pulled his wallet from the breast pocket of

his blazer and extracted a slip of paper. So far, the addresses provided by his handler in Moscow had proved to be remarkably accurate.

The next name on the list was Alexander West, New Braunfels, Texas. He silently mouthed the boy's name. This was the job he had really looked forward to. This one would be personal.

He studied the address one more time, memorized it, and headed for the restaurant's exit.

* * *

The front door was locked, but the sliding glass door that opened onto the back patio was not. Borya Balakin entered Marcus West's home, quietly shut the door behind him, and listened.

The sun was setting and the living room was awash in red glowing light. The house was of a handsome construction, Borya thought, but ruined by its gaudy furnishings.

Voices were coming from upstairs: moans and indistinct murmurings. The Russian intruder headed up the staircase, unsheathing his combat knife when he reached the top of the stairs, and stealthily made his way down the upstairs hallway toward the origin of the voices.

The sound of a woman's voice grew louder in the form of high-pitched rhythmic yelps. Borya, the holy man, immediately recognized their sinful nature.

Keeping his back flat against the wall, he peeked through an open door into a bedroom. A naked man was lying supine in bed. He might have seen Balakin were it not for the fact that he was peering through a compact video camera which he held with one hand. The man's other hand was cupping the bare breast of the young woman who was straddling him, bouncing up and down, grinding her hips, emitting those infernal yelps while the man who was filming her repeated, "Smile for the camera, baby. Just like that. Smile for the camera."

Borya backed away, disgusted by what he had witnessed. He slid his combat knife back in its scabbard. One thing was certain: the boy, Alex, was not home. No parent could be so devil-may-care.

He walked past another bedroom, stopped, retraced his steps, and looked inside. This had to be the boy's room. The bed was made, the covering tucked snuggly under the mattress with such fastidiousness that one might have guessed it was a military cot. Borya didn't bother to inspect the contents of the room. There was nothing more he wanted to learn about his target.

He made his way back downstairs and walked into a study with a rosewood desk covered by a glass plate. A matching bookcase displayed cheap, transparent acrylic trophies engraved with the inscription, "Barron Realty Agent of the Month." There were three in all, with dates spanning over five years, the last one dated two years ago.

Another shelf held the framed photograph of a boy, no older than six or seven, flanked by a man and a woman. The woman exuded a noble grace. The man, not so much. A mismatch if Borya had ever seen one. The glass covering the picture had a hairline crack traveling diagonally from corner to corner. A telling feature, the Russian thought.

There was another photograph: same boy but with a much older couple, standing in front of a beach house. Borya picked up the frame. In one corner of the picture, an etched tag read, "Aransas Pass, 1988." Now there was a bit of intelligence that might prove useful.

Borya heard the sound of footsteps coming from upstairs. Only then did he realize that the woman's moaning had stopped. The Russian slipped out of the office and took his position in the passageway to the living room. He heard a man's voice shout out, "And get me a beer while you're at it!"

Borya shook his head. So, the fornication had come to an anticlimactic end. He had not heard the slightest evidence of a crescendo of passion. Not even a solitary ecstatic cry to signal that the sin was complete. And now this feckless boar was ordering her concubine to fetch him a beer? Marcus West was no gentleman.

Borya slipped into the kitchen and waited for the woman's arrival behind the door. As soon as she stepped through the doorway, he pounced on her and snapped her neck before she had the chance to make an utterance. It was a good kill. There was no reason for her to suffer, after all. Her only sin was that of being a whore.

He lay the naked woman's body on the black and white checkered tile floor, straightened her legs, and folded her arms across her chest. He found a white tablecloth in a kitchen drawer and draped it over her corpse, covering her from her shoulders to her feet. Borya tried to center the woman's head but wasn't able to. One of the woman's cervical vertebrae must have gotten wedged well out of alignment.

Borya took a moment to study the sinner's face. She was so young and fair. It was a pity she had immersed herself in such a predicament. He knelt beside her and with his thumb traced the sign of the cross on her forehead. Then, he got to his feet, opened the refrigerator door, and pulled out a bottle of imported beer. Slowly, he made his way back upstairs.

Marcus West was watching a replay of the video he had just recorded on the tiny screen of the VCR when Borya walked in on him.

"I got your beer," Borya said.

Marcus jerked, fumbled the camera, dropping it on the bed, and quickly stuffed a pillow between his legs to conceal his flaccid organ.

"Who the fuck are you?" Marcus said breathlessly.

"My name is Borya. You still want the beer?"

"Where's Faye?"

"She's not coming back. I think she was unimpressed by your performance. Is that what you're seeing on your little camera?"

"I'm calling the cops," Marcus said. He reached for his cell phone, which was sitting on the credenza. Borya hurtled the bottle of beer at Marcus, pegging him squarely on the side of the head. Marcus fell back in bed and let out a shriek.

"I'm sorry," Borya said. "I forgot to bring a bottle opener. If you like, I can pry it open with your teeth."

"Stay the fuck away from me!"

"Where is the boy?" Borya said.

"What?"

"Where is Alex? When is he coming home?"

"Who the hell are you?"

"Social Services. Have you been a good father, Mr. West? It doesn't look like it at first glance. No, it seems you've been downright neglectful."

"You're not Social Services. Get the hell out of my house!"

"I'd be happy to leave. Just tell me where I can find the boy."

This time Marcus scrambled to reach for something under the box spring. Borya had heard that every good Texan keeps a loaded gun under his bed. He thought it a preposterous claim but, just in case it was true, he quickly swooped in on

Marcus, grabbed his foot and snapped his big toe with one good twist.

Marcus howled in pain.

"See?" Borya said. "Now that was completely unnecessary. It's as though you're inviting misfortune. You know, my dear grandmother used to say, 'Never invite misfortune. Trouble never comes alone.'"

"What do you want from me?"

"Is Alex coming home tonight? Or is he with his grandparents?"

Marcus didn't reply. He was moaning softly as tears streamed down his cheek. But even this vermin, defeated and exposed, seemed compelled to put on a feeble show of dignity.

Borya was growing annoyed by Marcus' pigheadedness. He grabbed Marcus' hand and started pushing his middle finger straight back.

"Okay, okay, okay!" Marcus hollered in defeat.

"Yes?" Borya said.

"Okay, he's with his grandparents."

"In Aransas Pass?"

"That's right."

"Remind me what street the beach house is on," Borya said.

Marcus stalled. He seemed to be contemplating making a last stand. Borya nipped the man's contemplation in the bud by breaking his middle finger. Marcus burst out in sobs.

"The name of the street," Borya said.

Marcus sucked a few breaths through his teeth, then managed to mutter, "Sea Mist Drive."

Borya knew the man was telling the truth. He nodded and said, "Marcus, did you know you are a coward? That's what you are, a sniveling coward. You disgust me. I can't stand to look at your face anymore."

Borya grabbed the pillow from the man's crotch and pushed it down on Marcus' face. Marcus kicked and punched the air frantically, but Borya kept his grip steady, waiting patiently, with not a sliver of anger. In fact, he felt no emotion at all. At least until the flailing died down, and Marcus' body grew limp and offered no resistance.

Only then did his memory flash to the last time he was forced to kill in this way, snuffing out life with a lowly pillow.

Borya's left shoulder began to burn, as if a hot poker was jabbing him. It was not from the effort of smothering Marcus. He knew the pain was just in his head. The giveaway was its location. Precisely where that Ukrainian policewoman had shot him so many years ago.

To distract himself, Borya began to pray out loud. "Dear Father, on behalf of a man whose soul is departing and who cannot speak, please receive my prayer."

Borya continued to pray, always pushing down on the pillow, even well after it was clear there was no chance Marcus was still breathing. He had to do it this way to be sure the man was dead. Borya would not be checking the carotid pulse in Marcus' neck.

He was afraid that if he were to remove the pillow, what he'd see peering back at him might be the face of his infant son Misha.

CHAPTER THIRTY-EIGHT

Heading South

Jamie Lee peeled away from the curb and took a hard left turn out of Professor Kovalenko's neighborhood, generating enough centrifugal force to send Patricia slamming against the passenger side door.

"Hold on, now," Jamie Lee said, in the way of an apology.

"I have to get to my son," Patricia said. "Take me to my car."

"No time for that," Jamie Lee said.

"What do you mean, there's no time for that?" Patricia cried out.

Jamie Lee Foster reached between her legs, felt around under the driver's seat, and pulled out a red dashboard police bubble light. She handed it to Patricia and said, "I'll get you to him a lot faster than you can by yourself. Plug this baby into the cigarette lighter."

319

The power cord for the light was a jumble of
knots. Patricia untied them, one by one, her hands
shaking.

"That's the way," Jamie Lee said. "Now, plug it
in and set that big shiny cherry on the dashboard."
As soon as the emergency light was in place,
Jamie Lee pushed on the car's horn, straight-
armed it, keeping her hand there even as she
steered with her other hand. She swerved around
a long line of vehicles that were stuck at a traffic
light, charging down the lane of oncoming traffic.
Patricia held onto the dashboard, her knuckles
turning white. "I wish this thing had a siren,"
Jamie Lee said when she finally removed her
hand from the horn."

"You're going to drive me all the way to
Aransas Pass?" Patricia asked.

"Just tell me the way," Jamie Lee said.

From the back seat, in a steady voice, Kyle said,
"I-35 South, then 123 until we hook up with 181."

"Got it!" Jamie Lee said as she barreled back
across three lanes to make a right at the next
intersection. Some ninety seconds later, they were
in the fast lane of the interstate highway due
south, and Patricia breathed a sigh of relief.

She looked across from the passenger seat and
studied Jamie Lee's profile. Jamie Lee caught her
looking, flashed back a soft smile, letting go of the
gruff detective persona for a brief moment,
allowing Patricia a glimpse of something deeper,

something warmer. And Patricia understood. The reckless driving was Jamie Lee's unorthodox way of getting Patricia's mind off of what Professor Kovalenko had said. To give her a respite from her thoughts, however brief, before the enormity of his revelations engulfed her completely.

"You know what they say?" Jamie Lee said with a satisfied smile. "This Austin traffic will kill ya."

"Thank you for doing this," Patricia said.

"Don't you worry your pretty little head," Jamie Lee said. "Your son will be fine."

Kyle Wagner said, "Why don't you call him?"

He didn't utter what he was really trying to convey, but Patricia understood. To warn him.

She fished her cell phone out of her purse and dialed the number for her father's house. She listened to the dial tone, waited.

"There's no answer," Patricia said.

"Probably went out," Jamie Lee said.

"My dad has a fishing boat," Patricia said. "He likes to take Alex out on the bay."

"Well, there you go," Jamie Lee said.

In the back seat, Kyle said, "We'll try again in a little while."

The traffic was heavy, but Jamie Lee managed to maintain a good speed in the fast lane, using the left shoulder to pass the odd dilly-dallier who wouldn't move out of the way.

Jamie Lee's phone rang. She picked it up,

looked at the caller ID. "Finnigan," she said. As was her habit, she thumbed a couple of buttons and held the phone up for all to hear, keeping her eyes fixed on the traffic out front. "Finn! I got you on speakerphone."

"And greetings to you too," Finnigan said. "Did you have a chance to speak to the professor?"

"He didn't have anything useful to add," Jamie Lee said.

Patricia was starting to understand Jamie Lee's reticence. Some information needed time to leaven before being disclosed. Jamie Lee was right not to tell Finnigan that the teenage boys, these orphans from the former Soviet Union, were part of a diabolical scheme. That they had been genetically engineered to be elite warriors. How could Finnigan even process the concept? She could barely grasp the idea herself, and only because she was assured repeatedly by Kovalenko that her Alex was not like the other boys. His genetic material had not been manipulated. But there were some shady characters out there who did not know this. People who would be out to hurt her son. It was becoming clear that not all the recent deaths were the result of horrible accidents. She didn't know who was behind it, or how their plot was being executed, but she understood one thing: a ghastly culling was underway.

"Well, we just got some news from our friends in Galveston," Finnigan said. "The coast guard located the mayor's missing motorboat."

"And the missing kids?" Jamie Lee said.

"Unfortunately, yes," Finnigan answered somberly. "They got a hit on sonar at the bottom of Galveston Bay early this morning, out by South Deer Island. Sent divers down to look. They recovered two bodies from the boat's cabin. Family members identified them as Aubrey Hurst and James Preston Tully."

"Jesus!" Jamie Lee muttered. "Cause of death?"

"Post-mortems are in progress as we speak, but the unofficial word is that the boy's head was bashed up pretty good. Detective Foster, the press has not been notified yet."

"Mums the word," Jamie Lee said.

"One more thing," Finnigan said. "The families had put out a bunch of fliers asking for information on the missing kids offering a reward and all. Well, we found a copy of one of the fliers on the internet. Guess what it says in the description of the boy? A white patch of hair on his head. How do you like that?"

"You speak to the priest yet?" Jamie Lee asked as if to change the subject, no inflection in her voice.

"Had a nice chat with Father Ambrus," Finnigan said, in a more composed tone.

"And?" Jamie Lee said.

"We tried to get a description of Borya Balakin out of him. I hate to say it, but the good padre is a sketch artist's nightmare. Kept repeating that our person of interest looks like a saint. He wasn't sure if he actually saw a halo on the man's head or just imagined one. But he did show us some beautiful Russian church icons."

"Well, that's nice," Jamie Lee said.

"This Balakin fellow apparently bears a striking resemblance to a sketch of Saint Demetrios," Finnigan said.

Jamie Lee scoffed. "Well, let's put out an all-points-bulletin, then."

"Funny," Finnigan said. "It wasn't a complete wash. We did manage to get a general sense of the guy's size and physical attributes. Caucasian male, about six-foot-two, thin, but with broad shoulders. Fits our runner from the cemetery."

"And just about every other tall dude in South Central Texas who isn't a slob," Jamie Lee said.

"So, what's next?" Finnigan asked.

"I think we're at a dead-end," Jamie Lee said. "I'm driving Dr. West home. I'm going to take a few days off to think about it."

"Uh-huh," Finnigan said. The skepticism was thick in his voice even over the phone.

"I'll check in with you boys when I'm back at work."

"You do that, detective." Finnigan hung up.

No one said a word for a long stretch of highway. They drove past the town of Buda. Zipped past the exit for Mountain City, eating up the miles, making excellent time. At this rate, they'd reach the Gulf of Mexico in just a couple of hours.

All Patricia wanted now was to smother Alex in an embrace. Wrap her arms around him and hold him tight. More than anything, she wanted to do that. And to make a fresh start with her son, now that she knew so much more about his past. Now she would understand him better. She might avoid the false steps of the past, the misspoken words, the miscues, the blunders. There was just one hitch: she could never tell Marcus.

* * *

During Desert Storm, there'd be times when Kyle Wagner would feel wired for days on end; his entire body buzzing, his mind alert, his eyesight focused, every fiber tense and and tingling in rapt anticipation. It was a raw and primal mental state known to few humans in this day and age: the mindset of a predator zeroing in on his kill. In this edgy state of mind, Kyle became completely impervious to fatigue and hunger and torrid heat.

The feeling had not been rekindled that doleful morning at the high school gym when he reluctantly set the sight of his partner's hunting rifle on Carson Taggart. But now, sitting in the back seat of Jamie Lee's car, the old buzzing had been roused again.

It had started with a tautness of his sinews. A

dull ache in his bones. It wasn't a particularly uncomfortable feeling, but it was certainly disconcerting. He knew what it meant. It meant that his body was getting ready, his core tightening, the knots in his limbs uncoiling, his muscles engorging with blood. His physique was preparing itself, forewarned by a voiceless signal from his subconscious mind. The message, growing louder now, was an admonition, a warning of imminent danger.

Kyle tightened his shoulders, stretched his arms down below his knees, squeezed his hands into fists, letting the feeling wash over him, allowing the dormant warrior in him reawaken. He felt like an athlete regaining muscle memory after a prolonged period of inactivity.

He was startled by the sound of his cell phone ringing. Staring at the caller ID, he wondered why his boss, the chronically surly Sheriff Rolf Mayer, would be calling him.

"Where are you?" Rolf Mayer said in place of a greeting.

"What can I do for you, Sheriff?" Kyle said.

"I wanted to be the one to give you the good news."

Kyle sensed a discrepancy between the sheriff's words and the underlying tension in his voice.

"The County Board of Supervisors had an emergency meeting this morning," the sheriff continued. "You've been reinstated, Kyle. As of ten o'clock this morning, you are no longer on administrative leave."

Kyle Wagner was silent.

"Kyle? You there? You heard what I said?"

"It seems premature," Kyle said as he gazed out the window.

"I went to bat for you. Twisted a few arms to get this done."

"Why?" Kyle asked.

"You're the best we have, son."

Kyle had never heard the sheriff express that opinion. It rang flat.

"Something happened," Kyle said "What is it?"

"Come by my office. You can pick up your service weapon, and we'll talk about it."

"I can hear you loud and clear right now," Kyle said.

"Look, Kyle, we're stretched real thin. We got the Feds here looking into the school shooting, and they've got the whole department jumping. And now ... Now we've got two dead bodies in a house in Canyon Lake. Looks like a double homicide. Christ! I need you here, pronto! Some of these other deputies ... Well, they're fine men, but when it comes to this type of stuff, they're way out of their depth."

"You have an ID on the victims?"

"Yeah. We have a woman by the name of Faye Green. And a man, Marcus West."

"Can you repeat that?" Kyle said, his eyes

shifting to Patricia. She was looking out the front windshield to the road ahead, her facial features unchanged.

"Faye Green. Marcus West. It's eerie, Kyle. I've seen my share of murder scenes over the years. But this ... This is different. Call me crazy, but to me, it looks like a professional hit."

"When did it happen?"

"Coroner was vague. He said they died sometime yesterday. We expect to get a more precise time of death from the ME in San Antonio later today."

"Next of kin?"

"We're working on it," Rolf Mayer said. "How soon can you be here?"

Kyle recognized the outlet malls of San Marcos flying past across the interstate to his left.

"I'll be there in thirty minutes. In civilian clothing."

"Hell, come in pajamas if you have to," Rolf Mayer said before hanging up.

Kyle held his phone in his hand, kept his fingers clutched around it tightly.

From the driver's seat, Jamie Lee said, "That didn't sound good."

"I'll need you to drop me off in New Braunfels," Kyle said.

"You're ditching us?" Jamie Lee said. "You gotta be kidding."

Kyle said nothing. He was trying hard to think

about how best to handle the situation. He looked up and caught Jamie Lee's gaze fixed on him in the rear-view mirror.

"Jesus, Kyle!" Jamie Lee said, looking alarmed. "You're freaking me out. What the hell happened?"

"Patricia," Kyle said. "I don't quite know how to say this."

Patricia West turned in her seat. Her eyes narrowed slightly as she seemed to be studying his features.

"Does it have to do with the school shooting?" Patricia said.

Kyle shook his head. "It's about your ex-husband."

"Marcus?" Patricia said, looking confused. Then her eyes widened. "Oh, my God! He's dead, isn't he?"

CHAPTER THIRTY-NINE

Stormy Skies

The sky had turned a slate gray that morning.
Out on the gulf, dark billowing clouds towered
over the horizon. Grandma Betty had gone off to
buy groceries while Grandpa Wyatt fired up his
ride-on mower to trim the front lawn. They were
each preparing for the coming storm in their own
way.

A storm is coming.

Those were the very words Carson Taggart had
uttered in what Alex West thought was an overly-
melodramatic tone the day before the school
shooting. At the time, it had seemed like just one
more incomprehensible conversation they had had
in the last few weeks.

One afternoon, after school, Carson approached
Alex and asked him, "Have you ever seen your
birth certificate?"

"My what?"

"Your birth certificate."

"I don't think so," Alex said.

"Why not?"

Alex shrugged. "Why would I care to see my birth certificate?"

"What are your parents hiding from you?"

That seemed like an odd thing to say.

"Have you seen *your* birth certificate?" Alex asked.

Carson nodded. "My dad left the document safe open one day. I thought I'd sneak a peek. Didn't know what I might find in there."

"So, what about it?"

"What?"

"Your birth certificate," Alex said. "What did it say?"

"I couldn't read it. It was in a different language. Jesus! A whole different alphabet. Russian, I think."

"Then how do you know it was your birth certificate?"

"Because it had a translation attached," Carson said. "I was born in Odessa. That's in Ukraine. I had to look it up on the internet. I found adoption papers in the safe too."

"Did you talk to your parents about it?" Alex said.

"Hell, I already knew I was adopted. I just always figured I was, you know, an American. They never told me otherwise."

"You *are* an American," Kyle said.

"You know what I mean."

Carson looked rattled. He seemed like he wanted to get something else off his chest but was wavering.

"We got a lot in common, you and me," Carson said.

Anyone who might have seen the two boys together would have found Carson's comment outlandish. For starters, the two looked completely different, with Carson's shoulders towering just about at Alex's eye level. And not only was Carson much larger in size than Alex; he was so much more confident, outgoing, relaxed in a crowd. Nonetheless, Alex saw some truth in Carson's words, for he had also felt that the two of them shared an intangible common denominator, a silent understanding. But he was never able to put his finger on what the connection between them might be.

"We like the same video games," Alex said, as a way of voicing agreement while lightening the tone of the conversation.

Carson gave him a light punch in the shoulder. It was a gesture of comradeship. Of brotherly love. "You should check your birth certificate. See if it's in Russian. Maybe we're twins." When he was some twenty feet away, Carson called back, "We're fighters, you and me!"

They both laughed as Carson turned and

walked away.

Alex looked out the window of the second-story bedroom of his grandparent's beach house. Out over the gulf, the black clouds that started forming that morning had moved in closer. The wind was picking up blowing whitecaps off the choppy water.

Alex sat down on his tidily made bed, picked up *The Art of War*, opened the cover and looked at the title page. Under the name of the author, in an elegant script written in red pencil, it said, "For Alex."

He had received the book on his twelfth birthday, wrapped in brown paper and twine. The anonymous sender had left it on the Adirondack on the front porch of his house, in the same way that, four years earlier, again on his birthday, Alex had received a copy of Russian fables: frightening stories featuring shape-shifting creatures. The same inscription was scribbled in red pencil on the title page.

Alex had no idea who the sender could be, why they were sending him books to read, or why they would want to remain anonymous. But something told him these books were important. That he should read them carefully, learn the lessons they bestowed in earnest.

He flipped through the pages, settled on a dog-eared leaf, and read a passage he had underlined more than a year ago:

If your enemy is secure at all points, be prepared for him. If he is superior in strength, evade him. If your opponent is temperamental, seek to irritate him. Pretend to be weak, that he may grow arrogant.

This wasn't very helpful. For starters, Alex didn't have the faintest inkling as to who his enemy might be, or even if he had one. All he had was an unsettling feeling, a clinging sense of foreboding. He turned more pages, pausing to read those sentences he had marked.

Attack him when he is unprepared. Appear when you are unexpected ... Know the terrain ... Know when to fight — when not to fight ... Hold out baits to entice the enemy — feign disorder and crush him.

Alex didn't know why, but in the last couple of days, he felt compelled to learn these lessons by heart, to burn into his memory cells each admonition until it became second nature to him.

Downstairs, the phone rang in the kitchen. Alex got up, trotted down the stairs, and walked into the kitchen as the phone kept ringing. He waited for the answering machine to pick up and play Grandpa Wiley's brief message. When the message ended, and the machine beeped, he heard his mother's voice. He reached to pick up the phone but stopped himself when he detected something was off in her voice. He tried to make out what was wrong. It was as though she was working too hard to maintain a calm tone. This made Alex's ears perk. He leaned over the answering machine, placing his ear closer to the speaker.

"Dad? Mom? Alex? Anyone? Please, pick up." There was a pause. "I guess no one's home. Dad, can you please, call me? Immediately. I mean, as soon as you get home. Or whenever you hear this message. Please. It's really important. Okay, then. I'm waiting for your call." There was a short pause, then, "Alex? *Peace be to France!*"

"*Peace be to France?*" Alex mumbled. Something was not right. At least she didn't say, "*Welcome to Rome.*" That was their code for imminent danger, get out now!

The machine stopped recording, and a small red indicator light on its display started flashing.

Alex played the message over. He replayed it a second time, listening carefully. On the third replay, he finally had a word for the emotion he had detected in his mother, the feeling she was trying so hard to hide: terror. But she spoke in code. Did that mean that she didn't want Wyatt and Betty to know?

His thoughts quickly shifted to Carson Taggart, whose voice was now ringing in Alex's ears. *A storm is coming.*

Alex ran into the living room, looked out the

front window. Grandpa Wyatt was maneuvering his ride-on mover around the base of a pecan tree, headphones covering his ears. Alex jogged back to the kitchen, went out the back door, and sprinted across the back yard towards the boathouse. He climbed the spiral staircase, walked past the trapdoors covering the openings above the boat slips, and made his way to the wooden chest. He opened the chest, reached inside, and pulled the spear-fishing gun out, held it up to study its parts.

It was quite a simple design, really. Two sets of thick rubber bands, fastened onto either side of the muzzle, joined at the rear by a thinner cable known as the wishbone. To load the gun, the rubber bands had to be stretched, and the wishbone fitted into a notch on the triggering mechanism.

He placed the handle of the spear-fishing gun against his chest, grabbed the thick rubber bands with both hands, palms up, and pulled back. He found he wasn't quite able to stretch the bands far enough for the wishbone to slip into the notch. He tried again, this time palms down. Now he was able to generate enough force to engage the wishbone into the triggering mechanism.

Alex looked at the speargun with a sense of awe. The words of Sun Tzu echoed in his mind.

All war is deception. Appear weak when you are strong, and strong when you are weak.

The boy placed the mahogany stock of the speargun against his shoulder and peered down the weapon's sight, keeping his finger off the trigger.

Grandpa Wyatt had said that the speargun was powerful enough to harpoon a Mako shark. Alex wondered if the old man was pulling his leg. He moved the muzzle of the gun side to side, conjuring up imaginary sharks swarming around him. He tried to find something specific to aim at. On the opposite wall, there was a wood knot in one of the wall panels which could pass as the cold, black eye of a hungry Mako.

Alex pointed at the eye, and before he had a chance to think it through, he moved his finger onto the trigger and squeezed it. The spear flew out from the gun at an astonishing speed, piercing the wooden panel with a great thunk.

Alex's jaw dropped. He could feel beads of sweat forming on his brow. He swallowed hard and mumbled, "Holy crap!"

The boy trudged over to the spot where the spear was sticking out of the wall at a near-perfect ninety-degree angle, his jaw still slack.

The tip of the spear had penetrated mere inches from the wood knot that, up close, looked nothing like the eye of a Mako shark. But the accuracy of his shooting failed to elicit even the faintest sense of pride or joy.

Alex tried pulling back on the spear to dislodge it. It was stuck pretty good. He tried giving it one hard yank. The arrow barely budged. Growing frantic, Alex tried wiggling the spear up and down, see if he could work the tip out somehow. Then he put one foot against the wall, grasped the shaft of the arrow with both hands, and pulled back with all his weight.

The spear came free, sending Alex tumbling backward. He landed onto the nearest trap door. The boy lay his head on the floor and breathed a sigh of relief. Not just because the spear came loose, but also because had the trap door been open, he'd have fallen through and would have made quite a splash. He let out a faint whistle and smiled. But his relief was short-lived. It ended abruptly when he caught sight of the jagged crater left in the wall where smooth polished wood should have been.

He jumped to his feet and walked over to it. Put his finger in the hole. It was the size of a chicken egg.

Oh shit! Wyatt's going to kill me!

He knew the right thing to do was to tell the old man. Fess up to his sins. He swallowed hard.

No, he wasn't ready to do that yet.

He looked around the attic. Caught sight of the folded blue tarp on the floor in the far corner, next to the wooden chest. He strode over, picked it up, and carried it to the damaged wall. He looked up, noticed a set of hanging hooks on the wall.

Alex unfolded the tarp and hooked it to the wall. It didn't look so good, but it did cover the gash. That would have to do for now.

He put the speargun back in the wooden chest, carefully lowered the heavy lid, then raced back to the house. The incident left the boy so shook up, it's small wonder he'd forget all about telling Wyatt about his mother's phone call.

CHAPTER FORTY
Grand Am

Arkadi Volkov glanced at the speedometer of
his Pontiac Grand Am, the car he bought second
hand at an auction with the money earned from
twisting pretzels. The needle of the speedometer
hovered just below the eighty mile-per-hour mark.
A good speed. Just a tad faster than the flow of
southbound traffic on Interstate 35, but not so fast
to get him pulled over. Or so he hoped. He
scanned the shoulder of the highway ahead for
black-and-white Texas Highway Patrol vehicles.
Then, he checked his rear-view mirror.

He didn't care so much about getting a ticket.
Most of all, Arkadi did not want to be delayed. Of
course, there was the matter of the loaded 45
caliber Glock in the glove compartment, two
additional loaded magazines stowed under the
passenger-side seat he would have a hard time
explaining to a nosy officer. Things could get

complicated.

A large highway sign signaled that the first exit for San Marcos was two miles away. He had better pay attention now and not miss the ramp for Highway 123 South. Otherwise, he'd end up snared in New Braunfels and have to jog down highway 46 through the town of Seguin and lose precious minutes.

At this pace, he'd arrive in Aransas Pass in a little over two hours. He knew his destination well: the beach house on the bay, Wyatt and Betty Holmes's residence. Over the last dozen years, he had spent many a day staking it out, studying the habits and movements of its inhabitants. Just as he had studied the house of Marcus West. And after their divorce, the home of Patricia West.

Though he had never been inside Wyatt Holmes's house, he knew its layout well from studying architectural blueprints he had downloaded from the internet. Just two weeks ago, he checked the locks once more. The front door and back kitchen door were still fitted with Schlage 3/4 trim single cylinder locks. Arkadi had purchased the same model and practiced picking it late into the night until he could roll the tumbler in a matter of seconds, blind-folded.

The boathouse was the only unknown. It was a custom-built job for which Arkadi was unable to find the floor-plan. He had had to rely on scouting it from across the channel. He knew it had two boat slips, a bar on the far wall, and a winding metal staircase that led to a windowless attic or loft. Pretty straightforward, Arkadi thought. Not worth the risk of breaking in to take a better look.

Arkadi glanced in the rear-view mirror once more. He frowned. The red flash of a police emergency light caught his eye.

He eased his foot off the gas pedal and kept steady, trying to appear inconspicuous. He flipped on his turn signal, glided over one lane as the vehicle following him gained ground in the fast lane.

Strange. No siren.

He took a better look.

The flashing light was mounted on the dashboard of a Ford Taurus. He recognized the car. It belonged to that woman detective. It was the same car he saw in the parking lot of the cemetery at Olga's funeral.

Arkadi slunk in his seat as the car was about to overtake him. He watched as the car eased by, saw Patricia West sitting in the passenger seat, her eyes fixed straight ahead.

Arkadi allowed himself to savor the sight of her. He always thought she had a good profile, regal and steadfast, like that of a lioness, with a faint pulsation of tension in the jaw muscles, which only served to punctuate her resolve. It was a profile Arkadi had shamelessly gawked at over the years through the lenses of his high-powered binoculars under the pretense of reconnaissance. And now, she was so close.

What if she turned her head? If she happened to look over and recognize him? What would he do then? Would he smile and wave at her? Like a silly circus bear!

He saw the Sheriff's Deputy in the back seat. The one that shot the Taggart boy. He was looking at Patricia in a way that stung Arkadi with a pang of jealousy.

Jealousy, of all things! Arkadi, old boy, you really are an exceptional imbecile!

He had been preparing for this day for the better part of thirteen years. And now he was letting soppy feelings cloud his judgment, like a pathetic, sniveling schoolboy. He had better snap out of it, focus on the task at hand.

Arkadi steered his car into the wake of traffic created by the undercover police car and picked up speed, careful to maintain a discrete distance to avoid detection.

They were in San Marcos now. The exit to Highway 123 south was no more than three miles away. Surely, the detective's car would be shifting to the right lane soon, preparing to turn off. But it never did. It missed the exit altogether, continuing south towards New Braunfels.

Arkadi took his foot off the gas pedal to give himself time to think.

Why were they going to New Braunfels?

Taking Highway 46 was a roundabout route.
Surely they knew better.

Or perhaps Arkadi had received faulty
intelligence. Maybe the boy was not with his
grandparents, after all. Maybe, he was in New
Braunfels with that sorry excuse for a father. He
let his brain process the situation. He quickly
calculated the odds of each scenario and drew up
the best possible contingencies for each. Then he
pressed down on the accelerator, yanked the
steering wheel to the right, cut across two lanes of
traffic and barely made it to the exit.

Always rely on your intelligence, Arkadi.

Hadn't he already learned that lesson once, the
hard way?

* * *

"Pull into that parking spot," Kyle said.

Jamie Lee had already turned off the dashboard
emergency light, slowing down on San Antonio
Street before entering the parking lot of the Comal
County Sheriff's Department. Kyle directed Jamie
Lee to a secluded spot on the far edge of the lot,
behind a tall sycamore. Patricia West was too
preoccupied to wonder why Kyle didn't want to
be dropped off at the front door of the building.
Her head was abuzz.

Jamie Lee kept the car's motor running. She
looked in the rear-view mirror with an expectant
look, as if wondering why Kyle hadn't budged
from the back seat. Almost to prod him, she said,

"We'll keep in touch, yeah?"

Kyle wasn't looking at her. His eyes were fixed on Patricia. He asked her, "Do you know how to shoot a handgun?"

Patricia hesitated before replying. "My father would take me to the range from time to time when I was a teenager, but I wouldn't say I —"

"Good enough," Kyle said. He lifted the right pant leg of his blue jeans, revealing an ankle holster, ripped back its Velcro strap, and pulled out a pistol that was dwarfed by the size of his hand.

"Well, aren't *you* a sneaky one!" Jamie Lee said.

Kyle ignored the comment. "This is a .22 caliber. Easy to use. Virtually no recoil. The magazine release is here." He pushed a tiny lever letting the magazine fall into the palm of his other hand, handed the loaded magazine to Patricia, who hesitated before taking it. "This is how you chamber the first round." He pulled back on the gun's slide. "The safety's right here. All you have to do, when you're ready, is point the gun and squeeze the trigger. Nothing to it." Kyle released the slide, grasped the pistol by the barrel and held it out for Patricia to grasp.

"I don't want your gun," Patricia said.

"Your ex-husband is dead," Kyle said. "I want you to be safe."

"The cowboy's right," Jamie Lee said. "We don't know what we're liable to run into down at your folk's house."

"What about you?" Patricia asked Kyle.

"I'm about to get my service weapon back," Kyle said. "Believe me, I'm set."

Patricia took the gun from Kyle's hand, reluctantly.

Kyle exited the vehicle, stepped up to the rolled-down driver's side window and bent down. He said, "You ladies be careful now." He tipped his cowboy hat and headed for a side door into the building.

Jamie Lee followed him with her gaze. "He's got a good walk," she said. "A real cowboy strut."

"Let's go," Patricia said.

CHAPTER FORTY-ONE

Canyon Lake

Bobby Briggs was standing guard at the front door as Kyle Wagner walked up the path to Marcus West's residence, perched high on a hill in Canyon Lake.

Bobby looked defeated. He had his thumbs hooked onto his belt in his usual stance, but his arms were slack, his shoulders slouched. The Sheriff's Deputy looked as though he had been lugging a heavy weight around his neck for some time now.

Bobby tipped his Stetson when Kyle greeted him.

"I waited for you," Bobby said in a reverential tone. "I didn't touch anything."

"Have they moved the bodies?" Kyle asked.

"Like I said," Bobby replied, "I didn't touch anything, and I sure as hell didn't let anyone move the bodies until you got here."

Kyle nodded.

"I did take a good look around the house," Bobby said. "Not much to see, really. Except for the two dead bodies."

The Sheriff's Deputies crossed the threshold and walked into the home. The front foyer emptied onto a spacious living room which had a glass screen door which led to a large back patio.

For a crime scene, the room seemed downright undisturbed. There was no sign of a struggle, no overturned furniture, no blood spatter on the walls, not even so much as an an off smell. The false serenity of the home bothered Kyle. He thought about what his superior had told him over the phone, that the murders looked like a professional hit.

"Where are the bodies?" Kyle said, becoming impatient.

"Woman is in the kitchen, man upstairs," Bobby said.

Kyle walked across the living room and entered the kitchen, where a crime scene photographer was snapping pictures of a young woman with a white table cloth draped over her body.

The photographer stood up and said, "See the angle of her neck? Don't need an x-ray to know it's broke. Never seen anything like it. Have you?"

Kyle turned to Bobby. "You said the man's upstairs?"

"Follow me," Bobby said.

They went back through the living room where crime scene investigators were now packing cardboard evidence boxes with samples collected in plastic bags. They headed up the stairs. In the upstairs hallway, a technician, a lanky guy with a pony-tail and John Lennon spectacles, was dusting the handle to a bedroom door.

"You finding any fingerprints?" Bobby said.

"You kidding?" the investigator said. "The place is covered in prints. Looks like our killer didn't have the good sense to wipe anything down before leaving."

"Maybe he didn't have time to do it," Bobby suggested. "How soon can you run the prints on IAFIS?"

Kyle said, "You're not going to find a match for this guy on any computerized database," before the technician had a chance to answer.

Bobby and the technician exchanged dumbfounded glances. Kyle walked into the master bedroom, where the naked body of Marcus West lay on the bed, a pillow covering his face. A VCR wrapped in a plastic bag was sitting on the credenza.

"Has anyone checked the tape in that video camera?" Kyle asked no one in particular.

A technician kneeling on the carpet next to the closet replied. "It's a homemade sex tape. A pretty good one. Starring the dead girl downstairs."

Kyle headed out of the bedroom, saying, "I

need a minute," as he passed a dazed Bobby Briggs. He hurried down the stairs, went out the sliding glass door onto the back patio, and pulled his cell phone out of his back pocket. He hesitated a moment before dialing the number for Patricia West.

CHAPTER FORTY-TWO

The Beach House

It had started raining. Borya Balakin turned up the collar of his jacket and moved a step closer to the trunk of the Magnolia tree under whose shadow he had been waiting. The air tasted sour, its smell a mix of peat and ozone. It triggered in Balakin a childhood memory: running hand-in-hand with his mother after getting caught in a downpour at Kuzminki Park in Moscow.

It was strange to remember her like that now, so full of life. For when Borya's thoughts turned to his mother, the memory that surfaced was inevitably that of the last glimpse he had had of her: sallow and withered, roiling in a hospital bed, a pink scarf askew on her hairless head.

That day, on the way to the hospital, his father, the Colonel, had informed little Borya that the doctors had abdicated the last glimmer of hope. Mother was losing her battle. She'd capitulate any

351

day now. Any hour, perhaps. The only thing left to do was to go to the hospital and bid her a final farewell. Borya was not to make a spectacle of it. As usual, the Colonel expected him to behave like a fine little soldier.

When he entered the cramped hospital room, Borya hardly recognized his mother but for her eyes. There was a fierceness in her expression, as though she could already feel the clutch of death pulling her into the abyss. Borya bowed stiffly and approached the hospital bed to plant a kiss on her cheek. "Farewell, mother," he said, just as his father had instructed him.

His mother said, "Don't leave me, my dear."

She took hold of his hand and squeezed it. It frightened Borya. He tried to withdraw, but she tightened her grip on him.

The thought dawned on him that she might try to take him with her. That she might die at that very moment as she clung to him, and would still not let go, even after sighing her last breath. She would never let him go — she would drag him straight down into the abyss with her.

Borya started sobbing as he struggled to pull away. The sobs gave way to a high-pitched wail. The Colonel stepped in. He pried his dying wife's fingers off the hand of his son, one finger at a time, having to exert considerable force, until Borya, who was still pushing away, collapsed on the floor.

Out in the corridor, in front of a gathering of doctors performing their rounds, the Colonel slapped Borya once, hard, across the face, splitting the boy's lip and making it bleed.

His father didn't talk to him for the rest of the day. Rarely exchanged more than a few words at a time with him until Borya enlisted in the army at the age of eighteen, like a fine little soldier.

Years later, after Borya had climbed through the ranks and become an officer, a Soviet Army psychiatrist advised him that the incident at his mother's deathbed was the root cause of all his neuroses. His anxiety stemmed from an inferiority complex brought about by the utter humiliation at the hands of his father, whereas his aloofness towards the opposite sex stemmed from the fact that any physical contact with women revived in him a paralyzing fear of dying. It was the defining childhood trauma that had been ruling his psyche throughout his adult life, according to the doctor.

Borya Balakin thought the therapist's assessment was plausible. He even had accepted it as accurate, until years later, when he found the redemptive power of the savior. Only then was he able to grasp the one undeniable truth. His afflictions were not medical in origin, but spiritual, brought on by his indifference to God.

That day he vowed to dedicate the rest of his life to carrying out God's will. The irredeemable sinner thus embarked on his quest for redemption.

From the shadow of the Magnolia, Balakin noticed that the light from an upstairs window of the beach house he had been keeping watch on had gone dark. Only the downstairs lights remained lit. It was getting late in the evening. He imagined that the occupants of the home were gathering for supper. It was what he was waiting for, to have all three of them assemble in the same room so that he could contain the situation.

He would take out the man first. He was old but still looked fit, and carried himself with a mien that suggested that he might have served a stint in the military in his youth. Not to be taken lightly. Besides, this was Texas. The odds were excellent that the old man kept a gun in the house.

Then he'd go for the boy. The old woman was not a priority. She could even live once the job was done, for all he cared. After tonight, witnesses hardly mattered.

Balakin unsheathed his walnut-handled Kizlyar combat knife and headed for the rear door of the house.

* * *

Jamie Lee veered right onto Harrison Avenue in Aransas Pass and was flying past Newbury Park when Patricia's cell phone rang. It was Kyle Wagner.

"Where are you?" Kyle asked.

"Just a few minutes from my parents' house," Patricia said.

"Stand down," Kyle said.

"What?"

"Put Jamie Lee on the phone."

Patricia passed the phone to Jamie Lee. "He wants to talk to you."

"Talk to me, cowboy," Jamie Lee said.

"You need to stand down. Call for back-up. This guy's bad news."

"Well, so am I, honey. So am I."

"You can't take him on," Kyle said.

"You saw the crime scene?" Jamie Lee said, glancing over at Patricia.

"I'm standing on Marcus West's back porch right now."

"And?"

"It's not a crime scene," Kyle said. "It looks more like the site of a well-executed military operation."

"That's our left turn right here!" Patricia shouted.

Jamie Lee stepped on the brake pedal and swerved left onto Goodnight Avenue. The car fish-tailed then righted itself.

"What're you talking about?" Jamie Lee said unfazed.

"The guy that did this, he's no criminal. He's got to be para-military. I'm guessing former special forces."

"All the more reason to get to the kid as fast as we can," Jamie Lee said. "We're almost there already."

"If this guy beat you there, it's already too late,"
Kyle said. "If he's not there yet, you better call
back up first. Lots of it. You'll need a SWAT
team."

"Anything else?" Jamie Lee said.

"A neighbor spotted a white Nissan Altima
with a rental car company sticker on the
windshield parked near the house around the
estimated time of the murder," Kyle said. "Listen,
Jamie Lee, I can't stress enough how dangerous
—"

"What? What? Sorry, you're breaking up."
Jamie Lee hung up. She passed the phone back to
Patricia. "Bad reception down here."

"What did he say?" Patricia asked.

"He said for us to keep our eyes peeled for a
white Nissan Altima. A rental."

* * *

Hours had passed since Alex had created that
gaping hole in the boat-house wall. Miraculously,
Grandpa Wyatt had yet to notice. Of course,
Wyatt had no particular reason to go up into the
boathouse loft today, but that would change when
he'd take delivery of the fishing boat with its new
twin Evinrudes. The proper thing to do, Alex
knew, was to fess up, assume full responsibility,
and start making amends. That's what the old
man expected. Alex decided to do just that. *After*
dinner. Wyatt could get grumpy when he was

hungry.

It was dinner time now. Alex walked out of the boathouse and trudged up the lawn toward the back entrance of the house. When he was a few feet away, he noticed that the kitchen door had been left partially open. The hair on his neck bristled. Wyatt and Betty would never have left a door open on purpose. Not for a minute. Wyatt wasn't about to flush good money down the toilet by air-conditioning the back yard. And Betty had a disdain for mosquitoes that was nearly pathologic.

Something was amiss. Alex was sure of it.

He approached the door cautiously. Crossed the threshold mindful of each step, trying hard not to make a sound. As he passed the kitchen, his ears perked up.

From the living room came the sound of furniture turning over. Then a loud thump. Alex stopped in his tracks. He swallowed hard. After a moment of reflection, he proceeded toward the living room as stealthily as possible.

Through the connecting doorway, he could see Betty lying lifeless on the living room carpet, a dark stain surrounding her torso. Wyatt was sitting on the floor, his back up against the white leather sofa. There was a wide gash on his grandpa's forehead, his nose was busted and bleeding profusely. A man holding a large knife towered over him.

From his vantage point in the kitchen, Alex couldn't see the man's face, but he managed to catch the briefest glimpse of Wyatt's gaze, who quickly redirected his eyes away from him.

Alex heard the intruder say, "Where is the boy?"

"Okay, okay," Wyatt said. "You win. The boy's upstairs. The first bedroom on the left."

Alex knew that Wyatt was a born warrior. He would never just surrender. The old soldier would fight till the death if he had to. This was not Wyatt giving up. No, it was an extraordinary act of bravery on his part. He was helping Alex escape. There was no bedroom on the left upstairs. The old man pulled a bluff, just to buy Alex a little time so that the boy could make a break for it.

Alex understood what his grandpa wanted him to do. The boy wanted to move, but his feet felt glued to the floor. He remained in place, paralyzed, drawn in to watch as the man reached down, grabbed Wyatt by the hair, and slit his throat.

Alex thought of grabbing a kitchen knife, stabbing the assassin in the back. But the words of Sun Tzu echoed in his head.

Know when to fight, when not to fight. Know your enemy. If he is superior in strength, evade him.

Alex began to take a few tentative backward

steps as the assassin made his way up the stairway. Only when the intruder was out of sight did Alex dare to turn. He ran out the back door into the night and sprinted towards the boathouse. He had to get to the loft and arm himself with the speargun. It would be his only chance to stay alive.

* * *

The old man had lied to him. Borya Balakin checked each room upstairs, inspected every closet, looked under every bed. He checked the bathrooms, pulled shower curtains out of the way. There was no sign of the boy.

But he knew his mark couldn't be very far. He couldn't be with his mother, and he sure as hell wasn't with his father. He had to be somewhere at the beach house. Hiding by now, no doubt.

Balakin went back downstairs, searched each room. He entered the garage and checked inside the parked cars, opening their trunks just to make sure. He even looked inside a disconnected freezer next to the water heater.

It was essential to be thorough. To eliminate each room as he went through it. He didn't want to return to the same spot twice.

Three minutes later, with still no sign of the boy, he stepped back into the kitchen. He flung open a broom cabinet, looked inside the pantry. Finally, he pushed open the rear door and looked out across the lawn. Through the dark curtain of falling rain, Balakin could make out the outline of a two-story building next to the boat canal.

The boathouse. That's where the little monster's hiding.

CHAPTER FORTY-THREE

The Boat House

Arkadi ditched his car behind a tall hedgerow off the driveway of Wyatt Holmes's neighbor. He prowled around the side of the beach house he had studied so carefully, heading for the back kitchen door, lock picking set in his back pocket, Glock in his hand, slung low behind his thigh.

He had come half-way around the house, his boots sloshing in the wet turf when he saw a figure darting towards the boathouse. It was Alex. He was sure of it. Even in the darkness, he could recognize the boy by the way he moved.

Arkadi began chasing after him, but a misstep on the slick grass sent him flat on his back.

Well done, Arkadi. Shoot yourself in the foot while you're at it.

He quickly got back on his feet and raced to the boathouse. He had waited for this moment for so long, he could hardly believe it was about to happen.

* * *

Alex climbed the metal staircase into the loft and jogged breathlessly to the wooden chest in the far corner. He opened the lid and pulled out the speargun. The boy cradled the gun's stock against his chest and began to load it, pulling on the thick rubber bands hands down, the only way to generate the necessary force. On the first attempt, he couldn't get the wishbone to fall into the notch of the triggering device. His grip faltered, and the rubber bands almost sprung back. That would have been disastrous.

He tried again. He pulled on the rubber bands with steady force. This time the wishbone latched into place. The speargun was armed.

Alex closed the wooden chest and knelt behind it, pointed the arrow of the speargun in the direction of the spiral staircase. His heart was racing, but his hands felt remarkably steady. He took a deep breath and assessed the situation.

Know thyself, know thy enemy; a thousand battles, a thousand victories.

What exactly did he know? He knew his enemy had a knife while he was armed with a speargun. Alex would have the advantage at a greater distance, which meant he couldn't allow his enemy to close in on him.

He knew his opponent was bigger and stronger than him. That he was ruthless and had already

killed in cold blood. And he realized he'd have
only one shot to stop him. If he missed, he'd be
cornered. Luckily, Alex also had the element of
surprise on his side.

If the enemy is superior in strength, evade him.

As the words rang in his head, Alex realized
that he hadn't allowed himself an escape route.
That could be a fatal mistake.

He placed the speargun on the floor, shuffled to
the trap door closest to him, and pulled it open.
He looked down at the slip below. The wooden
canoe was moored there. If he'd have to make a
jump for it, he had better take care to land in the
water and not in the canoe.

He heard the sound of footsteps coming from
the boardwalk outside. The murderer was getting
close now. He looked in the direction of the spiral
staircase.

This was it. Time to get in position.

But his eyes caught sight of the blue tarp
hanging over the divot he had gouged in the wall.
It gave him an idea.

*All warfare is based on deception. Hold out baits to
entice the enemy — feign disorder and crush him.*

He pulled the blue tarp off the wall, spread it on
the floor, covering the hole of the trap door.

There was a slight creaking sound coming from
downstairs. The door had been opened. Then
Alex heard a click as the door shut again.

Alex tugged on the corners of the tarp to make

it at flat as possible. He could hear footsteps coming from below. Then a pause. More footsteps. Their tone changed. The killer was coming up the staircase.

Alex took his position behind the wooden chest. Lifted the speargun and aimed it.

The man came up into the loft, moving slowly. He was as big as a bear. The far corner of the attic was too dark to see his face clearly. Of course, he hadn't caught sight of his face inside the house either, only glimpsing the back of his head.

The man spoke in a soft tone. "Alex. I can see you. What do you have there? A speargun? Why don't you put it down? It makes me nervous pointed like that at me."

He recognized that voice. It didn't sound like the voice of the killer inside the house, but he couldn't be sure. Still, he knew he had heard that voice before.

The man took a couple of tentative steps towards him, out of the shadow. And Alex realized something was terribly wrong. The man didn't have a knife in his hand; he had a gun. The advantage of distance was crushed.

"Alex. Sasha. I don't have time to explain. But you'll have to trust me. I'm here to protect you. I'm coming over to you now. Please, put down the speargun."

And then Alex saw his face. He put it together with the voice and recognized him at once, even though the memory was from a long time ago. It happened at a park. This was the man with the funny-looking dog. The man who talked to him with such kind words and somehow knew his name. Alex didn't know who this intruder was, but he was positive that this wasn't the killer.

Alex tried to warn him. He shouted, "Stop!"

The man said, "Don't be scared, Alex. I'm not going to hurt you. I would never hurt you."

Again, Alex shouted, "You have to stop! Don't take another step!"

But it was too late. The stranger had already stepped onto the edge of the tarp. He took one more step, and the tarp caved in beneath his feet. The man dropped, feet first, pulling the tarp down with him.

Alex waited for the sound of a splash, but instead, he heard a bone-crushing thump followed by a loud groan. He dropped the spear gun and crawled across the floor to peak down through the trap door. The man was lying on his back in the canoe clutching his leg.

Alex said, "I tried to warn you."

The man laughed, "Good one, Alex! That was a smart move. I think I broke my ankle."

"I'm sorry."

"Do you know who I am?"

"You're the man from the park. The one with the dog."

"My name is Arkadi." Arkadi groaned again as

he palpated his ankle. "So I see you read the books I sent you. It makes me happy. Makes me very proud."

"There's a man in the house. He killed my grandparents."

"His name is Balakin. Listen to me, Alex. He's a very bad man. He wants to hurt you, and he will stop at nothing. You must run. I will try to keep him here."

"He only has a knife," Alex said. "You have a gun. You can shoot him."

Arkadi looked around him. "I think maybe my gun went in the water." He chuckled. "Oh, that was a very good trick with the tarpaulin, Alex. Know the terrain. Deceive the enemy."

"You taught me," Alex said.

The man's expression changed. He flashed Alex a wistful smile. "There are so many things I would have liked to teach you."

"I can shoot Balakin with my speargun."

"No," Arkadi said. "You have to escape. I will hold him here as long as I can."

"But your ankle is broken. He'll kill you."

"I have died before, dear Sasha," Arkadi laughed. "I'm getting used to it. It's really not that big a deal for me anymore. But you — you must live. Please, go before it's too late."

There was the sound of footfalls coming from the boardwalk.

"It's too late," Alex said.

* * *

Patricia directed Jamie Lee through the residential area. They turned onto the street that dead-ended at her parent's house. Half a block away, a white Nissan Altima was parked on the shoulder of the road.

"You better pull out that little pea-shooter Kyle gave you," Jamie Lee said. "Better make sure it's loaded too."

Patricia took the 22 caliber pistol out of the glove compartment where she had stowed it. She grasped the slide firmly and racked a round in the chamber with a loud *ka-chunk.*

Jamie Lee said, "That's the right spirit, girl!"

The detective stopped the car in front of the neighbor's house. The neighbor was standing in the rain, holding an umbrella, talking in a cell phone, staring at a green Pontiac Grand Am that seemed to have jumped off the curb somehow and landed on his lawn.

Jamie Lee and Patricia got out of the car.

"Mr. Henderson," Patricia called out to the man under the umbrella. "Is everything alright?"

"Some yahoo decided to park his car on my lawn," Mr. Henderson said. "I'm calling the towing company."

"You better stay here, Dr. West," Jamie Lee said. "I'm going in the house." She un-holstered her sidearm and disappeared around the hedgerow.

Patricia turned to the man. "Mr. Henderson, hang up the phone. Now! Call the police. And ask for an ambulance."

"What do I tell them?" Mr. Henderson said.

"There's a break-in in progress at my parent's house. The man is armed and dangerous."

Mr. Henderson began to frantically dial the phone. Patricia squeezed the grip of Kyle's gun. She couldn't just stand there and wait. She could feel the adrenaline coursing through her veins, her heart pumping faster, forcing lifeblood to engorging muscles. Her body was beckoning her to move. To run. To fight.

To hell with Jamie Lee's instructions. Patricia started running to her father's house.

She could barely feel the weight of her own body as she moved over the lawn. Her mind seemed more focused than ever. She caught sight of the boathouse and immediately understood that's where Alex would be hiding if he was still alive. It was more than a hunch. It was her subconscious mind prodding her, outracing her conscious thought processes, performing dozens of operations in a fraction of a second, processing hundreds of discrete data points to come to an intuitive conclusion. It was the perfect embodiment of the tacit knowledge she had written and lectured about.

Patricia veered to the right and picked up her pace.

* * *

Arkadi grasped the side of the canoe to try to lift himself out of it. He was still partly wrapped in the tarp. As he pulled it away, the back of his hand struck something hard and smooth. He ran his fingers across it. It was a wooden oar. Now, this could certainly come in handy. He lifted himself up, using the wooden paddle to help balance him on his one good leg, and managed to swivel around and sit on the dock.

"Hide, Alex," he said. "Don't make a sound."

Using the oar again, Arkadi managed to clamber to his feet, and, despite the wrenching pain, he tried to strike as natural a pose as possible. If Balakin knew of his injury, he would zero in on it. Arkadi would be finished in seconds flat.

The door to the boathouse opened. Borya Balakin stepped in and came to a dead stop. His eyes sparkled as he took in the sight of Arkadi standing on the dock. A thin smile came across his face.

In Russian, Balakin said, "Going for a canoe ride, Arkadi? In this weather?"

"It's an excellent canoe," Arkadi answered in Russian. "Very strong. Made of incredibly hard wood."

"They told me you were dead," Balakin said. "I didn't believe them. I could still feel your presence."

369

"Come a little closer," Arkadi said with a smile. "And I'll let you feel the presence of my boot up your arse."

"Where's the boy?"

"Who?"

"Your little Sasha."

"Long gone," Arkadi said. "What took you so long to get here?" Arkadi flicked his eyes to get a brief glimpse of the position of the combat knife in Balakin's right hand.

"Gone?"

"He took the motorboat. He's well across the bay by now."

"Is that so?" Balakin said. "Strange. I didn't hear the sound of motors." Balakin started pacing toward the dock.

"Come closer," Arkadi said, "so I have reason to shoot you."

"Shoot me? With the oar of a boat? Is it loaded?"

"Have you ever known me to be unarmed?"

"The boy has to die. You know that, comrade. His life is an abomination. Every breath he takes is a sin against God."

"You are not God," Arkadi said. "It's not up to you to decide."

"You are right," Balakin said. "But I am not the one who decided. It has already been decided for us."

"You keep bad company, Major Balakin,"

Arkadi said. "You always have."

"That's the pot calling the kettle black, Private Volkov. The problem with you is you never could follow orders."

"And you're problem is that you followed them too well. But we're not in the Army anymore."

"Oh, but I am," Balakin said. "I'm a soldier in the Army of God."

Balakin had barely uttered the phrase that Arkadi lifted the oar and swung at him.

Balakin ducked just in time to avoid the blow.

Arkadi swung again, this time connecting with Balakin's forearm. The knife fell out of his hand, clattering onto the dock. Despite the blow, Balakin swiveled his body in a low pirouette and kicked the legs out from under Arkadi.

Arkadi landed on the floor with a cry of pain. His injured leg felt like it was on fire.

"Oh, dear," Balakin said. "I do believe you're injured. It's your left leg, no? But I couldn't have done that just now."

Arkadi reached for the knife, but Balakin stepped on his hand just as his fingers grazed the grip. Balakin shifted all his weight on his boot. Arkadi felt his ring finger snap. He winced but didn't give Balakin the satisfaction of as much as a groan.

Instead, Arkadi took a couple of deep breaths. Then he rolled on his back, kicked his legs up in the air, lifting his pelvis and driving the boot of his good foot into Balakin's chest. It unbalanced Balakin just enough to get him off Arkadi's hand, but not enough to send the killer in the water as Arkadi had hoped.

Balakin scooped down and retrieved the knife.

Arkadi was on his back now. He lifted his shoulders off the wood deck and began scuttling backward on his elbows, dragging his injured leg, thrusting with both arms and his sole good leg. He moved in the direction of the bar. Maybe there was a knife there. Or a corkscrew. Anything he might use as a weapon.

Balakin stalked him in a deliberately slow prowl. With the combat knife, he slashed the front of Arkadi's thigh. He jabbed again, plunging the blade in Arkadi's flank.

Arkadi yelled wailed with pain.

"Now what, Arkadi?" Balakin said. "Have you run out of ideas? You used to be so clever."

"Here's an idea," Arkadi said as his shoulders bumped into the side of the bar. "Go to hell!"

"No, Arkadi," Balakin said. "That's where I'm sending *you*." He lifted the knife and prepared to plunge it into Arkadi's heart.

* * *

Alex had backed away from the trap door, clutching the speargun close to his chest. First, he heard the door of the boathouse creak open. Then he heard voices talking in a foreign language. He figured the two men were talking in Russian. It

sounded like Russian, anyway. What the hell
other language could it be?

It started as a normal conversation with a
somewhat even tone. But soon, the voices became
more agitated.

That's when he started to consider his options
for escape. Jumping through the trap door into the
water was only a last resort, in case the assassin
happened to come up into the loft. But as long as
Arkadi had him occupied, a more feasible
alternative would be to sneak down the metal
staircase and slip out the door. He could run to a
neighbor's house. Turn and shoot if the assassin
gave chase. Take that one shot. Make it count. He
had nailed the side of the boathouse pretty good,
after all.

Alex started moving toward the staircase,
placing his feet as close to the far wall of the loft as
possible to avoid any creaking of floorboards.
When he reached the top of the stairs, he heard
what sounded like a scuffle. Then louder thuds
and the sound of scraping on the wooden deck.
He hesitated a moment, gathered his courage, and
started descending the stairs.

He saw Arkadi on his back, slithering like a
crab towards the bar. The assassin was following
him at a leisurely pace, slashing the air with his
knife.

As if someone had whispered in his ear, the
words of Sun Tzu echoed in his mind: *Attack the*

enemy when he is unprepared. Appear when you are unexpected.

Alex lifted the speargun and aimed.

The man brought the knife up. He tightened his grip on the handle as he prepared to plunge the blade into Arkadi's chest.

Alex squeezed the trigger of the speargun.

Almost instantaneously, the assassin let out a howl.

The harpoon had come to rest in Balakin's right shoulder. The assassin reached back with his left hand to feel what had stabbed him. He spun around wild-eyed and caught sight of Alex.

The assassin lunged toward the boy, so suddenly, Alex no longer had time enough to open the door and slip out. Instead, he ran toward the end of the dock. He knocked fishing poles off their racks, trying to trip up the assassin. It helped to slow him down just enough.

But now, Alex was cornered. Balakin knew it. He stopped and began speaking in English.

"Alex. This is not your fault. But understand, the situation cannot be remedied any other way. This is God's will. Please know that I will pray for you. Just as I prayed for all the others."

Alex glanced in the direction of Arkadi, wondering, "What others?"

Arkadi had managed to get to his feet. He was limping badly, holding onto the wall for support, grimacing as he tried to move in behind the assassin.

"I'll say a prayer even as I hold you dying," the assassin said.

Then Alex heard another voice, loud and hard-as-nails.

"Get the fuck away from my son!"

On the other end of his dock stood his own mother, pointing a gun at the assassin in a two-handed grip.

* * *

The man with the knife stopped, turned around. The other man, the one Kyle had chased down at the cemetery, the one she had chased into a canyon so many years ago, looked to be in bad shape. He was leaning onto the bar in the corner, hemorrhaging. She had a pretty good idea, by now, as to which one of the two men was Balakin, and a healthy suspicion of who the other man must be. What if she was wrong? There was one way to find out.

Patricia shouted, "Drop the knife, Balakin!"

The man chuckled. "So, you know my name."

"And I know you killed Olga. And those boys," Patricia said.

"Ah, yes, well, I'm almost embarrassed to tell you I killed your parents as well," Balakin said. "It's really too bad. They looked like decent people. They died honorably, but for what? Oh, well, collateral damage, as we say. I shall put them in my prayers. But, on the bright side, I *did* kill your husband, a most vile man. I don't know what you ever saw in him that would have impelled you to marry him. You really should thank me for that one. I did you a favor. Now, let me do you another favor. Let me rid you of this vile boy."

"Shut the hell up and drop the knife!" Patricia shouted, her eyes welling with tears.

"Your hands are shaking, Dr. West," Balakin said. "I hope they don't shake like that when they're holding a scalpel." Balakin started taking slow steps toward her. She knew she'd have to shoot the bastard. But Alex was standing on the dock behind him. He'd be in harm's way if she began firing now.

Balakin was getting closer. It was time to act. In as clear and steady a voice as she could muster, she shouted, *"Welcome to Rome!"*

Alex got the message loud and clear. He dove into the inky waters of the boat slip as Patricia fired her first shot.

Balakin stopped. He said, "See, you missed."

Patricia saw Alex's head surface. He was swimming toward the wooden canoe. She said, "That was a warning shot."

Balakin almost doubled over in laughter, regained his composure, waited a couple of seconds, then moved in on her again.

Patricia fired another round. This time, Balakin jerked, as if he had been jolted with an electric shock. It brought his advance to a halt. The man reached down and dabbed his flank with his fingers, then brought his hand up to peer at them.

His expression changed. His eyes were now filled with rage. The next moment, he lunged at Patricia.

Patricia fired off yet another shot, but almost immediately, the hand of her aggressor latched onto her throat and started squeezing.

She tried to bring the gun around to shoot him once more, but Balakin managed to grasp her wrist. He banged her hand against the wall of the boathouse to make her drop the gun.

Patricia tried to hold onto the weapon, but she was finding it hard to breathe. Her chest heaved, the air now barely moving through her windpipe. Her grip on the gun was weakening. Finally, she dropped it. She had no choice. There was nothing more she could do now. She would have to let go. There was no strength left in her.

As she began to lapse into oblivion, she detected a shadow, a blurred movement out in front of her. The injured man who had been leaning on the bar was standing behind Balakin, hoisting a wooden oar. He swung and landed his blow on the side of Balakin's neck. Balakin fell on his side, stunned.

With her aggressors grasp released, Patricia crumpled to the floor. She gasped. Life-giving air flooded into her starved lungs. The sudden surge of oxygen jostled her back to life. Her mind still in a fog, she tried to assess the situation. Balakin was stumbling back to his knees. The man that had knocked him down was sprawled out on the floor. Alex was nowhere to be seen.

She started feeling her way around the floor, looking for Kyle's handgun, becoming frantic in her search as Balakin slowly got back to his feet. The gun was nowhere to be found.

Balakin stretched his spine, rubbed the side of his neck where the oar had pounded him, then lumbered toward Patricia again. He said, "Doctor, doctor! This is getting tiresome. Why can't you accept God's will?" He lifted his knife and said, "Give my regards to your dear parents."

A shot rang out, loud and close. Patricia smelled the reek of gun powder. She looked up.

Jamie Lee Foster was standing above her, pointing her smoking service weapon at Balakin. Jamie Lee squeezed the trigger again. Balakin collapsed lifeless on the deck.

The detective moved her gun in the direction of Arkadi, aimed it at his chest.

"Dr. West," Jamie Lee said. "Please tell me I shot the right guy."

Patricia managed to say, "You shot Balakin."

"And who's this handsome fella?" Jamie Lee said.

From the other side of the boathouse, Alex's voice called out. "That's my father."

CHAPTER FORTY-FOUR

Hanging On

Two burly paramedics began loading the gurney onto which Arkadi lay strapped into the back of an ambulance.

"I have to go with him," Patricia said, looking at Alex sheepishly.

"Go, mom," Alex said.

"You run right along," Jamie Lee said. She put a hand on Alex's head and tousled his hair. "Don't you worry about this little man. I got his back."

Patricia hugged Alex for the third time in five minutes. Then she turned and started running toward the ambulance. "Meet me at the hospital!" she called back.

Patricia stepped inside the vehicle and sat on a padded bench next to Arkadi's gurney. One of the paramedics shut the doors behind her. The siren came alive, and the ambulance started moving.

The temporary dressing on Arkadi's flank was turning crimson. Without hesitation, Patricia opened the hatch of an overhead cabinet, took out a package of sterile gloves, donned them, and began to change the dressing. When the new dressing almost immediately became saturated with blood, she applied more pressure to the wound.

"I believe I am dying, Patricia," Arkadi said.

"Nonsense." Patricia said. "You'll be fine."

"It doesn't matter anymore. Now that Alex is safe."

"You're not dying," Patricia said.

"I imagine you'll want to interrogate me now," Arkadi said. The man's eyes were piercing, probing, but he no longer appeared the least bit menacing.

"I have questions, yes," Patricia said.

"When did you know?"

"That you're the father of my son?" Patricia said. "It hit me when I saw you in the boathouse."

Arkadi smiled. "Not a moment too soon." He looked down at his wound. "Better apply more pressure there. What I have to say might take a while. I don't want to bleed out before I've finished."

"You've been watching over him," Patricia said.

"For more than thirteen years," Arkadi said. "Watched him grow from afar. I got a little careless that day in the park. I let myself get too close to him. I couldn't help it. And then you chased me away like a mother bear protecting her cub." Arkadi sighed and looked at the ceiling of the ambulance. "That was something!"

"And you know about those other boys?" Patricia said.

"He is not like the other boys," Arkadi said.

"That's what Professor Kovalenko said. But then how—"

"I was an army soldier long ago, young, confident, hungry. I was an excellent fighter, but a little hard-headed. My lack of discipline got me in a spat of trouble from time to time. One day, a captain came to recruit me for what he said was a top-secret mission. I thought it was a trick seeing as I was confined in a Russian Army prison at the time, arrested for insubordination: assaulting an officer of all things. So, how could I refuse his offer? Next thing I know, I'm given a hot meal, a cold shower, and put on a train to to Odessa. There were a half-dozen other soldiers already there when I arrived, mostly privates, a couple of officers."

"Was Borya Balakin one of them?"

"Major Balakin was the most senior ranking guinea pig."

"Guinea pig?" Patricia said.

"That's what it felt like. They quartered us in a make-shift barrack surrounded by razor wire, right next to the military hospital."

"I've been there," Patricia said. "At that hospital."

"Yes, I know. Soon they were running tests on us. X-rays, EKG, physiologic tests, tests of endurance, psychological batteries. Of course, they also tested our blood, urine, stool."

"And semen?"

Arkadi exhaled. "This is what happened, Patricia. On the other side of the hospital, there was a dormitory. I got a good look at it one day when they were marching us out of the hospital after a long day of tests. But this dormitory did not house soldiers. It housed women. Young, beautiful women."

"Keep going," Patricia said.

"Her name was Natalia," Arkadi said. "She was only nineteen. Very fresh. Charming. And very pretty. Alex is the spitting image of her. It might be hard for you to believe but I was a bit of lady's man back then."

"How did it happen?" Patricia said. "How did you get her pregnant?"

"Razor wire is useless if there is a faulty padlock on the gate. And a carton of Turkish cigarettes and a bottle of cheap vodka goes a long way in bribing Russian sentries."

"Did anyone find out?"

"Kovalenko knew. I told him."

"What did he do when you told him?" Patricia asked.

"You have to understand that a strong bond had formed between me and the professor by then. He became the father figure I never had. The professor was pragmatic. He said that seeing as Natalia was already fertilized *extra-vitro*, as it were, there was really nothing more to do. It would be our secret. Kovalenko's heart was never in the project. What he was forced to do still troubles him to this day."

"So, you didn't get in trouble?"

"Not for that," Arkadi said. "But when Natalia died in childbirth, I went a little crazy. Yes, I behaved very badly, and was sent back to prison. This time, they told me I would never get out. Not alive, at least. But I didn't care. The thought of dying did not trouble me after Natalia was gone."

"But you had a son," Patricia said.

"Yes. A son I did not deserve. One I would never be able to see," Arkadi said. "And then a miracle happened. The Soviet Union collapsed. I was released. Kovalenko and his cousin, Olga, managed to arrange my passage to America through some contacts they had in the State Department."

"And you kept an eye on Alex ever since," Patricia said. "Knowing that one day Balakin might come."

"His own son was born very sick. Balakin interpreted that as a message from God, a

punishment for having taken part in this
monstrous experiment. So, as a form of penance,
he murdered his own son. He was immediately
arrested by Ukrainian authorities, shipped to a
hell-hole of a prison in the Crimea, but not for
long. By this time, Major Balakin had become
extremely devout, and he had always been
severely obedient. The order came from the
Kremlin to break him out of jail. The operation
was successful and he was shipped off to a far-
away convent outside of Moscow. He would be
protected there but kept under the thumb of the
very person who started the experiment."

"That would be General Rostov," Patricia said.

"Kovalenko told you, yes?" Arkadi said.
"Balakin would become a sort of insurance policy.
Rostov knew how to manipulate him, using
Balakin's intense fervor in God as leverage.
Major-General Rostov soon left the Army but
continued his climb up the ranks of political
leadership until he was in the very inner circle of
the Kremlin. Of course, amidst all the confusion
surrounding the collapse of the Soviet Union, his
controversial program had been shut down. This
made Rostov furious, enraged that his experiment
had run aground, and that the boys — *his* boys, as
far as he was concerned — were no longer in his
clutches. Even worse, they had been sent to safety
in America. You see, he worried that the
experiment would turn out only too well, and that

the American military might develop an interest in these boys. He was afraid that maybe Kovalenko would start his own program here in the United States."

"Is that why Professor Kovalenko stopped doing research?"

"After the program fell apart, the professor was quite fed up with genetic research, to be sure. But retiring from research was his way of sending a message back to Moscow. He hoped that if he signaled to Rostov that all his research activity had come to a complete close, Rostov might forget about the boys and leave them alone. But men like Rostov never forget, and that psychopath still had one ace up his sleeve."

"Borya Balakin," Patricia said.

"The holy man." Arkadi scoffed. "His insurance policy. Balakin was still in Rostov's clutches. Seeing as the disgraced Major had already proved himself by murdering his own son, Rostov knew Balakin would have no qualms about killing the other boys to fulfill his twisted idea of penance. Rostov decided to bide his time. To wait and see. If the need arose, he would activate his insurance policy."

The ambulance slowed.

"You did it, Arkadi," Patricia said. "You saved your son."

"No Patricia, *we* saved *our* son." His face lit up in a smile that brought tears to Patricia's eyes. She

grasped Arkadi's hand, squeezed it once and
quickly released it.

Arkadi looked at his wound. The bleeding was
subsiding. Arkadi seemed to want to say
something but hesitated.

"What is it, Arkadi?"

Arkadi shook his head. "Perhaps, it's too much
to ask for ..."

"No, Arkadi. It's not," Patricia said. She
marveled at how she could have been so wrong
about this man. "After all, Alex is your son."

CHAPTER FORTY-FIVE

Austin

Patricia and Alex strode up San Jacinto Boulevard in Austin, Patricia in a snazzy suit and leather briefcase, Alex wearing a rugby jersey and a Detroit Lions cap he seemed to be unable to take off for the last week. They stepped onto the outdoor patio of a coffee shop where Arkadi was waiting at a wrought iron table, with Volya the fox tucked between his feet. Arkadi shot up when he saw them and buttoned his smart-looking blazer, adjusted the knot of his tie. He looked as nervous as a teenage boy picking up his date for the prom.

"I hope you haven't been waiting long," Patricia said as they approached him.

"Good morning, Patricia. Hello, Alex," Arkadi said.

"What's up, dad?" Alex said.

The two exchanged a fist bump that came off so

smoothly it seemed as though they might have
practiced it a thousand times. It made Patricia
smile.

"I took the liberty of ordering coffee for you,
"Arkadi said. "I hope you don't mind." He picked
up a bouquet of wildflowers wrapped in craft
paper and held them out to Patricia. "These are
for you."

"Arkadi, you really didn't have to," Patricia
said.

"For your first day at your new job," Arkadi
said. "Congratulations, Professor."

"Thank you, Arkadi." Patricia leaned into him
and planted a peck on his cheek.

Arkadi was beaming. He pulled a chair out for
Patricia. Waited for her to be seated before joining
her at the table while Alex knelt to play with
Volya. On the table were three cups of coffee, a
platter of pastries, and a parcel wrapped in brown
paper tied up in twine.

"I didn't know they had such nice pastries
here," Patricia said.

"Actually, I took the liberty of baking those this
morning," Arkadi said.

"You really didn't have to," Patricia said.

"Don't listen to her, Arkadi," Alex piped in
from under the table. "You just keep on baking."

Arkadi and Patricia chuckled.

"I have a little something for you too, Alex,"
Arkadi said.

Alex stood up. He looked at the package, smiled, and said, "Gee, I wonder if it's a book."

"You've seen this wrapping before, yes?" Arkadi said.

"Is it Von Clausewitz?" Alex asked.

"No. The war is over, son," Arkadi said. "Go ahead. Open it."

Alex tore off the packaging. He pulled the book out and read the title, "The Meditations of Marcus Aurelius." He quickly opened the book and flipped to the title page, smiled, and said, "For Alex."

Alex leaned down and gave Arkadi a hug.

Arkadi covered his mouth with his fist, looking overwhelmed by emotion.

"I see you're not using your cane," Patricia said.

"The ankle is all better," Arkadi said.

Patricia eyed him suspiciously.

"Those doctors treat me like a baby," Arkadi said in his defense.

"I'm sorry about Professor Kovalenko," Patricia said.

"He went in peace," Arkadi said. He glanced at Alex and looked back at Patricia.

Patricia nodded. It was meeting Alex that replenished the dying professor with the peace he so desperately sought.

"How is your new apartment?" Arkadi asked.

"A little cramped," Patricia said. "How about your new home?"

"The professor's house is too big for me,"
Arkadi said. "But, it makes Volya happy."

"Dr. Kovalenko cared about you a great deal,"
Patricia said.

Arkadi nodded. "He had no heirs. I don't
deserve such gifts."

"I think you earned it," Patricia said.

"I bought a new wardrobe," Arkadi said.

"I noticed!"

"But I kept my old leather jacket. I don't know
why I can't get rid of that old thing."

"I think I understand," Patricia said.

Arkadi held the platter of pastries in front of
Patricia. She selected a tart with forest berries.
Then he passed the tray to Alex. He picked up the
largest pastry on the dish: a huge cheese Danish.

Patricia smiled and shook her head.

"He's a growing boy," Arkadi said with a
chuckle.

"You could at least take your cap off at the
table," Patricia said.

"Why?" Alex said.

"It's not polite," Patricia said.

"Who says?" Alex said with his mouth full.

Patricia reached over to Alex, yanked the cap
off his head. Alex quickly snatched it back,
popped it back on his crown. But not quite fast
enough. Something had caught Patricia's eye.

She turned to Arkadi and said, "Arkadi?"

Arkadi looked at her for a moment. Then he

turned to Alex and said, "Excuse me, son." He gently lifted the cap off Alex's head, studied the boy's hair. It was hard to notice, but it was definitely there: a round patch, no bigger than the size of a pencil's eraser, of thin, wispy, white hair.

Arkadi slowly pushed the cap back on Alex's head. He put his hand on Alex's shoulder, squeezed it, turned to Patricia, and, in an unruffled tone, said, "I really don't mind if he keeps his cap on."

THE END

ACKNOWLEDGMENTS:

I am hugely indebted to my wife, Dr. Emma
Diaz de Leon, for her thorough, thoughtful
critique which resulted in a radically transformed
(and improved) story line. Wise husbands always
listen to their wives.

I would also like to thank all my Russian and
Ukrainian friends who coached me on all matters
related to life in those countries. Thank you,
Vladislav, Peter, Maria, Natalia, Alex, and Victor.

Any remaining errors are, of course, my own.

DID YOU KNOW?

Trofym Desinovich Lysenko was a Soviet agronomist and biologist whose pseudo-scientific theories resulted in the starvation of millions.

Dmitri Belyaev was a zoologist and geneticist who successfully bred docile Siberian Silver foxes which, in the process, acquired dog-like physical features.

Joseph Stalin was the premier of the Soviet Union from 1941 to 1953.

Colonel-General Boris Gromar completed the withdrawal of Soviet troops from Afghanistan in 1988.

All other characters and events discussed in this novel are fictional.

A MESSAGE FROM THE AUTHOR:

As a reader, you have tremendous power. Even as millions of books become available for purchase online, and it becomes increasingly difficult for a title to stand out, a single good review can result in the sale of hundreds of books, which in turn can propel the title up Amazon's ranking chart. For independent authors such as myself, there is no greater gift than an honest review and rating.

I hope you enjoyed reading SING THE RAGE. If you did, will you give me a little hand? Please post a review on amazon.com. Then copy and paste it on goodreads.com. Don't forget to recommend my book to your friends, both in person and on social media. Recommend it to your enemies, too. I don't mind.

Do you belong to a book club? Suggest SING THE RAGE for your reading and I will make a brief appearance at your meeting via Skype (if my schedule allows). You can ask me questions, give me feedback, even make comments on my hair style, if you like.

And if you'd like to give me personal feedback of any kind, please send me a note at peterpeds@gmail.com Finally, visit my web page: medicalthrillerwriter.com and follow me on facebook

Thanks!
Peter Palmieri, January 7, 2020

Sing the Rage

OTHER BOOKS BY PETER PALMIERI:

THE ART OF FORGETTING — A romantic medical thriller set in Chicago. Winner of the North Texas Book Festival

BLOOD MOON — If John Grisham were a physician, and The Firm a medical thriller, this is what it would read like. A gripping tale of corruption and redemption set on the Texas-Mexico border.

SEE ONE, DO ONE, TEACH ONE — A collection of short stories about doctors and patients, including the award-winning story, *A Long Stretch of Highway.*

SUFFER THE CHILDREN — Non-fiction: a disturbingly candid critique on the state of Pediatric medicine in the United States.

Made in the USA
Columbia, SC
22 January 2020